THE CHILDREN OF THE GODS
Book 10

DARK WARRIOR'S LEGACY

I. T. Lucas

D1526389

NOTE FROM THE AUTHOR:
<u>**This is a work of fiction!**</u>

Names, characters, places and incidents are products of the author's imagination or are used fictitiously and are not to be construed as real. Any similarity to actual persons, organizations and/or events is purely coincidental.

The Children of The Gods

TABLE OF CONTENTS

CHAPTER 1: NATHALIE

"Where are you going?" Andrew murmured when Nathalie kissed his cheek, checking once more that he was indeed sleeping and not unconscious. Ever since his transition had started with him lying unconscious in bed, she'd been having mini panic attacks every time she opened her eyes to see his closed.

Relieved, she kissed him again. "Go back to sleep. I'll be right back."

Hoping to do her laundry while avoiding the butler, Nathalie had crawled out of bed at five in the morning. Funny. For years, she'd been waking up when it was still dark outside, and this would've been considered late for her. Getting used to good things was easy, and not having to wake up before the sun came up was definitely at the top of her list of good.

A bundle of dirty clothes under her arm, she tiptoed to the kitchen in search of the laundry room. Opening each one of its three doors, she discovered that one led to a secondary elevator, another to the dining room, and the third one to a large pantry.

"Figures," Nathalie muttered. Kian and Syssi probably used a service, and there was no laundry facility in the penthouse.

Unless one of the doors off the main hallway was hiding what she was looking for. On the remote chance that it did, Nathalie tried the one directly across from the guest suite.

Damn, it was the butler's, and he wasn't sleeping. He was sitting in a BarcaLounger, not much different from the one he'd brought for her father, and watching some British show on the tube. His bed looked like it hadn't been slept in at all, but that was probably because he'd made it as soon as he'd woken up. Perfectly, like a display in a department store.

Well, he was the butler; of course his bed would look like that.

"Can I help you, madam?"

Shit, if she asked him where the washer and dryer were, he would insist on doing her laundry himself. It was better not to mention it at all and avoid an argument.

"No, thank you. My mistake, I'm sorry to disturb you. Good day." She quickly closed the door before he had a chance to answer.

Well, not a big deal.

She was going home to check on the boys and could drop her dirty stuff there, change, and pack a bag with fresh things for the next day or two. The only problem with that plan was that, in the meantime, she was stuck wearing her clothes from yesterday.

"Good morning, Nathalie. What are you doing up so early?" Kian's voice startled her.

How the hell did he walk without making a sound?

With a hand over her chest, she turned around and plastered a smile on her face. "I was looking for the laundry room," she blurted before thinking it through. Not that she had a better explanation for the evidence under her arm.

Kian wouldn't offer to do her laundry for her, but he might suggest his butler.

As if reading her thoughts, Kian chuckled. "I'm sorry to disappoint you, but the entrance to the laundry facility is through Okidu's room, and he wouldn't let anyone set foot in there. If you're out of clothes and you don't want anyone doing your laundry, I suggest you borrow some of Syssi's."

That was awfully perceptive of him, not a trait men in general were known for and especially not Kian's type. She put her hands on her hips and narrowed her eyes at him. "Are you reading my thoughts?"

He shook his head, then winked. "I would never do so without your permission."

"So how did you know?"

A soft smile tugged at the corners of his lips. "Syssi had the same problem. She didn't like the idea of anyone handling her intimates. But she soon realized that resistance was futile."

Nathalie grimaced. "Ugh. I don't know how she does it. I can't even think of anyone touching my intimates, as you said so politely."

Kian dipped his head. "Thank you. My mother would've loved to hear it. She tried her best to teach me manners but had limited success. Come to the kitchen, and I'll tell you how Syssi solved the problem. I need my morning coffee."

She did too. "Thank you."

After dropping her bundle back in her room, Nathalie joined Kian in the kitchen and sat on one of the counter stools, watching him pull out the thermal carafe from the coffeemaker and pour its contents into three cups.

"I have it set on a timer, so the coffee is ready when we wake up," he explained.

Apparently, Kian wasn't the only early bird in the house. Syssi was too. "Do you guys always wake up so early?"

Kian pulled the creamer out of the fridge. "I used to get up even earlier and go to the gym, but Syssi doesn't allow me to get out of bed before her. She'll be here in a moment." He handed Nathalie the cup, then put the creamer and a small plate with sugar cubes on the counter.

"Thank you." Nathalie dropped two cubes into her coffee and poured a little creamer. From the first sip, she recognized it as the same brand of coffee Syssi had made for her before. It was so good that Nathalie was considering trying it in her café even if it was on the pricey side. The coffee might be well worth the added cost if she gained a few more regulars thanks to it. People would come back for coffee that good.

Kian rounded the counter and sat next to her, took a couple of sips from his cup, then put it down. "I apologize for not offering breakfast. We usually eat after our morning exercise."

Was it her imagination, or did Kian just wrinkle his nose?

"Okidu will make some later." He shook his head and reached for his cup, dipping low as he took another sip.

Oh, shit. He must've smelled her dirty clothes.

Mortified beyond words, Nathalie stayed seated by sheer force of will when everything in her demanded that she bolt out of there. After only one day of wear in an air-conditioned environment, her clothes should've been still

4

good today, but evidently she'd been wrong. Kian was smelling something unpleasant, and it wasn't the coffee.

She took a few quick sips, burning her tongue in the process, and put the cup down. "I should get going. I need to go home and check on how things are going over at the shop." She got up and took a few steps back. "I hope to be back before my father wakes up, but if I'm not, could you please tell Okidu to serve him breakfast? Otherwise, he might try to cook it himself and set the kitchen on fire."

"Don't you want to hear how Syssi solved the laundry problem? It may save you the trip."

Hell no.

She wanted to be out of there as soon as possible and not come back until she was showered and wearing fresh clothes. There was nothing more embarrassing than an offensive body odor.

"I would love to hear all about it, but maybe some other time. I really need to check on the boys and see if they need anything. I've been gone for too long."

Kian shrugged. "I'll wait for you here until you're ready to go. The elevators are controlled by a thumbprint, and you'll need one of us to escort you down to your car."

Great. Now she was going to be stuck with him inside a small, enclosed space.

Can this day get any worse?

Shut up, Nathalie. Of course it can get worse.

She was stupid. It wasn't her fault that she didn't have clean things, and Kian wouldn't judge her because of it. He would understand. And anyway, wasn't he supposed to be ancient? He'd lived in an era when people rarely bathed. A little body odor shouldn't be a big deal to him.

Back in the guest suite, first thing she did was to

5

check on Andrew. Poor guy. She'd woken him several times during the night just to check that he was responding. No wonder he didn't even twitch when she sat on the bed. He was exhausted. Lifting his limp hand, she kissed the back of it. His eyes popped open, shining with an eerie blue glow—the kind she'd seen in Kian's.

Scary and yet beautiful.

"Your eyes are glowing," she whispered.

Andrew smiled, and she was relieved to note that his canines still looked normal. After everything they'd been through recently, she couldn't handle more than one thing at a time. The extent of physical change Andrew had already undergone was staggering, and she hadn't been prepared for so much in such a short time. Thankfully, on the inside he was still the same old Andrew.

A wonderful, devoted, caring man.

"I'll be damned. I can see the light shining on your face. A useful trick in case of a power outage." He chuckled. "No need to go searching for a flashlight."

"Aren't they supposed to do that only when you're horny or stressed?"

"And your point is?"

She laughed. "You're right. You're always horny. I guess flashlights are no longer needed in our household."

He pulled her on top of him. "Only when I'm near you, my sexy lady." Reaching for the back of her head, he brought her down for a kiss, and a moment later she found herself pinned under him. Thank God he hadn't gained weight along with his other changes because he would've crushed her.

"Not now, Andrew. I need to go home, change, and pack a few clothes. I'm out of everything, and I'm wearing what I had on yesterday. I stink."

He sniffed her neck. "You don't stink, sweetheart. You smell great, like a ripe peach."

That was a relief. "Are you sure? Kian wrinkled his nose at me."

Andrew sniffed again. "I'm sure. But you do smell different. I told you that before. Have you gotten your period? That could explain it."

A wave of anxiety swept through her, and for a moment Nathalie couldn't breathe.

Kian had obviously smelled something that had caused him to react like that. And since he hadn't gone through any changes during their short acquaintance, it meant that she was the one emitting a different scent from before.

That, together with the nausea and Bridget's suspicions, all pointed to only one possible conclusion.

Damn. If it were true, she was so screwed.

Or rather the other way around. A snarky little voice whispered in her head that she had the cause and effect in reverse. After all, the screwing had to come first.

CHAPTER 2: ANDREW

As soon as Nathalie had left, Andrew jumped out of bed. Ever since Bridget had taken his measurements, he'd been itching to check himself out in the mirror. He'd grown bigger all over, which was great. The question was whether everything got bigger proportionally. Not the kind of thing he wanted to do in front of his fiancée. As much as he loved her, some things were too embarrassing to share.

Hell, he was embarrassing himself.

Only a delinquent attached so much importance to the size of his dick.

When he'd made love to her, Nathalie hadn't had any complaints, and that should've been enough. But damn his stupid ego, it wasn't. He had to know, and now that she was gone and wouldn't be back for at least an hour, he could finally do a thorough inspection without fear of getting caught doing something so juvenile.

Last night, before Nathalie had come into the

bathroom, he'd managed to get a quick peek in the small mirror over the vanity. But if he wanted to see more, he had to do it inside the walk-in closet. The only full-sized mirror in the entire damn guest suite was in there.

Padding to the door, Andrew locked it before embarking on his mission—exploration of his new and improved body. A precaution in case Nathalie came back early, or one of the others decided to pay him a visit.

In the closet, he turned on the light, closed the door, and then stood in front of the mirror.

"Not bad," he told his reflection.

The two small scars on his face had faded completely, and the only evidence they were ever there was the missing hair in his brow and in the scruff over his upper lip. He had no doubt that in a few days the hair would grow and cover the small lines bisecting his upper lip and his brow.

Stretched over his frame, his skin was taut like a young man's. Hopefully, it would stay like that after adjusting to his larger frame. He needed to fill out more, though. Some of the muscle tone he'd had before going through the transition had been lost.

One of the things he'd hated most about his aging body had been the slight sag of his skin. All the iron pumping he'd done hadn't helped fill it up.

Did it feel as smooth as it looked? He ran his hand over his chest and his abs.

Nice. Everywhere he touched was taut, and what's more his old scars, even the big ones, were barely visible. In a day or two, they would probably be gone completely.

The ping of sorrow that followed surprised him. The old stab wounds and bullet holes told a history. So yeah, it was a history of battles, of losses and victories, of blood and

9

sweat, but it was his, and he owned it. To see it disappear felt like erasing the memory.

With a jolt, he moved sideways to bring his tattoo in front of the mirror.

"Fuck!" It had faded so much that only the outline was still visible.

He should snap a photo before it vanished so he could have it redone once his body stopped changing. Except, he couldn't remember seeing tattoos on any of the Guardians.

Andrew frowned. Perhaps it was impossible for immortals to mark their bodies—the self-healing mechanism preventing any lasting changes. He hadn't seen any of them with piercings either.

The thought of losing the tat spoiled his good mood.

As long as he carried the monument to his fallen friends on his flesh, Andrew felt as if he was carrying on their legacy. In a small way, it made the guilt of surviving while they hadn't tolerable.

And now it was fading.

With his shoulders slumped, he shuffled back to the bed and sat down. What the hell was he going to do if tattoos were a no-go for an immortal?

He must've brooded a long time because he was still sitting on that bed when he heard Nathalie trying to open the door.

"Andrew?" she said quietly with a note of worry in her voice.

Still in the buff, he padded to the door and stood behind it as he opened it for Nathalie, closing and relocking it after she'd stepped in.

She dropped two overstuffed plastic bags on the floor and turned to look at him. "I see you've been waiting for me." A smile curved her lips, but after a quick once-over, it was replaced with a frown. "Not excitedly, though."

He'd better spit it out quick before she started thinking some nonsense like she wasn't turning him on anymore. "My tattoo is fading away."

"Let me see." Nathalie grabbed his elbow and turned him sideways. "It is. Do you know if you can get a new one?"

She hadn't forgotten its significance.

He'd told her about it almost at the start of their relationship, which had been as good an indicator as any that she was his one. Andrew didn't like to explain it to people. It was private. But there was nothing he wanted to keep secret from Nathalie if he didn't have to. It was enough that he worked for the government and couldn't tell her anything about his work. The least he could do was tell her everything else.

"I don't know. I suspect my body will keep repairing my skin and erasing it."

Nathalie looked at it closer. "We should take a picture before it is gone completely. I can still see the outline." She let his arm drop and reached inside her purse to pull out her phone. Snapping a few from different angles, she checked after each one to make sure it had come out all right. "What do you think?" She handed him the phone.

It was a relief to see that the white phoenix was clear enough for an artist to recreate, if not on his skin then on something else. Question was, on what?

"It's good. I can take it to a tattoo place, and they can use it to make a new one. I need to dedicate a budget for redoing it every few days."

"It doesn't have to be on your skin."

As if a picture on the wall could serve as a memorial. Maybe for someone else; not for him. "You know what it means to me. I need it on my body, always. That's how I keep them in here." He put his hand over his heart.

Her forehead furrowed, she closed her eyes to think.

Sweet Nathalie. That was what she always did when pondering a difficult problem.

"I have a solution." She lifted her hand in the air. "A pendant. We can have a jeweler create a replica in white gold, or silver, but gold is better because it doesn't tarnish. You can wear it without ever taking it off."

The woman was brilliant. He pulled her into his arms and swung her around. "My Nathalie is sexy." He kissed her. "And beautiful." He kissed her again. "And smart." Another kiss.

She laughed. "Put me down before you pull a muscle."

He did. "Can immortals pull muscles? I don't think so."

"Asked and answered yourself." She lifted one of the bags off the floor. "I stopped by your house and brought you your own clothes."

"Thank you. I hate to keep borrowing from Kian."

"I know. Now get in the shower and get dressed. Syssi is making us cappuccinos, and Okidu has his famous waffles in the warming drawer for you. Supposedly, they're heavenly."

Andrew took the bag. "I feel bad. I know Syssi has important work to do, but instead she hangs around here to watch over me."

Nathalie made a shooing motion with her hand. "After breakfast, she plans to go to the lab. So don't keep her waiting and hurry up."

"Yes, ma'am!" He saluted.

Ten minutes later, Andrew emerged from the bathroom and gingerly headed for the kitchen to join Nathalie and the rest of the gang. Everything he was wearing was too tight, too short, and pinched in various places.

Clothes shopping had just gotten pushed to the top of the list of things he needed to do once he was cleared to go. Shoes too. His feet must've grown overnight because the shoes that had barely fit yesterday didn't fit at all today.

"Oh, my God, Andrew!" Syssi exclaimed. "How much did you grow?" She turned to Nathalie. "Am I imagining it? Or did he get even bigger overnight?"

Nathalie giggled. "I don't think so. It's just his old clothes. They look ridiculous on him."

Syssi pressed a button on her cappuccino machine, and the thing started huffing and puffing. "Wait here. I'm going to bring you more of Kian's." She snorted. "You look uncomfortable."

"I am, but I don't want to take any more of his stuff. At this rate, he is going to run out of clothes."

Syssi let out a puff of air. "Don't worry about that. When Shai was in charge of buying Kian's wardrobe, he filled out his closet with stuff Kian wouldn't have a chance of wearing before they went out of style. I was thinking of packing some of it up and donating it to the old people's home I used to volunteer at, but then I realized that his things wouldn't fit anyone there. He's too big."

"Well, in that case, I'll be happy to take some off his hands. What's his shoe size?"

Syssi and Nathalie both glanced at his socked feet.

"Fourteen," Syssi said. "I can bring you a new pair of

flip-flops he doesn't like."

Andrew nodded. "It would be greatly appreciated."

"You know what they say about men with big feet," Nathalie said when they were alone.

Andrew quirked a brow, then glanced down at his straining jeans. "I don't know. Tell me."

She stifled a giggle. "Big socks."

"Ha, ha. Very funny."

She put her hands on her hips. "Come on, it *is* funny. I know you were expecting me to say something else."

"Of course I was, woman. I have a fragile ego that needs constant reassurances." His tone was joking, but he wasn't.

Nathalie sauntered up to him and wrapped her arms around his neck. "Andrew, my love, you're a perfect fit for me."

Damn, this wasn't the answer he wanted. "So what are you saying? I need to know. Did I get bigger all over, or not? It's not about vanity, but I don't want to look disproportionate."

It's very much about vanity.

A sexy smirk on her gorgeous face, Nathalie caressed his cheek. "You take my breath away, Andrew. You were always handsome, but now…" She fanned herself with her hand. "If you thought I was jealous before, you've seen nothing yet. I'm not going to let you out of my sight."

Good enough.

CHAPTER 3: CAROL

Poor Robert.
Hell, poor Carol.
They were both miserable.

The moment he'd come back from yet another unsuccessful job search, Robert had locked himself in the bathroom.

Gazing out the window at the *scenic view* of the hotel's parking lot, Carol wondered when he was going to give up. No one would hire a guy who couldn't produce proof that he was allowed to work in the States. All he had was a fake Australian passport. It was as good as having nothing at all.

Robert was growing desperate, and so was she.

But for different reasons.

Living in a hotel in Vegas would have been fun if she could've splurged on one of the big names. A fancy one with a nice suite like the Venetian would have been great. But her modest share in the clan's profits wasn't enough for living in style. She could barely afford a cheap room in the MGM. It wasn't crappy, but it wasn't great either.

Not exactly the type of casino high rollers frequented.

Which meant that she had no prospects of making the extra money she needed. Settling for some average Joe Schmo who could part with no more than two Benjamins wasn't going to happen. Besides, getting away from Robert wasn't happening either. Not for long enough to score with the type of client who could afford her.

The dude still believed that she was his destined mate.

Poor, delusional Robert.

He bored her to death, but she wasn't going to go back on her promise. No matter what. Two weeks down and ten more to go. She would try her best to make the schmuck happy.

The one bright spot was the sex. What an immortal male could do for her, no other man would. It was mind blowing. Not that Robert was all that great—the guy was just as boring in bed as he was everywhere else—it was mostly about the venom's aphrodisiac and euphoric effect, and the incredible stamina. The guy could go for hours.

Carol sighed and plopped onto the hotel's uncomfortable chair. "Robert! Are you done yet? I'm hungry." That should get him out of there.

He was a good man; always mindful of her, making sure she was comfortable, well fed, and sexually satiated. She would've been ecstatic if things had worked out better between them. Robert could have made a great mate and maybe even a father.

But when it wasn't meant to be, it wasn't meant to be. Round pegs didn't fit into square holes, and there was no

16

point in trying to force them.

Robert could make some other immortal female happy, just not Carol. She needed excitement, adventure, a variety of partners…

That alone was proof that this wasn't it. Carol had heard that after Amanda had hooked up with Dalhu, she no longer craved other dudes and was annoyed even when other men leered at her. Maybe that was what happened when an immortal female found her true love mate.

Obviously, Robert wasn't Carol's.

She could hook him up with someone else. Her bestie Sharon would be a good candidate. If the girl found accounting interesting, she might find Robert fascinating.

Nah. Not even Sharon would think that. The only type of woman who could tolerate Robert was someone who didn't mind a guy who had absolutely nothing to say.

"Come on, Robert! I don't want to be stuck in the long line to the buffet."

Finally, the door cracked open, and Robert came out showered and shaved and wearing a fresh T-shirt.

After George had FedExed her credit cards and her driver's license to the cheap motel they had stayed at the first night, she'd taken Robert shopping. They had found all they needed at the north side outlet. It was cheap crap, but at least there was enough of it so she didn't need to send him to the laundromat too often.

Slapping a smile on her face, she got up and kissed his cheek. "Let's go. You must be just as hungry as I am."

Robert nodded and followed her out of the room.

The line to the buffet wasn't too bad; she estimated about a half an hour wait. Carol had discovered early on that feeding Robert in regular restaurants was too costly. The quantities he consumed were huge, making an all-you-can-eat buffet a real bargain for her.

While they waited, Carol did all the talking—as usual. She told him about the latest Hollywood gossip, what happened on her favorite television series, and so on until she ran out of things to talk about. His responses were limited to an occasional nod, but she knew he listened. Or maybe he just liked the sound of her voice.

When they were finally seated, he insisted she go and load her plate first, while he waited for the waiter to take their drink orders.

Such a nice guy. Why oh, why couldn't she fall in love with him?

When Carol came back with a plate full of various foods that had no culinary association whatsoever, Robert gave it an approving glance and got up. From experience, she knew that was only his first round and that he would be going for a second and a third and a fourth. Not including dessert.

Returning with a plate full of ribs, he stuffed a napkin into his shirt collar and went to work.

"Robert, I need to talk to you about something. Are you listening?"

He grunted.

"I would like you to reconsider coming home with me. I can't afford both the mortgage payments on my house and the extended hotel stay, and you can't find a job without proper papers. All of that will be solved if you just come with me. I can get you fake documents that would pass scrutiny, we will be living in my comfy house, and I can ask around if someone has work for you."

Robert finished chewing on the rib he was holding,

put down the cleansed bone, and wiped his hands and mouth with a napkin.

"How do I know it's not a trap?"

"Do you think I would betray you like that? By now you should know that I keep my promises."

"I'm not questioning you. But what about them? Your clansmen?"

"I've been told that you're invited, but I can check again and ask to talk with someone in charge."

"They can lie to you."

Carol rolled her eyes. "You wouldn't be the first Doomer to cross over. There is a very positive precedent. A wonderful love story. She fought hard to get him accepted, and he went through hell for it, but there is a happy ending. They are together."

Robert frowned. "How did they meet?"

"I'm not sure. But there were rumors that he kidnaped her off the street. Personally, I don't believe that this is how it happened, but maybe."

"Let me think about it."

"Sure." A start. He was considering going home with her. She wouldn't mention hooking him up with someone else, not yet. It might spook him.

One step at a time.

CHAPTER 4: ANDREW

One big happy family.

Sitting at the counter and stuffing himself full of waffles topped with strawberries, Andrew listened to Syssi and Nathalie chatter about this and that. He wasn't paying attention to the words being said, just enjoying the soothing sound of their soft voices and occasional chuckles. Next to him, grumpy as usual, Kian had his nose buried in the morning paper, grunting from time to time about something in the stock market and shaking the paper.

It was fucking great.

His family. His fiancée, his sister and her husband, and an entire clan of immortals who had accepted him as one of their own.

A man could spend half his life imagining a future, building different scenarios in his head, and get it all wrong. His life could take a detour into a completely different territory, one that would make him happier than he'd ever imagined he could be. And the opposite was also true. Fate wasn't kind to everyone. He was as lucky as a man got to be.

"Andrew." Nathalie nudged him.

"Yeah?"

"Do you want to go shopping? William is keeping my dad busy, so we have a good couple of hours to ourselves."

"Sure." Not his favorite activity, but any time spent with Nathalie was good. Besides, he really needed new clothes that fit.

Syssi shook her head. "I don't think it's a good idea. Bridget said you should stay put for forty-eight hours."

"No, she said she would like to keep an eye on me for forty-eight hours. But she is not monitoring me every moment of every hour. True?"

"I guess. Let's call her to make sure."

"No!" Nathalie and he exclaimed at the same time.

Kian chuckled from behind the newspaper.

Syssi crossed her arms over her chest. Never a good sign. "What if you collapse in some store? Nathalie can't pick you up. People will call 911, and the paramedics will show up."

What a role reversal. Andrew used to be the worrywart, the older, overprotective brother. He'd never understood why Syssi had been mad at him for butting into her life. He'd only wanted to steer her in the right direction. Now that the shoe was on the other foot, he realized what a pain in the ass he'd been. Hiding his amusement, he took a sip of coffee and let Nathalie handle it.

"My father can come along. I mean Bhathian, not Papi. He is certainly strong enough to carry Andrew if needed," Nathalie said with a clear note of pride in her tone. Calling Bhathian Father hadn't always been easy for

Nathalie.

Discovering at the age of thirty that the man who'd raised her wasn't her biological father had been difficult for her. She loved Fernando dearly, and he loved her back. Even his dementia hadn't diminished his feelings for her.

Both Nathalie and Andrew wondered if Fernando knew she wasn't his. After all, her mother had married him at the early stages of her pregnancy. She might've deceived him. They wouldn't know until they found the elusive and mysterious Eva. Trouble was, the woman didn't want to be found and was very good at dropping off the face of the earth. She'd already done it twice.

Kian closed the newspaper and folded it into a neat rectangle. "Bhathian is teaching a class this morning. But if you can do your shopping fast, I could spare Anandur for an hour."

Andrew cast Kian a grateful look. "That would be great, thank you."

Kian nodded. "I'll send him up." He pushed to his feet and put his hand on Syssi's shoulder. "Ready to go?"

"Yeah. It's about time I got back to work." She leaned in to kiss Andrew's cheek. "Behave, and don't overexert yourself. I'm so profoundly relieved that you made it through the transition, but after all that stress, I can't help worrying about you."

Andrew pulled Syssi into his arms. "I'm fine. I'm better than fine. I'm spectacular, indestructible, and handsome as the devil himself. Nothing to worry about."

Syssi chuckled and punched his shoulder. "Careful, Andrew. By the possessive look on Nathalie's face, she is going to put you on a very short leash."

He cast a sidelong glance at his fiancée, confirming

that the monster of jealousy had indeed risen to the surface. "I don't mind a leash as long as you're the one holding it, baby."

That got him a smile.

Fifteen minutes later, they were sitting in Nathalie's car with Anandur complaining about the cramped backseat.

"We should've taken my car."

Andrew turned to the Guardian. "As if the Thunderbird has more legroom in the back than this old clunker."

Nathalie needed a new car, and he was going to take care of it as soon as he could. It wasn't about being a snob and wanting to show off that his girl was driving something fancy, it was about safety. His Nathalie was still a fragile human, and this older model didn't have all the safety features the newer cars had. It was not safe enough for his treasure. He turned to her. "You need a new car, baby. First thing after we get home, we are going to get you a decent vehicle. This old thing is a safety hazard."

Nathalie shook her head. "Don't be ridiculous. It's old, but it has very low mileage. The car runs perfectly."

"I agree that it runs well, but is it built to the newest standards? Does it have airbags everywhere?"

"No, but neither does Anandur's Thunderbird. Isn't she vintage?"

"She sure is," Anandur said.

"Yeah, but he is an immortal, and you are not. Not yet. And until you are, I'm going to wrap you in Bubble Wrap every time you leave the house."

Damn. It was such a scary thought. Anything could happen to her. She could get into an accident, get sick…

Andrew's gut clenched. What if she was already sick?

What if that new scent she was emitting was caused by disease? The immortals wouldn't know what it was because they were immune to all human diseases, and he doubted they bothered to familiarize themselves with all the different scents mortals produced.

Andrew was still getting used to the barrage of sensations assaulting him; the smells and the sounds, the sharpness of the visuals, it was all so overwhelming it was giving him a headache. The other immortals must've learned to block it.

Nathalie rolled her eyes. "Did the transition affect your brain, turning you into a mother hen?"

"I can't wait to turn you." Andrew rubbed the back of his neck. "I don't know why, but I feel like every moment that you're still human, you're in danger."

Nathalie's features softened, and she took one of her hands off the steering wheel to clasp Andrew's. "I know how you feel. I was going out of my mind waiting for you to go through your transition and praying for you to come out okay on the other side."

Anandur cleared his throat. "If you kids want to make out, just drop me off on the sidewalk."

Andrew ignored the peanut gallery. "I know my anxiety is irrational, but there is a nagging thought at the back of my mind that I've been too lucky and that my luck is not going to hold forever. I've survived missions that most of my friends didn't, and each time I asked God why? Why them? Why not me? Don't get me wrong; it wasn't as if I wanted to get killed. I was grateful for being spared. I just wondered why. I wasn't a better man. I didn't deserve to survive more than any of the others."

Nathalie brought his hand to her lips and kissed it.

"God saved you for me, so one day you'd come into my coffee shop and fall in love with me."

A sniffle sounded from the backseat. "It's so romantic. I'm tearing up."

Andrew smiled. "You're an angel, my Nathalie, but if God wanted to reward you for your good heart and your sacrifices, he should've arranged for a more worthy man than me. I sure as hell didn't do anything to deserve you."

"Oh stop it, you two. Now you'll start a pissing contest of who is less deserving and who loves who more."

Anandur was right. They were sliding into soppy greeting cards territory.

Andrew took a deep breath and put Nathalie's hand back on the steering wheel. "Safety first, baby, both hands on the wheel."

"Yes, sir!" She winked.

"Anandur, I wanted to ask you something." Andrew turned to look at the Guardian.

"What?"

"Can immortals get tattoos?"

The guy shook his head. "Not permanent ones. Our body considers it a wound and heals it. But if you really want one you can get a henna tat, though personally, I think they're girly and they don't last long."

Henna wasn't going to solve Andrew's problem. "I'll pass."

"That's what I thought."

CHAPTER 5: NATHALIE

"It seems we have the place all to ourselves," Andrew said as he removed the sticky note pasted to the door of Kian and Syssi's penthouse.

"What does it say?" Nathalie asked.

"It's from Okidu. He's gone grocery shopping, and we are to let ourselves in. The door isn't locked."

Handing her the note, he pushed the door open and motioned for her to go in, even though he was schlepping several large shopping bags that must've weighed a ton.

Always the gentleman, her Andrew.

She waited for him to get in and closed the door behind them. "Let's put these in the closet. I suggest we leave everything in the bags. Doesn't make sense to take it all out, only to put it back in when we go home tomorrow."

"Good idea. But I want you to try on the new dress

and put on that *Angel* perfume. I love the smell."

Nathalie felt her face warm up. Was he hinting at something? Should she take another shower? Probably. She'd sweated a little. Trying to keep up with Andrew and Anandur's long strides, she'd been running around the mall and not strolling leisurely as she would've if she'd been there alone. Shopping with two impatient guys hadn't been fun. Andrew hadn't even tried on any of the clothes they'd bought. The sales lady took his measurements and handed him stuff in his size and that was it. At least he'd tried on the shoes, but only after Nathalie threatened not to leave the store until he'd made sure they fit.

"I'm going to grab a quick shower. I don't want to try on a new dress on a sweaty skin."

Andrew dropped their shopping bags in the master closet. "But you showered this morning," he said as he walked out.

"I know, but I had one hell of a workout running after you and Anandur. I feel icky, and I don't want to stink up a new outfit."

"You can never stink." He pulled her into his arms, lifting her easily for a kiss. "You always smell sexy. In fact, I want a better sniff." Still holding her up, he walked over to the bed and sat down with her on his lap.

Did he mean it? Only one way to find out.

Nathalie relaxed in Andrew's arms, snuggling up to him. "What exactly did you have in mind?"

He chuckled. "You know what I want, woman."

She had a clue, but she wanted to hear him say it. "I don't. Tell me."

With a wicked smile on his handsome face, he pulled her shirt up over her head and unclasped her bra before she even had a chance to blink. "How about I show you instead?" He started working on her zipper.

Apparently, the man had meant every word. Andrew's voice was husky with desire, and she knew he wasn't faking it. He prided himself on being a good liar when needed, but he couldn't fool her.

Nathalie was so attuned to him, knew him so well, that there was nothing he could hide from her.

"Andrew, this is gross. Let me shower first."

"No." Lifting her up a little, he pulled her pants and panties off with one hand. He was so strong now, holding her up on one palm as if she was a small child and not a healthy woman who wasn't exactly thin. Nevertheless, the size of his muscles didn't give him the right to boss her around.

"No?" She lifted a brow.

"You're clean, baby, and you smell fantastic to me. If you shower, your natural aroma will be replaced by artificial soap smell. I would much rather smell you."

"Are you sure? Does the smell of soap bother you now?"

He shook his head. "Only if it's a strong scent."

"Fine. I'll rinse myself without using soap, but that's all I'm willing to compromise on."

Andrew pinched her butt. "Stubborn woman. Have it your way. I'm coming in with you."

She could live with that.

Andrew picked her up and carried her into the shower. The thing was the size of a small carwash.

"It's cold," she complained as he laid her down on the curved bench.

"It will warm up in a moment."

While Andrew fiddled with the water temperature dial, Nathalie gathered her long hair in a tight bun, securing it by tucking the ends inside it. As the shower filled with steam, he got rid of his clothes and stepped in.

The man took her breath away; all six feet and three inches of him and his beautifully sculpted lean muscles. Or perhaps it was the steam. Nah, it was the man. Her body warmed up from the inside, and the moisture between her legs had nothing to do with the overhead spray.

Andrew's nostrils flared. "Oh, baby, spread these lovely legs of yours and let me get a lungful."

Nathalie's knees parted of their own accord, and Andrew's erection sprang to attention. He sat on the bench beside her, and she reached for him, gently rubbing the hard length. Was he bigger than before? She didn't think so. In fact, she hoped nothing changed in this part of his anatomy. The fit had been perfect before, and thankfully it was still perfect after his transition.

Andrew ran a finger between her folds. "So wet," he groaned.

The sensation was electrifying, and her hips jerked up. "Put it in," she whispered.

He did, and the moan that escaped her throat was loud. For a change, there was no need to keep things quiet, and Nathalie loved the freedom of making as much noise as she wanted and saying whatever she wanted. There was no one else in the apartment. "Make love to me, Andrew. I need you inside me."

He smirked. "I will. But first, I want a taste of that sweet pussy of yours. Spread wide for me, baby."

Oh. That was so naughty.

Andrew got between her legs and lifted them over his

shoulders, exposing her even further, then dipped his head and gave her slit a long lick. "Delicious."

Nathalie closed her eyes and let pleasure overtake her. It was a bit selfish to lie on her back and let Andrew take care of her, but she had every intention of returning the favor later. For now, she would take everything he offered and enjoy every little bit of pleasure guilt free.

He was going slow, letting her simmer, licking at her folds and lapping at her juices but avoiding her clit. Impatient, Nathalie craved his fingers inside her and his lips on that most sensitive spot, but he was in no rush.

Her breasts heavy and full, her nipples stiff and in need of a good pinch, she ached for Andrew's hands on them, but unfortunately he had only two and they were busy elsewhere. Unbidden, Jackson's tentacle porn popped into her mind.

Oh, the possibilities. Nathalie chuckled softly.

In the real world, however, Andrew wasn't about to sprout extra appendages, but she had her own two hands. Nathalie cupped her breasts, thrumming her nipples with her thumbs.

Not the same as Andrew's rugged hands. Not even close.

Closing her eyes, she imagined Andrew's long fingers on her achy nipples, pinching, first lightly, than a little harder... "Ouch!" It hurt, and she hadn't applied much pressure at all.

"What's the matter, baby?" Andrew lifted his head. "Did I hurt you?"

She shook her head. "No, I did it to myself. My nipples are so damn sensitive."

"I told you. You're about to get your period. Your

breasts are always tender a couple of days before you're due."

"Yeah, you're right, that must be it. Now go back to what you were doing." She pointed at the junction of her legs.

Andrew chuckled. "Your wish is my command."

CHAPTER 6: ANDREW

Andrew would never admit it to Nathalie or anyone else, but he liked it when she got all bossy with him. Other than Bridget, his ex-girlfriends had been guarded around him. He'd known he'd intimidated them, not intentionally, but between the scars and the secrets and his less than cheerful demeanor, women had trodden carefully around him.

It had been fine for the short-lived relationships he'd had—the distance hadn't bothered him. In fact, it had had its advantages. Fewer questions asked, fewer demands on his time, fewer opportunities for friction.

Nathalie was possessive, jealous, and bossy. If anyone had told him that he would love it, Andrew would've laughed in their faces.

The thing was, Nathalie was possessive and jealous because she loved him as much as he loved her. And the bossy part? It meant that she was comfortable with him and that he didn't intimidate her.

"Come on, Andrew, stop teasing, I'm so close." She rubbed her core against his mouth.

He lifted his head. "Do you want me to make you come? Or do you want me to take you to bed?"

She smiled with hooded eyes. "Take me to bed, big guy, and fuck me long and hard."

Damn, Nathalie talking dirty was hot. They really needed to get their own place so she could always let go like she was doing now.

"Give me ten seconds." Andrew jumped up and turned the water off, then grabbed one of the big towels stacked inside a big niche by the tub. He lifted Nathalie off the bench and wrapped her in the towel, all in one smooth move, then carried her to the bedroom.

"I love it that you carry me all the time," she said into his chest.

"Only when I want sex. It's a bribe." He deposited her on the bed and used the towel she'd been wrapped in to dry himself off. The thing was still wet, but it was good enough. Going back for another one would've taken too long.

Nathalie lifted up on her elbows. "Do I look like a woman who needs to be bribed?"

Andrew got on top of her and nuzzled her neck. "You don't, baby. It just makes me feel manly. Admit it; it's a turn-on."

Nathalie wrapped her arms around his neck. "Yes, it is. But everything about you turns me on. You're a very sexy man." She narrowed her eyes. "My sexy guy."

"Only yours. And you are mine. Only mine." For some reason, the statement carried a different meaning for him now. Before, it was a declaration of love; now, it was possession, and he felt it with every molecule of his new body.

It seemed that these immortal genes were advanced in some ways and primitive in others. On the one hand, the longevity and mental abilities were light years ahead of human evolution, but the urges and instincts were almost animalistic in nature. Not to mention the intensity. Compared to this, on a scale of one to ten—with what he was feeling now being ten—his pre-immortal human urges were at a two.

Nathalie was his mate, she belonged to him, and he knew without a shadow of a doubt that he would kill anyone who threatened to take her away from him. Tear the perpetrator to pieces with his bare hands...

Andrew shook his head. It was insanity. He had to control those animalistic urges before he became a mindless savage. How the hell did the other immortal males handle the intensity of their emotions? Was he having trouble because he was new to this?

After all, he hadn't grown up among them. The severe punishments imposed on the young immortals for breaching the clan's code of conduct made sense to him now. As their powers emerged following their transition, and puberty hit them full force with its avalanche of hormones, there was no other way to keep them in check.

Human teenage boys were hard enough to control; young immortals, who were just getting into their powers, were probably a nightmare. Between the insatiable sex drive and the predatory instincts, they could easily turn into monsters.

Jackson and Vlad seemed like well-adjusted, reasonable guys, but then restraint had been drilled into their heads for years, and the threat of a whipping was a formidable deterrent.

Maybe sating his sexual need would calm the other urges. He needed to be inside his woman. "Are you ready for me, baby?" He kissed her neck, fighting the urge to sink his teeth into the softness.

"Why don't you check for yourself?"

She was soaking, but he made himself go slow, prepping her with his fingers first. It had been a tight fit even before his transition, and if his cock had indeed grown bigger, he might hurt her.

When all three fingers slid in and out of her with ease, he deemed her ready and poised his shaft at her entrance.

Nathalie panted in anticipation. "Now, Andrew…"

He surged into her.

"Yes…" she groaned.

Andrew pulled out and pushed back again. "Like that?"

"Aha…don't stop." Her arms wrapped around him, holding him tight, Nathalie closed her eyes and let the pleasure take her.

God, he loved this woman. Loved the way she trusted him completely.

Love, he realized, that soft, tender feeling was the antidote to the madness. It allowed him to slow down and take his time pleasuring his sweet Nathalie.

Problem was, in no time at all lust overpowered love, and the savage need returned full force.

Nathalie took it all, meeting his pounding thrusts and spiraling out of control along with him. Her climax erupted, detonating his seed, together with an overwhelming urge to bite—a primitive need to mark her as his own.

Clinging desperately to his sanity, to his humanity, Andrew forced his teeth away from Nathalie's neck, licking and sucking the spot he'd nipped until his cock finally stopped shooting into Nathalie's spasming sheath.

It felt like he'd emptied a gallon of his essence into her. Good that she was on the pill. Otherwise, he would've gotten her pregnant for sure.

Except, right now, still surrounded by her welcoming heat, connected to her body and soul, he wished he could've put a child inside her.

Given their respective ages, there was no reason to wait.

I'm an idiot.

Of course there was reason to wait. Nathalie hadn't transitioned yet, and giving birth was dangerous even in today's world. He would not risk her life for anything.

Andrew lifted his head and winced. He'd made a mess. Teeth marks marred Nathalie's neck, clearly visible under the purple bruise of the hickey he'd left.

"I'm sorry, baby." He smoothed his finger over the bruise. "Does it hurt?"

Nathalie's expression was one of bliss, not pain, but it might have been the post orgasmic endorphins numbing the pain.

"Nah, just a little and it was worth it." She smiled. "And to think I was so afraid of the bite. It's really not so bad, it adds to the excitement."

Should he tell her the truth? Yeah, he should.

"I don't want to scare you, but this was more of a nip than a bite. My fangs didn't come out yet, and my glands are not producing venom, but the urge to bite is strong. I tried to be as gentle as I could because I can't give you pleasure this way. Not until I produce venom. The bite on its own is no fun."

"Well, I liked it. It was kinky."

Andrew felt his cock swell up again. Being immortal had its advantages, but he had to remember that Nathalie was still human. He didn't want her to get sore. Gently, he started to withdraw.

Nathalie grabbed his ass. "Where are you going?"

"Back to the shower?"

"Nah-ah. We are not done here."

"We aren't?"

"Nope."

CHAPTER 7: ROBERT

It was humiliating.

Just like the other illegal workers standing next to him on the corner of a building supplies warehouse and baking in the Las Vegas heat, Robert waited for some random jackass with a pickup truck to stop and offer him a job for the day.

A day's worth of manual labor; that was all he could hope for. That was his future. That was what he'd abandoned the Brotherhood and the only home he'd ever known for.

It would've been all worth it for the right female, but he was coming to the sad realization that Carol wasn't the one.

He'd betrayed his brothers for a slut.

She'd fooled him with her big innocent eyes and her soft blond curls and her beautiful, angelic face. He'd made a bad bargain and was getting no more and no less than he'd asked for.

Carol's slutty predisposition didn't mean she was without honor, though. She was going to stick to the deal she'd made with him, giving him the three months he'd asked for but not a day more.

After that, he would have absolutely nothing to show for his sacrifice.

A brief gust of hot desert wind ruffled his shirt, providing a little relief by drying some of the sweat dripping down his back.

Robert glanced at the group of men standing a few feet away from him. They kept their distance, sensing that he was different, dangerous, and not only because he topped the tallest of them by a full head.

The men knew he didn't belong with them. Except, his situation was the same as theirs—short on money and desperate for work.

He pulled out his wallet and counted what little was left of his cash; a couple of twenties, a five, two singles and some change. Carol offered to give him pocket money, but he would rather starve than take it. Her paying for all their expenses was shameful enough.

He would've loved a cold Coke, but water would have to do. The warehouse people had been kind enough to leave a cooler for the day laborers. Robert grabbed a paper cup, filled it with cold water, emptied it on a oner, then repeated two more times before crumpling the cup and throwing it into the trash bin.

A pickup rolled to a stop. The driver eyed the group of men, then pointed at Robert. "You, tall guy, ever installed sprinklers?"

Robert nodded. He knew what they looked like. That should be good enough. He'd figure it out on the job. It wasn't as if he could afford to turn down an offer.

"Then come on, get in."

Robert didn't even ask how much the guy was willing to pay. At that point, he would've accepted anything. He walked over to the passenger side of the truck and got in.

"Robert." He offered his hand.

The guy's eyes widened in surprise as he shook what was offered. "Don, but my friends call me Donny. I never expected to find an American here. Mostly it's illegal workers." He put the stick into drive, and the truck lurched forward. "I don't usually hire guys off the street, but two of my boys didn't show up this morning. The bums called in sick, but it was just a lame excuse. They were probably hungover." He winked at Robert.

Robert returned a tight-lipped smile. "I'm actually Australian." Interacting with humans wasn't something he was good at. Hell, he sucked at interacting with immortals and mortals alike. Lucky for him, the guy was a talker.

"Down under, ha?" Don imitated Robert's fake Australian accent. "What brings you here?"

"A woman." It was partially true.

The guy nodded with an expression of compassionate understanding. "A man would do all kinds of stupid things for the right woman; follow her half around the world if need be. I hope she is worth it."

Robert rubbed a hand over his sweaty neck. "I don't know."

"Is she trouble?" Don asked, looking eager. It seemed Don loved listening to gossip.

"Not really. She just isn't the kind of woman I thought she was."

"So you didn't meet her before traveling all the way to the States? Was it an Internet romance?"

"Yes, exactly." Robert liked the way the guy asked a

question and immediately offered an answer. Coming up with lies on the spot wasn't one of his strong suits.

Don shook his head. "My friend's wife left him for a guy she met on the Internet; an Australian like you. Three kids and twelve years of marriage didn't mean shit to her. She gave it all up for a guy she chatted with on the Internet. He came here and they got married and everything. Two years later, she divorced that dude as well. But at least he got a Green Card out of it."

"What's a Green Card?"

Don regarded Robert as if he was missing a couple of screws. "How can you be in the States and not know what's a Green Card?"

Robert shrugged. It hadn't been part of his briefing.

"It's a piece of paper that says you are a legal resident of the United States. It means you get treated almost like a citizen. You can work legally, pay your taxes, stuff like that." Don drifted off as they arrived at the construction site.

This Green Card was exactly what Robert needed, but there was something he was missing in this story.

"I don't understand. How did he get a Green Card out of the divorce?"

Don rolled his eyes. "Not from the divorce, from the marriage. You marry an American woman, and you get a Green Card." He enunciated each word as if he was talking to someone who had trouble understanding English.

"Yes, of course. It makes perfect sense. I guess standing in the sun all day fried my brain." Robert attempted a smile.

That seemed to appease Don, and he clapped him on his shoulder. "The Vegas sun would do that. Lucky for you, we are installing sprinklers in the basement today. Compared to the outdoors, it is nice and cool there."

As the crew supervisor explained what needed to be done, Robert understood why Don had picked him out of all the guys who had been waiting at the warehouse. The sprinkler system was being installed up on the ceiling of the basement, and Robert's height was an advantage. The added benefit Don hadn't anticipated was Robert's strength and endurance. He was fast, efficient, and untiring. It didn't take long for the crew to realize that he could do the work of three men with ease.

An hour later, the supervisor stopped by Robert's ladder and looked up. "If you want the job, it's yours, son. It pays well."

That got Robert's interest. "How much?"

"Twenty-five an hour."

He had no idea what was considered good pay for this kind of work and didn't really care. He would've happily shoveled manure for half of that. Problem was, his lack of papers.

Robert wiped the sweat off his forehead and frowned.

The supervisor put his hand on the third rung and leaned in closer. "Don't worry about the paperwork. Don will make it happen for a guy like you."

"Thank you."

Glancing at all the work Robert had managed to do in the past hour, the guy smiled. "No, thank you!"

After a while the repetitious work became automatic, and Robert's mind was freed to mull over the important information he had gleaned today. If Carol agreed to marry him, he would get that coveted Green Card. It seemed that fate had brought him to the right place at the right time.

Las Vegas was, supposedly, the best place for a quick

marriage.

Ever since Carol and he had made their residence in the MGM, he had seen many couples dressed in fancy attire walking through the lobby and the casino. Carol had explained that they were wearing traditional bride and groom outfits. She'd also explained the benefits of getting married in Las Vegas.

The problem would be convincing her to do it. She didn't love him, and Robert had lost hope that she ever would. Still, she could do it as a favor. After all, it wasn't as if her true fated mate was going to show up anytime soon.

They could get a quick Vegas wedding and then go their separate ways.

Robert let the hand holding the heavy wrench drop by his side. Saying goodbye to Carol was going to be tough. He didn't love her, but he'd gotten used to having her around.

Was caring for a person not good enough?

They liked each other and the sex was like nothing he'd ever experienced with a mortal woman. Carol admitted the same. It wasn't perfect, they weren't each other's one true love, but what they had was better than going through life alone.

Much better.

Tonight, after he got back from work, he was going to have a talk with Carol.

Robert groaned. It wasn't going to be easy. By now he had a pretty good idea who Carol was and what she was all about. Even if she agreed, he knew what her conditions would be.

After his three months were up, she would demand the freedom to screw whoever she wanted, whenever, wherever, and he had a big problem with that.

CHAPTER 8: NATHALIE

"I'm hungry." Nathalie stretched lazily. Exhausted after their marathon sex session, she had fallen asleep in Andrew's arms while he carried her from the shower back to their room.

Andrew propped himself on his elbow and leaned, dipping his head to plant a soft kiss on her lips. "I'm starving, but we need to get dressed before venturing out to the kitchen. Syssi and Kian are back."

Impossible.

They'd gotten back from their shopping trip shortly after lunch. Kian and Syssi should've been still at work. "How long was I asleep?"

"Over three hours." There was a very satisfied smirk on his face. "I tired you out, didn't I?"

"You're insatiable. If I didn't pass out, you would've kept going."

A frown replaced his smirk. "I'm such a selfish prick.

I was curious to see how many times I can go and forgot that I needed to be mindful of you."

Nathalie punched his forearm. "I'm not fragile. And I could've stopped you at any time, but I didn't want to. I was curious too."

"Aren't you sore?"

"Yeah, but I didn't feel it before."

"The endorphins."

Nathalie smiled sheepishly. "It was worth it. I lost count of how many times I orgasmed."

That erased the frown from Andrew's face, but only for a moment. "Do you want me to bring you Advil or Tylenol?"

"Don't be silly." Nathalie swung her legs over the side of the bed and got up. "I'm fine." She rubbed her belly. "But I need to put something in here."

Andrew arched a brow.

The scoundrel.

Nathalie shook her head and pointed a finger at him. "I meant food. God, you've such a one-track mind."

"I'm a man, sweetheart," Andrew said as he padded to the closet. He leaned over the shopping bags and pulled out a new pair of jeans and a pack of boxer shorts.

She followed him inside. "That's your answer to everything?"

Andrew tore open the pack and pulled out one. "No, just anything that has to do with sex."

"What kind of sex?" He'd better not fantasize about other women.

He winked at her as he pulled the boxer shorts over his muscled thighs and covered his tight ass. "All the things I could do to you, where, when, and how."

Good answer.

Nathalie leaned against the doorjamb and watched Andrew's beautiful body move with the same elegant fluidity she'd noticed about the other immortals.

It was fun teasing him about his dirty mind, but that didn't mean she wanted him to stop. Nathalie loved that Andrew was always hungry for her. He made her feel desired, beautiful.

"I love you," she said.

His jeans halfway zipped, Andrew paused and reached for her. Nathalie went into his arms, placing her palms on the taut skin of his pectorals. He was still shirtless, and she was still naked, and the skin to skin felt incredibly good.

"I love you too." He kissed her lips softly, an almost chaste kiss. "If you want to eat, you need to get dressed, baby. Seeing you naked makes me forget I have any needs other than being inside you."

Reluctantly, she left the shelter of his arms. "You want me to try on that dress?" Another red number he'd claimed would look fantastic on her. If it were up to Andrew, she would be wearing nothing but red. Correction, she would be wearing nothing at all. Which was fine by her. Problem was, they seldom had the privacy to indulge in prolonged nudity.

Nathalie sighed. They needed to find a solution that would allow them to live as a couple and still provide for her father's needs.

"You don't have to wear the dress if you don't want to." Andrew misinterpreted her sigh.

"It's not about the dress." She pulled on a pair of black undies. "I was just thinking that we need to find a way to live as a couple; to have the privacy to be intimate with each other outside the bedroom, or walk around naked if we want to."

"Where there is a will, there is a way. We'll find a solution."

As Nathalie finished dressing, she thought about Andrew's reassurance. It was the same as saying everything would be fine. There was no way to predict with surety that indeed all would be well. No one could promise that. They needed to brainstorm solutions, maybe even get Kian and Syssi to brainstorm with them, and come up with a plan.

That's how things got done.

When they finally made it to the living room, they were met by three pairs of amused eyes. Kian sat on the armchair he favored, his laptop resting on his knees, while Bridget sat across from him on the sofa, her doctor bag on the coffee table.

Syssi closed the book she'd been reading and smiled. "Hi, you two. You slept through dinner. Your plates are in the warming drawer." She pointed toward the kitchen. "Okidu is not here, so help yourselves."

"How did you know we were sleeping?" Andrew asked as he walked over to where she pointed.

Nathalie's snort was echoed by Kian's.

"This is one thing your transition didn't cure. You still snore like a jackhammer," his brother-in-law said without lifting his head.

Andrew flipped him off, but Kian's eyes were glued to the screen of his laptop, and he didn't see it. Or pretended not too.

After Nathalie had helped Andrew with the silverware and the napkins, they sat down to eat at the kitchen counter.

"When you are done eating, I want to do a check up

on you," Bridget said.

Andrew nodded with a full mouth. He was shoving food into it as if someone might take it away from him. Good thing that the plates Okidu had prepared for them were the size of platters and piled with enough to feed a family of ten. Humans, that is. Immortal males? Maybe one and a half.

When they were done, cleanup and all, they joined the others in the living room.

Bridget checked Andrew's vitals and took a blood sample. She also took a few measurements to see if he was still growing, making notes of everything on her tablet.

"Stand up, I want to check your height." Bridget took him by the elbow and walked him over to the nearest wall.

Nathalie smiled sadly. She remembered her mother checking her height and marking it on the kitchen wall. Eva had not allowed that wall to be repainted. Ever. There was no doubt in Nathalie's mind that her mother loved her, and yet she had left, never to be heard from again. The home they had shared, along with all those happy moments embedded in its walls and its floorboards, had to be sold, the memories of growing up with two adoring parents gone with it.

She couldn't understand how her mother could've done it. Even if she was on the run, she could've sent a postcard, or called from a public phone and let Nathalie know she was still alive. Didn't she know how devastating it was for her daughter, not knowing if her mother was dead or alive?

Hopefully, Bhathian would find Eva, and Nathalie would get the answers she desperately needed.

Bridget retracted the measuring tape and put it back in her pocket. "If there was any growth, it's minimal.

Tomorrow, stop by the clinic so I can take accurate measurements."

"Yes, ma'am."

"How are you feeling, any pains, aches, discomfort?"

Andrew chuckled. "I wouldn't know. The pain meds you gave me are great. I feel the swelling in my gums, but it's like uncomfortable pressure, not pain."

Bridget patted his arm. "Smart man, following doctor's orders. Anything else?"

Andrew scratched his head. "The sharpened senses are very disturbing. I'm sure that without the meds I would've had a bitch of a headache. Sometimes it's so bad that I feel nauseated."

Bridget turned to Nathalie. "I forgot to ask, but are you still getting nauseous?"

Nathalie shook her head. "I'm fine. It was the stress."

Bridget nodded and turned back to Andrew. "I'm sorry, Andrew. You were saying?"

"That's about it." He scratched his head again. "I don't know if it's worth mentioning, but Nathalie smells differently to me now."

Nathalie felt her cheeks heat up. What was wrong with him? Why was he bringing it up?

He cast her an apologetic glance. "Don't get me wrong; she still smells amazing, just different. I don't know if it's me, or perhaps it's something else. Could she…" He hesitated and cast her another glance. "Could it be an illness?"

Bridget smiled, which was weird considering Andrew's obvious worry. "I think Nathalie is perfectly healthy, but I'll run a few tests. In fact—" She turned to Nathalie. "Why don't you come with me to the clinic now?"

"I feel fine, and I need to go get my father. William probably can't wait to be free of him."

Bridget lifted her doctor's bag and motioned for Nathalie to follow. "We can stop by William's on the way to the clinic and see what's the status there. If they're fine, we can continue to my examination room and run a few tests. If not, you can take your dad up, and we will meet tomorrow."

As usual, Bridget was the definition of no-nonsense.

"Sounds like a plan. Let's go." Nathalie followed Bridget.

"I'm coming too," Andrew said.

Bridget halted him with a hand on his chest. "No, there is no need for you to be there. Let the girl breathe, she'll be perfectly fine without you hovering over her."

Andrew looked a little miffed and lifted a questioning brow at Nathalie. "Do you want me to come with you?"

From behind his back, Bridget shook her head.

"I'll be fine. I think you've had enough of that clinic. Right?"

By Andrew's frown, he wasn't happy about her leaving his side, but for some reason, Bridget didn't want him to come.

"Text me if you want me to join you. Okay?"

"I will." She kissed his cheek.

As they waited for the elevator, Nathalie didn't dare risk asking Bridget anything. If Andrew's hearing had become as good as Jackson's, he would hear them even out in the vestibule. She waited for the elevator doors to close behind them and then for the lift to start its descent. "What was that all about?"

Bridget smiled and clasped Nathalie's hand. "I'm almost sure you are pregnant. I didn't know if you wanted

Andrew to be there when we found out the results or not, and I couldn't ask you in front of him. He provided the perfect excuse, and I seized it. Now you can decide if you want to find out first and then tell him, or if you want him to be there for the test results. If you do, you can text him to come down and join you before we start."

Nathalie pulled her hand out of Bridget's and crossed her arms over her chest. "I'm not pregnant. The nausea is gone, and besides, I'm not late. I'm due in a couple of days." Her breasts were full, and her nipples were sensitive—same as every month before menstruating.

"You smell pregnant. I didn't recognize it at first because pregnant immortal females emit a different scent, and I don't interact with human females enough to be familiar with it."

"So how can you be so sure if you don't know how a pregnant human smells?"

"I stood next to one in the sandwich shop across the street and then it hit me. I knew you were pregnant."

Oh, dear God, she couldn't be. No way. It wasn't part of the plan.

Bridget was smiling broadly as if she'd delivered the best of news.

"I can't be pregnant," Nathalie whispered, tears prickling the back of her eyes.

Bridget looked puzzled. "You don't want to be? Why the hell not? You're not a teenager, you're not destitute, and you have a wonderful man to raise this child with. Pregnancy is wonderful. It's a miracle. You're going to have a baby with the man you love! What could be better than that?"

With a ping, the elevator came to a stop, and the door slid open. Bridget pulled Nathalie out and practically dragged her to the clinic. Once there, she pushed her into a chair and handed her a box of orange juice.

"Drink. You look pale as a ghost. Though I can't understand why."

Bridget seemed angry, as if for some reason Nathalie's freak-out over the pregnancy was offending her on a personal level.

A few sips from the juice helped, and Nathalie took a deep breath. She didn't owe Bridget an explanation but she needed to voice her fears. "It's not that I don't want a baby, I do, just not yet. I'm stuck in a situation that I see no solution to. I have a tiny apartment above my coffee shop, which is perfect for keeping an eye on my father at all times but too small for the three of us to live there together, or for Andrew and me to have any measure of privacy."

Bridget shrugged. "So you need to move to a bigger place. I don't see how this is an insurmountable problem."

Easy for her to say.

But the truth was that things had changed a lot since Andrew and Bhathian walked into Nathalie's life, bringing Jackson, who brought Vlad and now another kid. It was no longer just her father and her without any support whatsoever.

Furthermore, moving her father from his familiar environment hadn't resulted in the meltdown she'd anticipated. Fernando was fine away from the shop. Never mind that he thought they were on vacation in a luxury hotel. As long as he was happy, Papi could believe whatever he wanted.

Perhaps she could just keep telling him that they were on a vacation—a very long one.

Nathalie lifted her chin. "You're absolutely right. I'm

no longer alone with no one to lend a shoulder when I need it. The boys are practically running the shop, William is keeping my dad busy for a few hours every day, and I have Andrew."

Bridget crouched in front of Nathalie. "And you have all of us and our not too shabby resources at your disposal. An entire clan is eager to help you in any way we can."

Choking on emotion, Nathalie nodded. "I still didn't internalize it. After managing on my own for so long, it's hard to expect and accept help."

"Understandable." Bridget pushed up to stand. "So, what will it be? Do you want Andrew to come down and wait with you for the results, or do you want to tell him after you know for sure?"

A tough decision.

On the one hand, she could've used the support; on the other hand, she wanted to spare Andrew the anxiety and stress. He'd been through enough. Besides, there was still a small chance that Bridget was wrong and Nathalie wasn't pregnant. Why make a big fuss for no good reason?

"Let's do the tests first. I don't want to tell Andrew and then discover that it was a false alarm."

Bridget cast her a disapproving look, but Nathalie didn't care if the doctor approved of her decision or not. It wasn't Bridget's call.

"Here, fill it at least halfway." Bridget handed her a plastic container.

In the bathroom, Nathalie did her best to aim straight into the cup, but it was easier said than done. Just another advantage guys had over girls. Mission accomplished, she closed the lid on the container, wiped it carefully with a paper towel, and returned to the exam room.

Embarrassed, she handed it to Bridget. It wasn't the same as depositing a pee container through a window in the lab's bathroom and having an anonymous lab technician pick it up long after she was gone.

Bridget took it with a gloved hand and walked to the other room. Nathalie frowned when she returned after a minute. No way she had the results already.

"I want to wait five to ten minutes to make sure. But it might be too early for a urine test to detect pregnancy. If it comes up negative, I'll do a blood test." The doctor handed her a magazine. "To pass the time."

As if.

She flipped through the pages while Bridget got busy with her laptop. After five minutes Nathalie could wait no more. "Could you go check?"

Bridget looked at her with an indulgent smile. "Sure."

The next few seconds were the most nerve-wracking moments of Nathalie's life.

When Bridget returned, the wide grin on her face announced the test's results, but Nathalie needed verbal confirmation.

"Congratulations, you and Andrew are going to become Mommy and Daddy."

Oh, my God!

Nathalie didn't know whether to laugh and clap her hands or cry. Mostly, she was terrified.

"Do you want me to call Andrew and tell him to come down here?"

Nathalie shook her head. "I don't want to tell him over the phone, and if you call him, he'll freak out. He already thinks I'm carrying a disease."

Bridget nodded. "Do you want me to come up with

you?"

"No. I'll be fine, but you can do me a big favor if you'd check on my father and bring him up. I'm sure William is tired of his company."

"I will. Now, chin up, and a big smile. You don't want Andrew to think you're upset about carrying his baby."

Nathalie grimaced. "I'll practice in front of the mirror in the elevator." She turned to leave then stopped. "I don't want you to think I'm not happy. I'm just scared."

Bridget pulled her into a gentle hug. "I know. It's going to be okay. In fact, it's going to be wonderful, and I'm saying it as a mother and as your friend, not your doctor."

Nathalie wiped a tear when Bridget let go of her. "Thank you."

"You're welcome. You can't understand it now, but you will when you hold your child in your arms for the first time. Nothing in your life experience can prepare you for that magical moment."

CHAPTER 9: CAROL

I found a job. I'll be back at 6, said the text from Robert.

Carol texted back. *I'm so happy for you. What kind of job?*

Installing sprinklers.

That's great. See you in the evening.

Carol dropped her phone on the bed and did a little victory dance. Not because she was happy that Robert had gotten a job, but because she was finally free of his constant supervision. Until now, even when he'd left the hotel room, she'd never known when he'd be back and hadn't dared visit one of the fancy casinos in search of a loaded high roller.

Freedom felt so sweet after being denied it for so long. Carol had spent her entire adult life doing as she pleased and answering to no one. Being shackled to a guy wasn't fun. Especially a guy like Robert. Spending time with him was as fascinating as watching paint dry.

She was sincerely glad for him; depending on her for money was making the guy miserable, and she didn't like seeing him moping around, getting more and more depressed with each passing day. He deserved better, and Carol desperately wanted to give it to him, but without sacrificing herself and her freedom.

Moving back to Los Angeles and arranging a job for him, maybe even hooking him up with one of her friends, was as far as she was willing to go to make him happy. She could also keep indulging him with fabulous sex, beyond the three months she'd promised, at least until she found him a substitute.

Not a bad deal if she said so herself.

He would be an idiot to turn it down.

Except, he had a job now.

Carol shrugged as she pulled her best dress off the hanger. Installing sprinklers wasn't the kind of job that would make him happy. A guy who'd been the second in command for the sadist wouldn't be satisfied with manual labor.

She pulled on the clingy black dress she'd bought in one of the hotel's stores and examined herself in the mirror, smoothing her hands over the stretchy fabric covering her feminine curves. She looked sexy, round in all the right places without crossing the line into overweight. Well, maybe a little, but this was exactly what men found attractive.

Guys didn't like sticks. They liked a woman who was soft and didn't poke them with her protruding ribs or wrap bony arms and legs around them. Those tall, skinny models looked great in clothes, but not so great in the nude.

A pink lipstick and some black mascara were all she

needed as far as makeup. Pushing her feet into high-heeled stilettos, she glanced at the mirror one last time before stepping outside.

As she walked through the crowded lobby, her hips sashaying and her blond curls bouncing, Carol felt the eyes of every male, regardless of age or ethnicity, follow her.

She let out a breath, feeling like herself for the first time since her abduction. This was her gig. A sexy-childlike seductress was what she did best. She was irresistible.

"The Wynn Hotel, please," she told the cabbie.

The drive was short, and as she entered the high-class casino, Carol felt giddy like a teenage girl in a shoe store. She approached one of the tables and started her usual act.

It had taken less than an hour of schmoozing with the rich guys for her to realize that she couldn't do it with any of them.

None were attractive. In fact, she found most of them repulsive.

Strange.

Powerful, successful men were attractive even if their physical attributes left a lot to be desired, and she usually found the high rollers sexy because of their personalities and their wallets. That being said, she had some minimum standards in that regard.

What she didn't tolerate were vulgarity and rudeness.

Yes, she expected to be paid, but she also needed to feel desired and appreciated. It was an integral part of the deal.

"It's been fun," Carol said as she squeezed her target's shoulder, keeping her ass out of his reach. His pinching fingers had no doubt left bruises on her soft derrière.

He caught her hand. "Where are you going? You're

my lucky charm."

"I have to go home and feed my five kids." Usually that line worked like a charm.

"You can go home later, after I fucked you long and good."

Right.

She doubted the jerk knew how to make it good for a woman. Flashing him one of her saccharine-sweet smiles, she patted his cheek. "Oh, baby, I was looking forward to a tumble with you, but it's getting late for me, and I don't want to interrupt your winning streak." She tried to pull her hand out of his grasp while using no more force than a human female would.

Evidently, the asshat wasn't getting her elephant-sized hints. He pulled on her hand with such force that she landed in his lap. "Give me five minutes to wrap this up."

This was getting sticky. She couldn't get off him without using her strength, and if she did, it would cause a scene.

Carol didn't want to do it, but the idiot was asking for it. Pretending she wanted to kiss him, she held his fat cheeks in her hands and looked into his eyes.

Feh. It was ugly inside his head. Really ugly. The guy was a cheating, lying, abusive jerk. She was lucky she'd changed her mind and hadn't gone up to his hotel room.

With a wicked smile, Carol reached inside his mind and implanted something that was going to ruin his way of life but make it better for everyone else. From now on, whenever he considered cheating, lying, or being nasty to his family or anyone else, the guy was going to get severe stomach cramps.

His face twisting in a grimace, he pushed her off his

lap. "Excuse me. Nature calls."

She smiled and patted his flabby arm. "Of course, sweetie."

As Carol sashayed away on her spiky heels, she wondered what else she could do with her time. Shopping with the killer heels on was out. Maybe she could watch a movie. But going to the theater by herself was just sad. If she were home, she would've pulled out a new gourmet recipe off the Internet, whipped up a meal and invited a few friends for dinner. But there was no kitchen in the hotel room.

On the way back, she stopped at the gift store and bought a bunch of new magazines and the latest Nora hardcover. Which was silly, since she read mostly on her phone. It was a bit of nostalgia, a throwback to simpler times.

She missed the feeling of holding a real book in her hands.

In the hotel room, Carol grabbed another shower even though she'd showered this morning, scrubbing herself all over and soaping twice. Just in case some of the jerk's scent had rubbed off on her when he'd pulled her onto his lap. If Robert smelled another man on her, he would go ballistic.

Carol snorted. For Robert, ballistic probably meant a frown and a grunt. She couldn't picture him raising his voice to her, or anyone else for that matter. He was so mellow it was hard to believe he'd had the courage to help her escape.

Still, one never knew. Immortal males were volatile and aggressive, even the more timid among them. Poked too hard, this gentle tiger might bite.

That was why she hadn't told Robert what had happened to those he'd left behind in the monastery. She knew he'd hated Sebastian, but it seemed he'd been on good terms with the others. Learning that they were either dead or semi-dead and buried in the catacombs in indefinite stasis, he might lose his temper.

Not something she was going to risk.

A little after six, she recognized his heavy footfalls coming down the long corridor, and a moment later his keycard opened the door.

The man who entered was not the same man who'd left the room this morning. It wasn't only the toothy smile he greeted her with; it was his loose posture, relaxed facial muscles, and fluid moves. She'd known his employment or rather unemployment status had been bothering him, but she hadn't realized to what extent.

"Hi." Carol laid the book she'd been reading on the nightstand and sat up cross-legged on the bed. "How was your day?"

Robert crossed the small room in two long strides and hauled her up, lifting her into his strong arms and twirling her around. "I got paid," he said when he finally let her slide down his body and stand on her own two feet.

Reaching for his back pocket, he pulled out a folded piece of paper. "Here, this is for you." He handed it to her.

Taking it, Carol lifted a brow. Had he written her a letter? That was awfully nice of him. She loved getting love notes, especially when they sang her praise. But when she looked at what was in her hand, she realized it wasn't a piece of paper but a folded check: Two hundred dollars written out to Carol with no last name.

"I don't understand." She lifted her eyes and took in the look of pride on his face.

"I didn't know your last name so I told Don, that's my new boss, to write my paycheck to Carol. You can add your last name." He pulled another piece of paper from his other pocket. "Don came up with a great solution to my legal status. He is going to write the checks to you, as if you are the one working for his construction company. And since you are a citizen it solves his accounting problem. But you need to fill in this form." He handed her the other paper.

That could work…

But wait, she didn't want it to work. She wanted to go back to Los Angeles, to her home and her friends and her old life.

Robert, like every typical male, was oblivious to her less than ecstatic reaction. "I'll shower quickly, and we'll go out to celebrate."

Carol managed a smile. "Sure, honey, and in the meantime think about where you'd like to go."

Hopefully, he wouldn't choose the buffet. She was getting sick of the greasy, mediocre fare.

He dipped his head and stole a brief kiss from her lips before heading to the adjacent bathroom.

Hmm, the smell of a man after a day of hard work was sexy as hell and it got her all hot and bothered. When he got out, she was going to start the celebration with an hour or two of wild sex.

Dinner can wait.

CHAPTER 10: NATHALIE

Nathalie paused in front of the penthouse door, took a deep breath, schooled her expression the way she'd practiced in the elevator, and knocked.

Syssi opened the door. "You don't need to knock. Just come in."

Nathalie nodded even though she had no intention of barging into anyone's home without knocking. But that argument would have to wait for another day. Now she had a single task on her mind, and it was gargantuan.

"Hi, sweetheart." Andrew took her hand. "Is everything okay?"

"Yeah, I'm fine. Healthy as can be."

His facial muscles relaxed. "Good." He walked her over to the kitchen counter. "You have to try this cake."

Nathalie glanced at the small porcelain plate with a slice of chocolate cake on top of it and felt her stomach roil. Evidently, the pregnancy alone hadn't been the cause of her bouts of nausea, only when combined with extreme stress.

"Maybe later. I need to use the bathroom."

"I'm not sure it will still be here when you come back. I had to guard this last slice with my life."

"Then bring it to our room." Andrew had just given her the perfect excuse for taking him with her.

"Yes, ma'am." Not letting go of her hand, he grabbed the plate and let her pull him along.

In their bedroom, Nathalie closed the door, then led Andrew to the bathroom and closed that one as well.

"Missed me so much that you couldn't wait another moment?" With a smirk, Andrew put the cake on the counter and reached for her.

She batted his hands away and opened the faucets at both sinks, then dragged him to the shower and closed that door as well.

Andrew laughed and started unbuttoning his shirt. "I see that we are going to be very clean today."

And the guy was supposed to be an undercover agent? Really?

"I just don't want them to hear us," she whispered.

"I know. Good thinking with the faucets."

So he understood what she was trying to do, just not the why. "Talking. I don't want them to hear us talking."

The worried expression was back. "Why? What's going on?"

Nathalie grabbed the end of her braid and twirled it between her fingers. "I suggest you take a seat." She pointed to the shower bench.

Andrew didn't move. "Just tell me. I can take whatever you throw at me."

Sheesh, what was he imagining that she was going to

tell him that he had gotten so defensive?

"It's not something bad, I hope. I want you to sit, so I don't have to stretch my neck while talking to you." The truth was that she wanted to see every nuance of Andrew's expression as she told him.

"Oh." Andrew backed into the bench and sat down, pulling Nathalie to stand between his spread thighs. "Now you can talk."

Seeing no point in prolonging the inevitable with a lengthy introduction, she leaned into him and whispered, "I'm pregnant."

Andrew's eyes popped wide, and he stopped breathing. Like a fish out of water, his mouth opened and closed a couple of times, but nothing came out or went in.

Nathalie patted his cheek. "Breathe, Andrew."

When he didn't respond, she patted him a little harder. "Come on, don't choke on me here. I'm freaking out enough as it is."

Instead of saying anything, Andrew pulled her into his arms in a crushing embrace. That was a good sign, right?

"How?" he mumbled into her neck.

Her strong, unflappable man was shaking like a leaf, and for some irrational reason, it amused her. "You know— peg A goes into slot B—" She demonstrated with her fingers.

"You are on the pill. I see you take it every morning."

"The pill is not a hundred percent effective, Bridget said so herself. And anyway, the how doesn't matter. Fact is that we are going to have a baby."

"We are going to have a baby," he parroted quietly, then louder, "We are going to have a baby!" He pushed up to his feet and lifted her up. Twirling her around, he repeated,

"We are going to have a baby!"

Lucky for her, the shower was so big that her airborne feet didn't hit anything.

She slapped his back. "Shh... they are going to hear you."

Andrew lowered Nathalie until her feet were back on the floor, but he didn't let go and sat on the bench, cradling her in his lap. "Do you want to keep it a secret?"

"No, of course not. I just wanted you to hear it before anyone else. And I don't want my father to hear it from Kian or Syssi either. I don't know how he is going to react. He's very traditional, and he's not going to be happy about his only daughter having a baby out of wedlock."

"So we get married. We can fly to Vegas today and be married by tomorrow."

Nathalie shook her head. "I don't want a crappy Vegas wedding."

"You're right. We have this huge family now. They won't be happy if we elope."

"No, they won't. Syssi said that she'd arranged her wedding in the span of two weeks. We can wait this long to tell my father." It would be awful to keep it a secret from him even for such a short time, but it was better than shocking him.

Andrew kissed her forehead. "No, sweetheart, we need to tell him right away. You can never know what will happen tomorrow. Your father is not well. If God forbid something happens to him between now and then, you'd never forgive yourself for not telling him in time."

She grimaced. "Way to spoil the mood, but you have a point. Besides, he already thinks we are married."

Andrew arched a brow. "Did he say something?"

"No, but he calls you son and doesn't make a fuss about us sleeping together. He would have if he thought we're living in sin."

"I think you are underestimating your dad. He married your mother while she was pregnant with you."

"I'm not sure she'd told him." Fernando had been a wonderful father to her. Still was, even in his impaired condition. His love for her was unconditional. Would it have been different if he'd known she wasn't his?

It was a question that would have to remain unanswered until her mother was found.

Andrew rocked her in his arms. "Tell me, baby, what kind of wedding do you want?"

She shrugged. "A big fancy white dress, preferably before I start showing, flowers, dinner, dancing, my father walking with me down the aisle..." She looked at Andrew. "Which one, though?"

"Neither. Syssi and Kian's was the first clan wedding and therefore created new traditions. The couple enters the ballroom together and walks up to the podium with Annani officiating over the ceremony. The "whole father giving away the bride" is so outdated, and besides, the clan females have no real fathers; they have sperm donors."

"Right. It makes sense for them, but I have a father; two of them."

"So does Syssi, one, that is. And the other thing that was out was the veil. Another outdated custom."

Nathalie snorted. "Look at us, planning a wedding inside a shower. We should go out and tell Syssi and Kian. And my father if Bridget brought him up already."

"About Bridget..."

"What about her?"

"I need to tell you something."

Here it goes. Nausea hit her fast and hard.

"We had a short fling before I met you."

"I knew it was her. I just knew it."

Bridget had seemed genuinely happy for her. There hadn't been even a hint of jealousy in her demeanor, but she'd gotten mad about Nathalie's lack of initial enthusiasm.

She must've at least still liked Andrew if not loved him.

Narrowing her eyes, Nathalie asked the one thing she needed to know. "Do you still have feelings for her?" Not that she was expecting an honest answer. Even if he felt something for his ex-girlfriend, he would never admit it.

"Of course I do."

Nathalie's mouth gaped open, but nothing came out. She closed it again and swallowed, wetting her suddenly dried out throat. "What?"

Andrew shook his head. "Not love. Not any romantic feelings, but we are friends. If she ever needs my help with anything, I'll do whatever I can for her. We parted on good terms."

She frowned. "Did you break up because of me?"

Andrew rubbed the back of his neck. "Yeah. I kind of dumped her over the phone."

Nathalie sat up straight. "Andrew Spivak, that was a horrible thing to do. How could you?"

Andrew patted her knee. "Don't judge me until you hear the whole story."

"I'm listening."

"I came into your coffee shop as a favor to Bhathian. The poor guy was afraid to even talk to you. I've seen your picture, and I knew you were beautiful, but I didn't expect you to enthrall me with one smile. I knew I was going to pursue you with everything I'd got and not stop until you were mine, but I didn't want to do it while still officially seeing Bridget. Problem was, she was out of town, attending her son's graduation from medical school in Baltimore. I couldn't wait. Lucky for me, while there, she also met someone and was relieved I called to let her off the hook. So it all ended well."

Nathalie raked her fingers through Andrew's sparse chest hair. "It must be awkward for you since she is your doctor now and takes care of you." It was quite disturbing to think that Bridget had seen him naked. Worse, she'd fondled his cock to put a catheter in and then remove it.

Ugh!

"Hey," Andrew grabbed her chin and made her look him in the eyes. "Don't go all jealous Godzilla on me. I'll admit that there were a few awkward moments, but most of the time it was easy to just slip into a friendly, professional mode. You have to understand, we never loved each other or even pretended to. Our so-called relationship was nothing more than several hookups."

Andrew was telling the truth, and Nathalie couldn't fault him for any of it. She couldn't fault Bridget either. The doctor hadn't shown any signs of jealousy or resentment toward her for stealing Andrew away from her. She obviously didn't feel that way.

So why was it so hard? Why the prospect of interaction with Bridget felt so uncomfortable?

"You're okay?" Andrew asked.

"Yeah. Any other revelations before we get out of here?"

"No, that's it. I just didn't want you to hear about it

from someone else and get the wrong idea."

It had taken him a while to come clean about Bridget and himself, not that there was much to tell, but he should've told her earlier.

"Am I that scary?"

Andrew's brows dipped low. "You? Scary? Why would you think that?"

"You were obviously hesitant about telling me because you were afraid of my reaction. I might be jealous and possessive, but I'm not unreasonable."

"And that's one of the many reasons I love you. I didn't tell you because it never seemed like the right time and, anyway, there wasn't much to tell. But now that we are rushing into a wedding, I wanted you to know. I don't want any secrets between us, other than the classified government stuff that I can't talk about."

Nathalie reached up and planted a wet kiss on his lips. "You are the best, Andrew, and I love you."

His big grin was her reward. She liked to see Andrew smile.

"How about you? Any last minute confessions?" Andrew asked.

She shook her head. "None."

As Nathalie's belly rumbled, she realized that the nausea was gone and that she was craving something sweet. Other than the sweet man holding her, that is.

"Let's go. I'm ready for that chocolate cake now."

CHAPTER 11: ROBERT

Carol was sprawled naked on the bed when Robert got out of the shower. His cock swelled, and his stomach rumbled at the same time. He hadn't eaten lunch and had been fantasizing about hitting the buffet, but when given a choice between sex and food—sex won.

Robert let the towel drop.

"Come here, big boy, and give me that magnificent cock of yours," Carol husked.

He hated when she talked like that, her true nature coming through loud and clear. But his cock begged to differ. The bastard loved her dirty talk.

Obligingly, he climbed on the bed and sat back on his haunches. His cock twitched as Carol seized it in her small, soft hand.

"Glad to see me?" She pushed up on her elbow and without preamble closed her sweet lips around the head.

With a groan, Robert pushed in. Not all the way,

although he knew she could take him, just a little further into the moist haven of her mouth. Even a slut like her needed some time to get ready before accomplishing such a feat.

Wrapping one of her soft, blond curls around his finger, Robert marveled at the silky texture. Everything about Carol was soft and silky smooth. He loved touching her all over, running his hands over every inch of her. As incredible as her mouth and tongue felt on his shaft, he wanted to touch her too.

Swiftly, he pulled out and lifted her, sprawling on the bed and positioning her on top of him, with her sweet-smelling slit right where he wanted it, and his cock poised within easy reach of her mouth.

She cranked her head around and gave him a sultry smile. "I love it, how exciting."

Yeah, he knew what she was really saying; finally something different.

He'd never been the type who'd liked to experiment with sexual positions. The one he loved most was the one the humans called missionary. In his opinion, nothing compared to face-to-face experience. It was intimate, and the closest he ever got to a woman emotionally. Even a hooker's face showed her pleasure and contorted in sweet agony when climax overtook her. For those few precious moments, she was giving herself to him.

As he gripped her ass cheeks, Carol moaned around his cock, and when he tongued her slit, she arched her back and pushed back like a cat in heat. Unlike human females, she was completely hairless there, and not because she shaved or waxed or did whatever else females did to get rid of pubic hair. Evidently, immortal females didn't have any.

She was even softer and silkier down there.

It didn't take long for her to reach her first orgasm, and in turn trigger his. By the time they lay exhausted on the bed, he'd lost count of how many he'd given her.

"Wow," Carol breathed. "You must've been in a really good mood. You've never fucked me like this before."

Leave it to Carol to spoil a compliment with insinuations of inadequate prior performance and vulgar language. If she'd said made love, instead of fuck, he would've been fine with the rest. Problem was, she regarded their coupling as fucking, while he regarded it as something more. Not love, he didn't love Carol, but he cared for her and liked her.

If only she weren't a slut.

If only she cared for him just a little.

She turned sideways and propped herself on her elbow. "Why the sad face? I gave you a compliment."

He was in no mood to discuss it with her. Besides, it was what it was. All the ifs were irrelevant.

"I'm hungry. Let's get dressed and go out."

Half an hour later, they were sitting in one of MGM's fancier restaurants. Carol refused to celebrate in the buffet and had chosen Italian cuisine. It was reasonably priced, so maybe they wouldn't end up paying more. He ordered a steak and asked for a basket of bread. One steak wasn't going to fill him up, but he wasn't going to order more while Carol was paying.

"You should've ordered an appetizer. This is not enough food for you."

"I ordered bread."

"It's complimentary,"

"Exactly."

Carol sighed dramatically. "You know, all of this

could've been a non-issue if you'd agreed to come home with me. I'm a great cook."

His mouth watered. That proposition was more tempting than all of her other ones. She hadn't told him she knew her way around the kitchen, and as someone who had never eaten a home-cooked meal, he was curious. Hell, he was salivating.

But that was his hunger talking.

Besides, he was employed now, and they might be able to rent a small apartment in town. One with a kitchen Carol could put to good use.

"We're here to celebrate my new job, one that has taken me forever to find, and you want me to give it up?"

"I'm tired of living in a hotel. I want my old life back."

Selfish woman. "So do I, but the difference is that I can't go back. My old life is dead."

Carol cringed. "I know, honey. I'm sorry. But I can give you a new life if you just agree to take the risk and come home with me. No one is going to harm you. The danger exists only in your head."

Their waiter arrived with the wine, and another one brought the bread.

Robert waited for them to depart before grabbing a slice of bread and stuffing it in his mouth. He chewed it quickly and helped it go down with a drink of water. "Even if I'm willing to take the chance, I'm not willing to sit around your house and do nothing. I'm a healthy male, and I need to work."

"You can do better than sprinklers."

"Like what?"

"I don't know. What have you done before?"

"I was second in command."

Carol shivered. "I don't know how you could've worked for that monster."

He shrugged. "We all do what we have to, to survive."

They hadn't talked about her ordeal, not even once since they'd arrived at Vegas. Robert didn't know what to say, except that he was sorry, and she'd never brought it up—for which he was grateful.

In fact, he was impressed with her.

She was one hell of a tough woman. Anyone who had gone through the kind of torture she had, even a hardened soldier, would have had nightmares. But Carol acted as if it had never happened.

Instead of being angry at the world for dealing her such a blow, she was cheerful. Instead of crying at night like she'd done in captivity, she was sleeping like a baby, snuggling up to him with her angelic face peaceful and content.

Damn, if only she weren't such a slut.

Who was he kidding, Carol was more than a slut; she was a whore.

He'd been around enough of them to recognize the calculating glances she cast at men who seemed wealthy, and it didn't matter if they were sixty and older, had more bald spots than hair, or flabby bodies and fat bellies.

He chuckled. A whore and an ex-Doomer. A match made in heaven.

"What's funny?"

"Nothing. I was just thinking…" He had to come up with something.

She made a hand motion for him to continue.

What were they talking about? Oh, yeah, his ruined

military career.

"For Sebastian, a second in command meant a glorified secretary. I was supervising deliveries, ordering materials, bringing meals to the girls. Basically whatever he told me to do. But I was good at it. Things got done on time, and it kept me off the battlefield."

She reached for his hand. "Not every man can be a fighter."

Hell, that wasn't the impression he wanted her to have of him. He pulled his hand away. "I was a fighter, and as Mortdh is my witness, I was good. I just hated every fucking moment of it. The whole fucking senseless carnage." He grabbed the wine bottle and filled his glass to the brim, then gulped it all down. It wasn't going to do shit for him; no amount of wine could affect an immortal. His body would process it too quickly. Something much stronger was needed to do the trick.

Carol looked at him with a pair of big sad eyes. "I'm glad you hated it. It means you're a good man."

No, he wasn't.

He'd been part of an organization that wasn't doing anyone any good, apart from itself, that is, and he'd had no problem with it. As long as someone else took care of the killing, he'd been content to be part of the Brotherhood. If not for Carol, he wouldn't have left. He'd despised Sebastian, that's all.

The most he would've done was request a transfer to another unit.

"If you say so."

"I know so. You saved me, risking your own life. If not for you, I would be as good as dead by now. Catatonic. My mind would've snapped."

He didn't know what to say to that and grabbed another piece of bread, then chewed it slowly to buy himself time to think.

"Come home with me, Robert. I owe you, and I don't mean the three months I promised. You saved my life by sacrificing yours, and I need to give it back to you. I'll find you a good job, and you can live with me for as long as you need."

Live with her... as if he was a mere roommate, then as soon as he had a job and earned enough to rent a place of his own, he was supposed to vacate the premises and get out of her life.

He would be all alone in the world.

If he thought he could go back to the Brotherhood without getting executed on the spot, he would've been on his way already.

Or the moment after he finished his damn meal.

An angry growl escaped his throat. "Where the hell is our food? Waiter!" He waved the guy over. "We've been waiting here for over half an hour."

The guy bowed politely, his voice trembling a little. "I'm sure it's coming out any moment now, sir. I'll go check."

"You do that, and if you're not back with our orders within the next five minutes, we are out of here." Robert saw himself fisting the guy's shirt and lifting him up—just to drive the point home. But he didn't. His self-control won.

"What's gotten into you?" Carol hissed when the waiter scurried in the kitchen's direction.

"I'm hungry." He took another piece of bread and shoved it in his mouth.

She crossed her arms over her chest and pushed her

chin out. "If you don't want to tell me, that's fine. But don't lie to me."

With a grunt, he grabbed another piece of bread and then did some thinking while chewing and swallowing until the last piece in the basket was gone.

If she wanted him to come with her to Los Angeles so badly, he could use it to his advantage.

"Fine. I'll tell you what. I'll come home with you on two conditions."

"I'm listening."

He lifted a finger. "One, you marry me." He watched her eyes peel wide open. "Two, you tell me the name of the Doomer who supposedly crossed over and was accepted by your clan."

Carol swallowed visibly, then leaned toward him and whispered, "Why on earth would you want to marry me? We don't follow human customs, and you don't love me."

"If I marry you, an American citizen, I get a Green Card, and I can work legally at whatever job I'm qualified for."

Carol's expression relaxed, and she slumped in her chair. "I see." She leaned toward him again. "I can get you papers that are scrutiny-proof. The best money can buy."

"I want the real thing."

She narrowed her eyes at him. "You know that it's not enough to get a marriage certificate. For at least two years, we actually need to live together, have a joint bank account, and whatever else married people do."

Robert smiled. "I know, Don told me."

"Shit," was all she said.

"You said that you owe me and that you're going to give me a new life. Were those empty words?"

"Sir, I apologize for the wait, but here are your orders." The waiter put the plates down. "Would there be anything else?"

"No!" Robert motioned for him to get lost, picked up his knife and fork, and attacked his steak.

The fish on Carol's plate remained untouched.

"Aren't you going to eat?"

"I lost my appetite."

Ouch. "Is being married to me so disgusting that you cannot eat?"

"No, it's not you, it's me."

Right.

He arched a brow and cut another big chunk of the steak. She was killing him, but unlike her, he found solace in good food.

"Don't give me that hurt look. I mean it, Robert. I like you, you're a good man, but both you and I know that we are not each other's destined mates." She glanced at the neighboring table to check if anyone was listening on their conversation.

Pushing her plate to the side, she leaned closer to him. "Eventually, I will want to hook up with other men, and I know it's not going to work while I'm married to you and we are sharing a house."

No, it was not going to work.

As long as they were together, they would remain monogamous. What reason did they have not to? It wasn't as if she had a lineup of immortal males to choose from, and even though he wasn't the world's greatest lover, he was sure as hell better than any puny, weak human.

Did she need the extra income? Was that it? Didn't the clan provide for its members? The rumors were that they were filthy rich, but as with everything else, the Brotherhood's propaganda might have been misleading.

Spearing another piece of steak with his fork, he leaned toward her. "Is this about money? Do you need to whore yourself out to cover expenses?"

Carol pushed back as if he'd punched her in the face, and then went redder than the wine in her glass. "Why—why would you say something like that? What made you think that I—" she stuttered.

He shrugged. "I figured it out as soon as we arrived at the first casino. You were eyeing rich men like juicy steaks, or in your case fat wallets, regardless of the attractiveness of their physiques. I've been around enough hookers to recognize that look." He shoved another piece of steak into his mouth.

She closed her eyes, breathed in and then out. Looking calmer, she asked, "And you don't mind?"

Robert finished chewing and wiped his mouth with a napkin. "As I said, we all do what we need to in order to survive. And if this is what helped you pay your bills, I'm not going to judge. But as long as we are together there will be none of that. I'll get work and pay for the household expenses. You don't need to go whoring while I'm around."

"I wish you didn't use that word. It's demeaning."

She was right. He'd done it purposefully. If she hadn't made him so mad, he would've thought of something that sounded better. "What word would you like me to use?"

"Courtesan. That was what it was called when I still did it to support myself."

That was a peculiar way to put it. "What do you mean? So you don't need to courtesan anymore?"

She smiled. "You can't use it as a verb. It was a title.

But to answer your question, when I held that title, the clan wasn't doing as well as it does today, and each of us needed to work. I like sex as well as the next immortal, so why not get paid for it, right?" She ignored his grimace. "In time, however, the title lost its glamor, and I lost the taste for it. I managed to accumulate some wealth and lived off it until the clan's finances improved. Now I do it only when it's an emergency, or for fun."

"For fun? How can money be fun enough to compensate for having sex with an ugly motherfucker?" Robert gritted through clenched teeth.

"Not all men who pay for sex are unattractive. Some are busy businessmen who have no time to go looking for it; others prefer the honesty and lack of expectation. After all, paying for it upfront is often cheaper than falling into the clutches of a cunning gold digger. And some just get a kick out of it. For me, I do it because there is a thrill in getting paid. It means that I'm beautiful and desirable enough for guys to spend a small fortune on."

Astonishingly, he could understand her motives, but it didn't mean he could tolerate her fucking other men while she was with him.

Carol waited for him to respond, but he took his time. She watched him finish the last of his tiny, grilled potatoes, pour the rest of the wine into their glasses, and lean back in his chair.

"Here is my deal. If you can guarantee my safety in Los Angeles, we will get married in a human ceremony, which I guess is not valid under your clan's law. We will live together as husband and wife for a minimum of two years, and during this time you will not fuck anyone else. All the money I earn from whatever job I get will be yours and should be enough to cover the extra income you were making."

She arched a brow. "How about you? Are you going to stay true to me as well?"

He didn't miss the mocking undertone but chose to ignore it. "Of course. Why would I want inferior human females, when I have an exquisite immortal one? It doesn't make any sense. And why would you want to screw rotten humans when you have an immortal male who can satisfy you like they never could? I get it that I'm not the best lover in the world, but I'm the best you are going to get. Unless I'm mistaken, and I'm not the only immortal male you can fuck."

Carol chuckled, but it wasn't with mirth. "No, I don't have any other immortal males to choose from. I find it funny, though, that the most I ever heard you talk was when you were berating me. I don't think this is going to work. I will not invite into my home and into my life a man who doesn't treat me with respect. My gratitude is not infinite."

Damn it all to hell, he'd blown it.

There were tears in her big blue eyes, and he had put them there. Robert reached for her hand, and surprisingly she let him clasp it. "I apologize. Can we go somewhere and start this over? I know we can make it work."

She wiped a tear from her cheek. "Because I owe you, I'm willing to listen, but I don't promise anything."

Thank you, almighty Mortdh. Not all was lost.

CHAPTER 12: ANDREW

Nathalie licked the last crumbs of cake off her lips, but a little smudge on her chin remained out of her tongue's reach. "It was good. No wonder you had to fight over it."

Andrew pulled her into his arms and licked the smudge for her. "Now your face is clean. How about I look for other spots that need a tongue bath." He waggled his brows.

Nathalie shook her head. "You're incorrigible. Let's get out of here. That little piece of cake just whetted my appetite. I want more chocolaty goodness. Maybe some strawberries too."

"Of course. I'm neglecting my obligations. Before I can feast on your delectable body, I need to make sure that you and the baby are properly fed so she can grow big and strong."

Nathalie arched a brow. "What makes you think we are having a girl? It's too early to know."

Andrew wrapped his arm around her waist, which was still as small as it was before, and walked her out of the room. "Remember Syssi's vision? She saw me playing with a beautiful girl who had long, luxurious, dark hair; like her mommy." He kissed the top of her head.

"Yeah, but maybe she would be our second or third child? The fact that Syssi didn't see anyone else in the vision doesn't mean there wasn't anyone."

"Hmm, I hadn't considered that." Andrew had been imagining his daughter for so long that it was impossible for him to think about the baby as anyone other than the girl in Syssi's vision.

When they entered the living room, Andrew was expecting to find Syssi and Kian, and perhaps Fernando. But Nathalie's adoptive father wasn't there. Instead, Bhathian was sitting on the large overstuffed chair across from Kian, and Bridget was sharing the sofa with Syssi.

"Here you are," Syssi said, "We thought you guys went for another nap."

Bridget smiled. "I'm glad you are taking naps. The body makes most of its repair work during sleep."

"Well, if it's under doctor's orders... Any cake left? Nathalie wants more."

"It will be ready in fifteen minutes. Okidu put another one in the oven. Would you like a cappuccino? And I can offer you some chocolate chip cookies while you wait for the cake." Syssi got up and walked over to her cappuccino machine.

"I would love some; the coffee and the cookies." Nathalie took Syssi's spot on the sofa. "Is my father still with William?" she asked Bridget.

"They are watching a show in the theater."

"I can't believe how wonderful William is with my dad. I need to bake him something special to thank him. In fact, I owe you all at least a year's supply of my best pastries, for all you've done for my dad and me, not to mention for Andrew."

Bridget patted her knee. "You don't need to get us anything."

"Speak for yourself." Kian winked at Nathalie. "I'm all for it; preferably fresh and still warm from the oven."

Bridget cast him one of her doctor looks; the one that said "I know things that you don't". "Aren't you supposed to be vegan?"

"I don't eat the cheese Danishes."

"And what do you think the other pastries are made of?"

Even before spending time in Nathalie's kitchen, Andrew had known what went into dough, and a lot of it wasn't plant based.

Kian closed his laptop and looked at Bridget. "From your mocking expression, I guess something I'm not supposed to eat."

Bridget chuckled. "Tell him, Nathalie."

"Butter, lots and lots of butter. And the better quality the butter, the better the pastries."

Kian didn't seem fazed by the newsflash. "In this case, I'm willing to make an exception for your pastries. They are worth the transgression."

Nathalie grinned. "I'm flattered."

Listing to Nathalie as she kept the chitchat going, Andrew rubbed a hand over his jaw. It didn't seem as if she was in a rush to make the announcement. They hadn't discussed who was going to deliver the news, and perhaps she was waiting for him to do it. Or she was planning on doing it herself but was waiting for the right moment. He'd give her a few more minutes. "I'll get the cookies if you tell me where they are."

"The pantry." Syssi pointed.

This was Andrew's first venture into the pantry, which he imagined would be the size of a small walk-in closet. The place was as big as his entire kitchen at home. The good news was that Okidu had it flawlessly organized and everything was clearly labeled. Finding the jar full of cookies was not a problem. In fact, it wasn't the only one; four more jars contained other kinds of cookies, and each was labeled with a name. He took two, the chocolate chip and the macadamia.

"Here you go, sweetheart." He placed the two jars on the coffee table in front of Nathalie.

Syssi gasped. "Oh, Andrew, you should have brought serving plates. You can't just drop storage containers on the table." She got up and rushed to the kitchen.

Women. Who cared about stuff like that? It wasn't as if he put a paper bag on the table. Not that there was anything wrong with that.

"It's fine," Andrew and Kian said in unison.

"Leave the jars, Syssi." Bhathian added his voice.

"You guys." She shook her head but abandoned her quest for fancy serving platters. "I swear, if not for us women, you would've still lived in caves."

Andrew couldn't argue with that. Kian and Bhathian seemed to agree, and no one said a thing.

"How are you feeling?" Bhathian asked. "All good?"

Damn, he was so sick of people asking him that. "As well as can be expected."

Bhathian nodded. "Growing pains, ha?"

"Yeah, that, and the enhanced senses. Too much input."

"You'll get used to that. In time, you'll learn to ignore it." Bhathian clapped his palms on his thighs. "Well, now that you're out of the woods, it's time for me to book that flight to Rio. I'm heading out on the first available seat I can find."

"Ahem," Nathalie cleared her throat. "I think you should wait a little longer."

Bhathian's bushy brows drew tight. "Why?"

She glanced at Andrew and smiled. "We are expecting."

The brows drew even tighter. "Expecting what?"

Bridget snorted. Syssi slapped a hand over her mouth. Kian looked just as puzzled as Bhathian.

"We are expecting a baby. You're going to be a grandpa."

Syssi erupted with a, "Yay! I'm so happy!" She pulled Nathalie to her feet, hugging her gently as if she was made from eggshells. "I need to be extra careful with you now." She patted Nathalie's flat belly.

"Congratulations." Kian pushed to his feet and offered Andrew his hand. They shook and then bro-hugged.

Through it all, Bhathian didn't respond. Not moving a muscle, he looked paralyzed.

Nathalie frowned and walked over to him. Crouching, she took his hand. "What's the matter? This is good news. Why aren't you happy?"

"I'm terrified," he admitted. "I don't want to lose you. I just found you, Nathalie. How could you do this to me?"

Talk about the wrong thing to say. Any other woman

would have gotten offended and turned her back on him, but not Nathalie. "Why would you lose me, Bhathian? What nonsense have you gotten into your head?"

"You're not immortal. And you can't transition while pregnant. Women die in childbirth, even in this day and age and with the best type of care." He turned to Bridget. "Am I wrong? Doctor?"

She shook her head. "It happens. Not a lot, but it still does. Last I read, one in every five to six thousand births ends with the mother's death, either during childbirth or shortly after."

Damn, that was way more than Andrew would've guessed, and it scared the crap out of him. And then there was the realization that Bhathian was right about Nathalie's transition. He didn't need Bridget's education to know that it couldn't be attempted while she was carrying a child. Now they would have to wait until after the delivery, and God knew what might happen during those nine months and then the birth itself.

"Nathalie is strong and healthy, Bhathian. You're panicking for nothing," Bridget said with complete conviction, which eased the tight vice squeezing Andrew's heart.

"And there is my vision," Syssi added. "I saw Andrew playing with his healthy, beautiful daughter. They looked so happy."

Bhathian pushed to his feet, his large body swelling with aggression as he got in Syssi's face. "Did you see my Nathalie in your vision?"

Kian was there in a flash. His hand on Bhathian's shoulder, he pulled him back. "Easy there. Syssi is not the enemy."

Bhathian hung his head. "I'm sorry, Syssi. I'm just so fucking worried... forgive my language, ladies... But I still have to ask, did you see Nathalie in your vision?"

"No, I didn't," she admitted, then quickly added. "But that doesn't mean anything. Andrew and the girl were playing in the park. Nathalie could've been sitting on a bench nearby, or stayed at home, or gone shopping."

He nodded. "I know. But I also know that the next nine months are going to be torturous for me."

"You should talk." Nathalie snorted. "Typical male. I'm the one that will get to be the size of an elephant, and you are complaining about how difficult it's going to be for you?"

"You're right. Come here." He opened his arms and Nathalie went to him. Putting her cheek on his chest, she sighed. He closed his arms around her with infinite care. "Whatever you need, I'm here for you. And you—" He pointed at Andrew. "—are a dead man should anything happen to her. Understood?"

"Yes, sir."

Nathalie let Bhathian get his fill, then pushed against his chest. Reluctantly, he let her go. "So what's the plan? Are you kids getting married or what?"

"We are, and the sooner, the better. I don't want to walk down the aisle with a big protruding belly." Nathalie glanced at Syssi who took the hint in an instant.

"Give me three weeks. With Amanda's help, we can have it done, including the most gorgeous custom-made wedding dress you can dream up."

"Six," Kian said.

"Why six? I did ours in two."

"Because we can't hold the wedding here. The enemy

knows where we are, and they will be sending new troops. Probably already have. I'm not going to risk bringing the entire clan here for the wedding. I propose we hold the reception at our Scottish stronghold."

Syssi's eyes sparkled, and she reached for Nathalie's hands. "Oh, Nathalie, it's going to be so beautiful. I'm already jealous. What Kian calls a stronghold is an old, majestic castle. You are going to have a real princess wedding."

Kian smiled. "It's not a done deal yet. I have to call Sari, get her okay, and see that she can have everything ready in six weeks."

"I feel uncomfortable about it," Bridget said quietly.

For a moment, Andrew thought she was going to say something about their prior involvement.

Nah, it wasn't Bridget's style.

"What do you mean?" Kian asked.

"All of us going to the wedding and leaving the keep unprotected. We've never done something like that before, and we don't have the procedures in place."

Kian waved a hand. "Don't worry about it. We will have it locked down and well guarded by our human security. Sari faced the same concern when she had to leave their castle behind and come to our wedding. Worse, they had to leave it exposed without the perpetual shroud they keep over their stronghold because everyone came here."

"Yeah, you're right. But we will need to keep it short."

"Naturally. Three days tops, that's all I can afford. If some of the others opt to stay longer, that's fine."

"Andrew and I will stay. A honeymoon in Scotland sounds amazing. Right, Andrew?"

As if he was going to deny her anything. "Sure, baby, whatever you want is fine by me. I just hope that I don't get fired for taking so many vacation days."

A hopeful expression on his face, Kian squeezed his shoulder. "You can always come work for the clan."

"It would be great if I can find Eva in time for the wedding," Bhathian said to no one in particular.

Nathalie turned around to face him and took his hand. "I don't want you to go crazy about it and take unnecessary risks. If you find her, great, if not, then not." She chuckled, but there was a sad undertone to it. "Instead of a mother and a father, I'll have two fathers at my wedding."

Andrew shook his head. "You know how it sounds...two fathers."

"Yeah, well, whatever." Nathalie suddenly looked bothered.

"What's the matter, baby?" Andrew picked up her hand and brought it to his lips for a kiss.

"I still want Fernando to walk me down the aisle. I know you have a different tradition, but this is something I always dreamt about, and I'm sure so did he." She glanced at Bhathian. "I hope you don't mind..."

"Not at all. It's important to you and Fernando, and it's your wedding day. You get to choose what you want to do. Right, guys?" He swept his eyes over everyone present, his stern gaze daring anyone to object.

"Yes, of course," Syssi hurried to agree.

Kian shrugged. "For all I care, you can get married on a beach in Hawaii, wearing swim trunks and a bikini. And I don't even care who will wear what. Though I have to admit that I'm not looking forward to seeing Andrew in a bikini."

Andrew rubbed his chin. "That's not a bad idea. I love

it. We can have a luau, with hula dancers and fire eaters…"

Three pairs of irate female eyes speared him.

"It was just a thought…" Andrew mumbled, looking at Kian for support.

With a smirk, the traitor shook his head.

CHAPTER 13: CAROL

Screw her promise. She should dump Robert now before he managed to soften her resolve.

Even after all he'd said, or rather the way he'd said it, she was letting him hold her hand as they made their way back to their room.

Carol, you are a soft-hearted fool.

In her defense, holding hands with a guy was a novelty, and it felt surprisingly good.

Her lovers from her courtesan days had never acknowledged her in public, and her modern-times hookups were of the *badabing badaboom* kind. No handholding or leisurely strolls involved.

In his other hand, Robert was carrying a shopping bag with the fruit-flavored vodka they'd bought at the gift shop. He'd wanted the plain stuff, but she'd told him that she hated it, and they'd compromised on a brand with a fruity flavor.

Carol smirked. If Robert thought to get her buzzed so

she'd agree to his terms, he was underestimating her the same way most males did. She might've not been educated or highly intelligent, but she was a pro at the art of negotiation.

Back in their room Carol took the only armchair, while Robert opened the fruit-flavored vodka and poured a glass for each of them. He handed her one, then lifted the chair from behind the desk and brought it next to her.

Carol took a sip, waiting for Robert to start his spiel.

"You know what I want. Tell me what you want," he started.

Not bad for a beginner, she had to give him points for tactics. Letting the other side state their demands first lowered their defenses. Except, she was so ahead of the game she could run circles around him.

"I'll start with something simple. You never ever use that offensive W word, or the P word either. In fact, I don't want you to mention my old occupation at all."

Robert raised his glass. "Deal."

She smiled sweetly. "Your turn."

"I've already told you the big items, but it seems you want to discuss the small ones first, so let's hear them all."

Carol scrunched her forehead as she thought what else she wanted from Robert. She couldn't ask him to change his dry and boring personality. That was who he was, and no amount of effort on his part would turn him into charming and worldly. These qualities were innate, not learned. Other than that she had no complaints. He was a good-looking guy, clean, respectful—most of the time—not selfish, not arrogant, and seemed to be a hard worker.

Fates, if only he weren't such a bore.

She shrugged. "That's all. Up until today you treated

me with respect and never got angry or raised your voice at me. I liked that about you, and I want you to continue treating me like this."

"I'm sorry I blew up before. Usually it takes a lot more to get me so angry, but without meaning to, you dealt me a harsh blow."

What was he talking about? "How so?"

Robert sighed and emptied the contents of his glass down his throat. "In so many words, you made it clear that once I can support myself, you want me out of your home. Out of your life too. I don't have a home anymore, Carol. I can't go back to the Brotherhood because I'd be executed on the spot. And if you cut your ties with me, I'd be all alone in the world. Doesn't seem like a fair reward for my good deed."

Poor guy, he'd misunderstood what she had planned for him. "Robert, I would never dump you like that. What I had in mind was to introduce you to some of my friends, my cousins, as it happens. Maybe one of them would turn out to be your true love mate? Ha?"

Robert was taken by surprise. "You would do that for me?"

"Sure. I don't want you to be lonely."

"What about you? Aren't you lonely?"

With a sigh, she put her glass down on the table. "As you said before, there are no immortal males I can pick and choose from. But I have a big and caring family, and some of them are close friends who I love hanging out with."

"It's not enough."

She snorted. "You're telling me? But what are my options?"

"Easy. Me."

"We like each other, Robert, but you don't love me, and I don't love you. Each of us has a true love mate somewhere out there in the world. If we stay together, we might miss the chance of finding that special someone."

For a few moments he didn't respond, sitting with his elbows on his knees, the empty glass clutched in his hands, and his head bowed. She didn't press. Robert wasn't a fast thinker; he needed time to figure things out. A good quality, since he didn't rush into things the way she often did.

Less chance of getting in trouble.

When he lifted his eyes to her, she was hit by the intense emotion she saw in them and braced herself for whatever conclusion he'd arrived at.

"You don't know for a fact that there is someone out there for each of us. We can spend our entire long lives searching for them and never find them. We have something here, Carol. It isn't the all-consuming love of a true mate, it's not a perfect match, but I suspect that this is as good as it's going to get. Let's not squander this opportunity for companionship. It must be better than having no one."

Damn, he had a point. But...

"It may be true for me, but you're giving up on an opportunity most immortal males would kill for. I just offered to introduce you to a bunch of immortal females who would love to get their hands on a handsome guy like you. One of them might be your true love match."

That shut him up. Not that she wanted him to stop talking. They were finally having a real conversation.

After a moment or two, he looked up at her with such a stubborn expression on his face that she knew what he was going to say before he said it.

"I'd rather hang on to what I have than give it up for a

dream. I don't need perfection. You're a beautiful, sexy female. You're nice to everyone. You have a good heart, and you're trustworthy. Doesn't get better than that. Not for me."

Carol couldn't help a smile. It was so sweet of him, but he was so misguided. Regrettably, she needed to shatter his illusions.

"Robert, sweetie, it's not going to work. I can't promise you fidelity, and I know you won't be able to compromise on that."

He looked so hurt that her heart ached for him.

"Why? What's so special about these humans that you would choose them over me? I know I'm not perfect, but I'm decent enough."

She sighed. "You might be, but I'm not. I'm just not the type of female who can settle down with one male. I need the variety, the excitement of the chase, of new partners. Every morning when I wake up, do you know what I think about first?"

"What?"

"Where I'm going to go prowling for hookups, and what I'm in the mood to cook. That's it. Occasionally, I invite my friends to dinner, and once or twice a week we go clubbing. That's my life. I have no other interests. I'm shallow, and I'm a pot head, which means I like to smoke pot in case you didn't know." Curiously, though, she hadn't had the urge to smoke or vape lately.

"I know what a pot head is." Robert got up and started pacing. "Are you satisfied with that? Isn't there anything else you would've liked to do?"

"Nope. I like my life the way it is."

He raked his fingers through his short, thick hair. "Fine, I see there is no changing your mind. After my three exclusive months are up, I move to a spare bedroom in your house, and you can do whatever you want with whomever you want. We will remain friends and roommates: nothing more. But the same holds true for me. If any of your friends want to hook up with me, are you going to be fine if I take them to my room?"

"Sure," she said without much conviction. "Roommates with benefits."

"What do you mean?"

"We can still have sex." She winked.

Robert shook his head. "I don't know. We will have to wait and see how it goes. But are you okay with the rest of the deal? The fake marriage and everything?"

Why not? It wasn't as if she was going to find her true love anytime soon. Two years were a blink of an eye in the lifetime of an immortal. "Yeah, I guess, unless I can get you legit papers some other way."

"You think you could?"

"I'm not sure. I'll have to call and make arrangements for your arrival. I want to get an okay and a guarantee that you will be treated like a hero and not an enemy."

CHAPTER 14: ANANDUR

"Would you accept charges for a collect call from Mexico, sir?" The operator asked.

Anandur frowned. He didn't know anyone there and wasn't aware of any clan member vacationing south of the border. Not that he'd checked the register lately. Perhaps one of the young ones had gone for a short visit to Mexico. Maybe he or she lost a wallet, or it might have been stolen. But why would they be calling his number?

"Who's calling?"

"She wouldn't give her name. She says she's your girlfriend."

Anandur's breath caught. "Put her through." The only one who considered herself his girlfriend was Lana.

"Anandur?"

The sound of her voice was such a tremendous relief that he had to sit down.

"You there? Anandur?"

"Yes, I'm here. Where are you? I've been worried sick about you."

"You miss me. I knew you liked me for me and not the information I give."

Yeah, he did, a little. "What's going on, Lana, is everyone okay? I have been imagining the worst. I was afraid that Alex found out about me contacting you and did something horrible to you and the others."

"He found out something, but we don't know what. He thinks the FBI is after him."

Anandur chuckled. "They might be."

"Are you FBI?"

"No, I'm not."

"So why you afraid Alex find out about you?" As usual, Lana was suspicious as hell.

"He knows me. We used to hang out in the same circles. Not the criminal ones, just socially. If he found out about me snooping around his business, he would have known my people are after him. And believe me, he is much more afraid of us than he is afraid of the FBI."

"Hmm, more than the FBI you say?"

"Definitely. By the way, I'm glad you're calling me from a public phone. He has listening devices all over that ship, and now that he is ultra-paranoid, even your burner phone is not safe."

"I know. He is very suspicious. We do everything to look normal for him. I went to buy supplies, and I call you. Did you talk to your boss?"

"Yes and he had a sweet deal for you, but you were gone before I could tell you about it."

"What deal?"

"How would you girls like to own and operate a

dinner cruise in Hawaii? Affiliated with a high-end hotel?"

"You joke?"

"No joke. Serious offer."

"Let me think." Lana was quiet for a few moments. "You help us start new? Papers and everything?"

He considered saying yes but ended up sticking to the truth. "I'm not sure we can get you real papers, but I can promise you that the fake ones will be top notch. I think it's not a big deal given everything else my boss is offering. You'll never get a better deal than that."

"I'm not complaining. It's a good deal, too good…"

Suspicious Russian.

"Why would I lie to you, Lana? To get away from Alex, you would've been happy with any help my boss offered. Am I right?"

"That's why it smells like fish. Why would your boss offer more? No one gives things for nothing."

She was right. But Kian was a businessman, and he saw opportunities where others didn't.

"You girls are an experienced crew and highly motivated to succeed. My boss is opening a new hotel in Hawaii, and when I told him about you, he saw an opportunity. You get what you want, and he gets a profitable side business for the hotel. Win-win."

"So the profit goes to him?"

"Part of it. Do you really want to negotiate the details now? You haven't escaped Alex yet."

"*Da*, I know. I will speak with others, and we make a plan. I'll call you from our next stop."

"You do that. And, Lana?"

"Yes?"

"Be careful. Super careful. Don't talk about any of it

on the boat or even near it. Check your pockets and your clothes for listening devices. I don't want anything to happen to you."

"I knew you like me. Tell me, don't be shy."

Hell, why not, he could make the woman happy. "I like you, Lana. Stay safe."

"I will. And I like you too."

Anandur rubbed his beard-covered chin. Alex had taken the boat to Mexico, which presented a problem. He had no idea how to plan a rescue and an extraction operation on foreign soil. Hell, he didn't know the first thing about it, especially since it involved a boat the size of a cruise liner.

This was a job for Andrew.

Question was whether the guy was operational. He'd just emerged from his transition and was still adjusting to his new body. For a fee, however, they could always turn to Turner, Andrew's ex-boss and commander.

A creepy fellow, but extremely effective at what he did.

CHAPTER 15: KIAN

"Do you have a moment?" Brundar walked into Kian's office and sat down on the chair facing Kian's desk.

"What's up?"

"Carol called. She wants to bring her Doomer home with her."

Kian had been expecting this. She couldn't keep living in a hotel in Las Vegas indefinitely. As someone who didn't hold a job in any of the clan's organizations, her share in the clan's profits was small. And as far as he knew, she didn't work outside the clan either. She had enough income to lead a comfortable life but not an extravagant one.

"What do you think?"

Brundar shrugged. "We don't know anything about the guy except that he saved Carol. It might have been a setup. Let her go free so she could lead him to us. On the other hand, Carol claims he still doesn't know we cleaned up his home base, which means he didn't try to contact them."

Kian rapped his fingers on the glass top covering his table. "I don't want him anywhere near here, not unless he is under lock and key or monitored twenty-four-seven. Can we ensure Carol's cooperation?"

Brundar shrugged. "She didn't spill under torture."

True, and it was quite remarkable, but in her home, surrounded by her friends, she might let her guard down and blurt something. Besides, she would have friends visit who were even less careful.

"I'm not comfortable with it. The only way I may consider it is if we bring him here and keep him guarded the way we did with Dalhu. Slap on him one of William's new locator cuffs, the kind that interferes with the cellular signal."

"Carol wants to bring him to her home."

"Can't allow it. If she wants to be with him, she will have to move into the keep."

Brundar leaned forward and snatched a notepad and a pen from Kian's desk, then scribbled something on it.

"Here is Carol's number. Call her." He pushed the notepad back toward Kian.

"Do I really need to deal with that myself?"

"You're dealing with it one way or another. It will be done faster without using me as a go between."

Good point.

Kian picked up the handset of his landline and dialed the number.

Carol answered on the second ring. "Hello? Who is it?"

"Kian. Are you alone?"

"Yes, Robert is at work."

"Good. You can't take him to your home."

"I can't keep living in a hotel in Vegas either, and I promised him I'd give him three months. And even after those are up, I need to make sure he is taken care of. The guy has nowhere to go. No identity, no papers, and no people to call his own. I owe him for what he sacrificed for me. I know I'm not an important member of the clan, and you don't have to help me, but I'm asking anyway. It's the decent thing to do."

Kian sighed. "I know, Carol, and I'm not turning my back on you or that Doomer. But we need to take precautions. If he comes here, I need him monitored around the clock, and that means he needs to stay here at the keep. He'll have to wear a locator cuff. If you want to be with him, you're welcome to move into the keep too. I want everyone to do so eventually, so it will only mean hastening the process for you."

"What about my house?"

"You can rent it. Make a few bucks."

"I'll run it by Robert, but I don't think he will go for it. He wants real papers, he wants a good job, and he wants a new life. That's not what you're offering him."

True. But what else could he do? It wasn't fair. If the guy was legit, then he deserved all that he'd asked for. Problem was, they had to make sure before they allowed him in.

"I'll give him something to do until we can be sure he is not still working on behalf of the Brotherhood. I'll have Edna probe him."

"Can I call you back?" Carol didn't sound happy.

Not that he blamed her. He wished there was more he could offer Carol. After what this poor girl had gone through, he would've loved to shower her with kindness. But safety always came first.

"Yeah, here is my cell number." He recited the digits. Kian never gave it away to anyone other than the Guardians, council members, and his mother and sisters. But he was making an exception for Carol.

It was the least he could do.

"Thanks."

It sounded more like thanks for nothing. But there wasn't much Kian could do about it.

Life wasn't fair.

CHAPTER 16: LOSHAM

Losham stared at the scorched earth of what used to be his son's base. Were Sharim's ashes scattered on the ground? Was he inadvertently stepping on his son's remains?

The fire department had concluded that it had been an accident; the gas tank catching fire and exploding for some reason. It had been an old building, they'd claimed, and someone had renovated it without pulling permits. The work didn't comply with current safety codes.

Bullshit.

Losham knew who was responsible for his son's death, and he was going to make them pay. Dearly.

He wasn't a violent man, and the use of force had never appealed to him. Losham's sharp mind was much more formidable than any weapon or military force. Like an invisible puppeteer, he could cause damage on an unimaginable scale just by pulling the right strings. But that was before it had become personal. Now he would've given anything for the military acumen and training of his brothers so he could hunt and kill each and every one of those responsible for Sharim's demise.

Careless of his Salvatore Ferragamo loafers, he kicked a stone. The shoes were ruined anyway, covered with ash and scuffed from the broken debris strewn about.

The remains of what used to be a fountain stood in stark relief against the canvas of the desolate landscape, showing remarkably little damage compared to the utter destruction of the rest of the compound.

Like a sad monument to Sharim's memory.

But there would be no other. No mourning was allowed in the Devout Order of Mortdh Brotherhood, no tributes to the dead, no memorials to friends lost.

Death was celebrated, not mourned.

Losham had never believed in any of the crap the Brotherhood's propaganda spewed. In fact, some of the ideas had been his. For him, it was a game of wits. Could he outsmart everyone, from leaders of countries to simple garbage collectors, leading them to believe in whatever the hell he wanted them to? Could he move the chess pieces with his ghostly hand and deal Annani, her clan, and humanity a checkmate?

It used to satisfy him like no mindless bloodshed ever could. But now he craved his enemies' blood. When he'd send Sharim over, the hunt for Annani's immortals hadn't been a priority for Losham. It had been all about gaining influence and playing the game. He'd left the "how" of the hunt up to his son.

It had been a mistake that had cost Sharim's life. Losham had trained him well, and his son had been a smart man. But no one could plan and plot like Losham. He should've given it more thought.

Annani and her tiny clan of average intelligence immortals stood no chance against Losham's brilliance. Once he devised a plan and put it in motion, they would be dropping like flies into his elaborate spider web.

He could've eradicated them from the face of the earth a long time ago, and the only reason he hadn't was his love of the game and his pride. With the clan gone, there would be no worthy opponent for him to outsmart.

"Sir, forgive me for interrupting your investigation, but we need to go. Your aircraft is ready." His assistant waved a hand toward the limousine parked outside the crumbled wall surrounding what used to be the monastery.

"Yes, of course." Losham lips lifted in his well-practiced smile.

Sadly, he had to lie to Navuh about the purpose of the trip. Showing grief for his son would've been viewed as a sign of weakness and lack of devotion to the cause. Navuh would've never allowed Losham to visit the site. The stated purpose of his trip was a vacation in Las Vegas. For the sake of appearances, he'd reserved the penthouse of one of Sin City's most luxurious hotels, and purchased the services of several pretty girls from the best escort service in town.

In secret, he'd chartered a private flight to Santa Barbara, planning to be back before anyone noticed he hadn't been sleeping off a night of debauchery in his room.

The only one Losham trusted with his secrets was his assistant, Rami, and that was because Rami had a secret of his own that only Losham was privy to. A secret that if found out would get him tortured and killed. The Brotherhood had absolutely no tolerance for gay men. Not even as guards for the harem.

CHAPTER 17: NATHALIE

Bridget put down her tea on the counter and crossed her arms over her chest. "How did your father take the news?"

Nathalie stirred sugar into her coffee, then added cream. "I didn't tell him yet."

Syssi had called for an emergency breakfast meeting to discuss wedding plans, inviting Bridget and Amanda. They had about an hour before Amanda and Syssi had to leave for work. With no patients waiting for her, Bridget wasn't in a hurry, and Nathalie could basically show up at the coffee shop whenever she pleased.

It was beyond wonderful, but old habits still had her waking up with a feeling of urgency every morning. She had to remind herself that everything was taken care of and she could take her time.

Bridget frowned. "Why not?"

"Last night, when William brought my father back to

the penthouse, he was so tired that I decided to save the wonderful news for today and tucked him in bed instead. He is still sleeping."

Cappuccino cup in one hand, her other arm crossed over her chest, Amanda asked, "Before we start throwing ideas around, do you have any preferences?"

Nathalie finished chewing a piece of toast and washed it down with orange juice. "As I told Bridget and Syssi yesterday, all I want is a beautiful white dress and my father walking me down the aisle. My girly fantasies never carried me past that point."

Amanda tapped her fingers on her bicep. "If you don't want to feel like a guest at your own wedding, you need to put some more thought into it. When you walk down the aisle, what do you see?"

Nathalie closed her eyes and tried to visualize. It wouldn't be in a small, community church as she had always assumed, so she imagined the dining hall of a medieval castle. Too big. She could almost hear the organ music reverberating from the stone walls.

"What's the frown about?" Syssi asked.

"I'm imagining the castle in Scotland, and all I can see is a huge dining hall that feels awfully empty, with every little sound echoing from the walls."

Amanda snorted. "Don't worry about it. The place is going to be packed, bursting at the seams with people. I don't know about the echo, but I can ask Sari to check the acoustics."

Nathalie's eyes widened. "How many guests are we talking about?"

Bridget grinned. "Everyone is going to come to your wedding; around five hundred and fifty people."

"Why? I don't know every person in the clan, and I'm sure Andrew doesn't know that many either."

Syssi patted her knee. "Yeah, it was a big surprise for me too. I hate big parties, and I freaked out when Kian told me he was inviting every member of the clan. But then he explained the significance of it, and I realized I had no choice. I couldn't be selfish about it and have my way. I had to bite the bullet. It turned out beautiful, though, and I didn't feel overwhelmed at all. I even managed to enjoy myself. You are an outgoing girl, not an introvert like me, you're going to love it."

"It makes sense in your case since Kian is Annani's son and one of the most important people in the clan. But why would everyone drop everything to come to Andrew and my wedding? They don't know us. We are not important."

Amanda smiled indulgently. "I see Andrew and Bhathian did a shitty job explaining the history and dynamics of the clan to you. I'll have to rectify the situation, but not now. Maybe I'll come back in the evening. The one thing you should understand is that every new Dormant female who is not a descendant of Annani represents a new hope for the clan. A new bloodline. So you are a very important member of the clan. Also, yours is going to be only the second wedding in the clan's history and therefore a huge deal."

"So why didn't you and Dalhu get married yet?" Nathalie blurted before thinking it through. "I'm sorry. It's none of my business."

Amanda harrumphed. "The thing about large, tight-knit families is that everything is everyone's business. No privacy whatsoever. Get used to it."

112

It didn't escape Nathalie's notice that Amanda hadn't answered her question, but she didn't want to push. Instead, she turned to Syssi. "Over five hundred people, huh?"

Syssi nodded.

Nathalie closed her eyes again. With the number of guests dictating the visual, the one that popped behind her closed lids was the scene from Hogwarts' dining hall in the *Harry Potter* movie.

The rest of the pieces fell into place. "If the castle's banquet hall is big enough, we can have long tables on both sides of the room with a big center aisle between them, and an altar on a podium at the far end so everyone can see the ceremony. I don't want big flower arrangements because they interfere with socializing. Food can be whatever as long as there is enough of it and it's tasty. As to the booze, given your Scottish heritage, we need a lot."

Amanda nodded approvingly and offered her hand to Nathalie for a handshake. "It's a pleasure doing business with you, Nathalie. Decisiveness is an admirable quality."

"Well, it's a quality that emerged out of necessity. Running a business basically by myself, with no time for anything, decisions had to be made quickly. I didn't have the luxury of thinking things over."

"Nevertheless, it's admirable." Syssi filled a tall glass with orange juice and handed it to Nathalie. "Drink! Vitamin C is important for a pregnant lady."

Nathalie took a sip. "Thank you for the compliment, but it's misplaced. You forget that I also had no one to answer to. If I screwed up and made the wrong decision, I might have had trouble paying my bills, but no one was going to berate me, other than me, that is."

Amanda shook her head. "You really need to learn to

take a compliment, Nathalie. The right answer is thank you, nothing more."

"That's what I keep telling her, but she never listens to her Papi."

Nathalie turned around and smiled. "Good morning, Daddy, did you sleep well?"

"I slept like a baby. The beds in this hotel are top of the line. We should buy the same kind of mattress for our home. Your mother always complains how lumpy ours is."

And just like that Nathalie's good mood flew out the window. When Fernando didn't remember his wife was gone, it was a sign he was going to have a bad day.

Should she wait with her news?

"Would you like toast with your eggs for breakfast, Papi?"

"Yes, I would. Thank you. Good morning to you, lovely ladies. Are you my Nathalie's friends?"

Damn, he'd forgotten who they were. Definitely a bad day.

"Yes, we are. I'm Amanda." She offered her hand and dazzled him with her gorgeous smile.

Fernando shook it. "Such a beautiful lady. You look familiar, have I seen you in a movie? Or maybe one of those Victoria's Secret commercials?"

Her father was such a flirt.

"No, sir. I wish. Regrettably, I'm not voluptuous enough for Victoria's Secret." Amanda winked.

Fernando actually blushed.

Bridget saved him by offering her hand. "I'm Doctor Bridget."

"Yes, yes. I remember you. I don't know from where, but I do. You're also a very pretty lady." He glanced down at

Bridget's impressive cleavage but refrained from making a comment. Good. It meant that his brain was still functioning. Never mind that he was probably faking remembering her.

"And I'm Syssi."

He shook Syssi's hand. "Another beautiful lady."

"Stop flirting, Papi, and sit down to eat." Nathalie put a plate on the counter for him.

"Thank you." Fernando paused his flirting to dig into his food.

"Has he always been such a charmer?" Syssi whispered in Nathalie's ear.

"Yes. When he was still running the shop, most of our clientele were ladies. Come to think of it, Jackson is a chick magnet as well. I swear, ever since he started working for me the female clientele has doubled, and not only the teenage girls. He charms grandmas just as well."

"Some guys just can't help themselves. They love women, and it shows. It's not necessarily a bad thing, though. I'll take a women lover over a women hater every day and twice on Sunday." Bridget took her coffee and headed for the living room.

"Yeah, unless you're the jealous type, and you're married to one," Nathalie said quietly. Her mother hadn't appreciated Fernando's innocent flirting.

Syssi and Amanda followed Bridget to the living room, leaving her alone with her father. She waited for him to finish his breakfast.

"Would you like some coffee, Papi?"

"Yes, please."

She poured him a cup. "There is something I need to tell you."

"What is it, precious?" Worry suffused his words.

"It's a good thing, Papi, a wonderful thing. Andrew and I are expecting a baby."

The bright smile that flitted through his face was immediately replaced by a frown. "Who is Andrew?"

Damn, most days he knew who Andrew was. She considered lying and saying he was her husband, but the lie couldn't pass through her lips. "My fiancé, daddy. We are getting married in six weeks."

He smiled and pulled her into a hug. "I'm so happy for you, my girl." He let her go with a mischievous grin on his face. "I'm happy for me too. I can't wait to hold my grandchild in my arms. But I'm not sure your mother will be thrilled about being called Grandma." He winked.

The best thing was not to correct him and just go with it. "She'll get used to the idea."

"Question is, will I? After all, I'll be going to bed with a grandma."

Unfortunately, only in your dreams, Daddy.

CHAPTER 18: AMANDA

Amanda glanced at her schedule for the day and sighed. It was going to be a rat race. There was so much she still needed to do in the two days before her scheduled trip to Hawaii.

They were taking the clan's largest jet to shuttle the girls and their escorts, Vanessa, Amanda, and Gertrude. Overkill on all accounts. The plane belonged to Annani's sanctuary and had to be flown from Alaska. Annani's people, who needed it on an almost daily basis, would have to manage without. Three escorts for a group of twenty-two kids made sense, but not for a same sized group of adult women. But the psychologist warned that the women's submerged memories might reemerge at any moment, and they might panic. According to Vanessa, a group that large required a minimum of three immortals with decent thralling ability.

"Is the next one here?" she asked Syssi.

Syssi glanced at the list of interviewees. "She is ten minutes late, I don't think she is coming."

"Good, I need a break. Join me for coffee?"

Syssi got up to her feet and stretched. "Sure." She turned to Hannah. "If someone named Mona shows up, come get us. We are in the kitchen."

Without lifting her head up from the monitor, Hannah gave her the thumbs-up.

In the kitchenette, Syssi put a fresh packet into the coffeemaker and leaned against the counter. "I can't believe how flaky these young ones are. Having a guaranteed source of income is spoiling them rotten."

Amanda nodded. "One didn't want to work full time, the other one expected an executive's pay, and this one made an appointment and didn't show up." She leaned closer to Syssi's ear and whispered. "I think we need to forget about hiring an immortal and settle for a mortal or two to handle the interviews."

Syssi pulled up two cups from the cabinet above the sink. "Not a bad idea. The questionnaire is vague enough. Paranormal abilities are strange, so it shouldn't come as a big surprise that some of the questions are a little out there." Amanda took one and held it out for Syssi to fill. "William is coming later today to show us his video game. If it's as good as he claims, we might not need to hire additional staff."

"Even if it's that good, it's not a substitute for a face to face interview. Besides, it only tests precognition and remote viewing. It can't test telepathy or any of the other paranormal phenomena."

Regrettably, Syssi was right. "We keep on looking then, but there are not that many unemployed immortals left. Shortly we will run out of names."

"I have an idea." Syssi put her cup down. "If I remember right, we have five high-school students and two local college students. Three of them are working for Nathalie, but we can offer the others part time jobs. Kids are always looking for an independent source of income, and they don't get their share in clan profits until they either graduate college or reach twenty-five years of age."

"Brilliant idea. I'll call Onegus and get their names and numbers."

"Yo! Amanda, Syssi, there is someone here to see you!" Hannah called from the other room.

Syssi lifted her cup. "Good. Ms. Mona decided to show up."

They headed back to the lab.

It wasn't Mona. It was William, and he was blushing like a red tomato.

Hannah cast him an indulgent smile. "So you're Amanda's cousin?"

"Unbelievable, ha? Look at her and look at me." He waved a hand over his rotund physique.

Hannah cocked her head. "I can see the family resemblance."

"You can?" Amanda and William said at the same time.

"Yes, of course. Don't you see it, Syssi? The blue eyes, the high cheekbones, the height."

Syssi glanced from Amanda to William and back, then nodded. "You're right. I didn't notice the eye color because of William's glasses, but it's the same shade of blue. Yeah, and you're right about the rest too."

What Syssi hadn't said was that William's cheekbones were not as pronounced because of his padding, and although he was only an inch or two shorter than Kian, his width made him look shorter. What Amanda couldn't understand, though, was why he was wearing glasses. Maybe it had something to do with filtering the glare from the monitors he was staring at all day.

William beamed. "Thank you. I'm flattered, especially since the compliment comes from such a beautiful woman."

Used to compliments, Hannah accepted William's graciously. Even before she'd lost weight, her pretty face, her confidence, and her witty sense of humor made her a very popular girl. Hanna never suffered from a shortage of suitors.

Which, unfortunately, didn't bode well for William. And anyway, there could never be anything more than a hookup between them.

"William, darling, you can come back and flirt with Hannah after you show us your game."

"Yes, right." He shifted the box he was holding under his left arm and offered his right hand to Hannah. "It was a pleasure to make your acquaintance, Hannah."

With a sly grin, she shook it. "Mine, too. Come see me after you're done with these two."

The girl had just made William's day. Hell, she'd probably made his year.

"I'll certainly will," he said.

Amanda shook her head. She'd better have a little chat with Hannah before the post-doc had a chance to toy with William. He was too sweet and naive, and she could easily shatter his fragile ego.

"Are you coming?" Syssi asked.

"In a moment. Help William set up the console in my office."

Syssi cast her a perplexed look. She knew perfectly well that William didn't need anyone's help with anything that had to do with electronics.

Amanda made a shooing motion with her hand. Syssi might be a seer, but unfortunately, she was no mind reader. "And close the door behind you."

Finally, understanding dawned on Syssi's face, and she winked, then did what Amanda had asked.

Amanda braced her hands against Hannah's desk and leaned, so her face was only a few inches away from the postdoc. "Hannah, sweetheart, you're an awesome girl, and if you really like William, I have no problem with some innocent flirting. But if you're just toying with him, don't. He is a sweet man, and I love him dearly. I would hate to see him hurt."

With an offended expression on her face, Hannah crossed her arms over her chest. "I never toy with guys. Have you ever seen me encourage someone I wasn't interested in?"

"Darling, I don't follow your love life that closely."

"I like William. He looks smart and kind, and he is very handsome."

Amanda rolled her eyes. *Yeah, right.*

Hannah narrowed hers. "You're lucky you're my boss, so I'm not going to say what's really on my mind. But just so you know, William has a gorgeous face. You just don't see it. You focus on everything that is less than perfect."

Ouch. Amanda could practically feel the slap on her cheek. She leaned back, getting out of Hannah's personal space. "You got me, and I'm sorry. But he is my cousin, and I don't really look at him that way; as a woman admiring a man, that is. Anyway, I'll leave you to your work."

Hannah's face softened. "I'm sorry too. I shouldn't have exploded like this. It's just that for years I had people look at me and see a fat girl and nothing else. My mother included. I can't stand it when it's done to others."

"I totally understand." Amanda turned on her heel and marched toward her office. She knew all there was to know about being objectified, but in her case, it was her beauty that was getting noticed. Hannah would not appreciate the comparison. People viewed Amanda's looks as a gift, an advantage, and in some ways they were, but not if you wanted to get noticed for who you were on the inside.

In her office, William was already done hooking up his game system to her monitor. "Ready for a demonstration, ladies?"

Amanda waved a hand. "Wow us."

"It looks like any other game. The objective of the spy is to reach a destination while overcoming obstacles on the way. He needs to survive the assassinations attempts; planes rigged with bombs, cars that are coming at him, and so on." He started the game and showed them a few moves.

"Someone with precognition or remote-viewing talent will be able to avoid the traps and choose the safe route. He or she will dodge a knife when it's thrown at them, not board a plane that has a bomb on it, and so on. Now, in most games, the players become familiar with the obstacles, and after playing it several times, they know what to expect. This game generates new scenarios all the time. A player will not encounter the same obstacle at the same spot in the game twice. It's always random. The only people who will do exceptionally well are those who have the paranormal ability to predict what will happen next."

Amanda put a hand on William's shoulder. "Excellent. It's violent and bloody enough to be rated M so, hopefully, we won't get kids. After all, we can only approach adults. Though we can take the kids' information to be used later when they reach legal age. The only problem is that we will get only guys. I don't see women playing a game like this."

Syssi nodded. "Is there a way to make the game attractive to females?"

William shrugged. "I wouldn't know. You need to tell me."

"We can have a choice of spy avatars and include female options," Syssi suggested.

Amanda had a few ideas of her own. "Get her a hunky counterpart. A hot British spy, or maybe a frenemy; a Russian spy."

William pulled his tablet from the box and started taking notes. "Got it. A female spy, and a hot counterpart. What else?"

Syssi smirked. "Get her a choice of disguises. Wigs, fashionable outfits, shoes. Girls like to dress up."

She was on to something. "Also a choice of flashy cars, and a condo to decorate, things like that."

William looked confused. "I'll need help. I know nothing about fashion or interior decorating…" His eyes widened. "Ingrid can help. Right?"

Amanda agreed. The interior decorator had a fabulous fashion sense. "Then it's a plan. What do we do once the game is ready?"

William shrugged as if it was too obvious to explain. "We sell it and rent it like any other game. To play, the gamers will have to be online, so we can collect the data. I'll have the software produce a daily list of top performers. With a certain threshold, naturally."

"Perfect." Amanda leaned and kissed his cheek. "You're a genius, William."

He pushed his glasses up his nose. "I know."

"And so modest too," Syssi teased.

They waited for William to pack away his equipment, then exited Amanda's office.

Once in the main lab William hesitated, casting a quick glance at the door and then at Hannah. When she smiled at him in invitation, he made up his mind and approached her.

"I was thinking," he started. "It's almost lunch time. Would you care to join me for a hamburger?" When he didn't get the response he was hoping for, William continued. "Or something else? What are you in the mood for?"

Hannah lifted a small cooler she had stashed under her desk. "I don't eat out unless I absolutely have to. I plan all my meals according to the guidelines of my diet and prepare them myself, so I know exactly what goes into them."

For a moment, William looked deflated but then remembered he was supposed to flirt. "You don't need a diet, you're perfect the way you are."

"Thank you. That's very nice of you to say. But this is the result of the diet. I've lost over sixty pounds. I could lose another thirty, but I'm happy where I am at. For now, I just want to maintain this weight."

"Good for you." He hefted his cardboard box. "Until next time, then." He turned to leave.

"Wait! I still want to have lunch with you. We can go out and sit on the grass, picnic style. You can share mine.

I'm a great cook."

Turning back, William looked like she'd given him the best of gifts. "Thank you, but I can't eat your lunch. I'll just take a bite to taste your cooking."

"Don't worry. I packed double in case I needed to stay overtime and eat dinner here. I have enough, and it seems I'm going home on time today."

"In this case, I'll be delighted. Thank you."

Hannah lifted her purse off the back of her chair. "You can stash your box under my desk and get it when we come back."

Amanda shook her head. The game was too valuable to be lying around for anyone to snatch. "I'll take it and lock it in my office."

William handed it to her. "Thank you, that would be better."

Hannah threaded her arm in his and walked him out. "So tell me, William, what do you like to do?"

"Isn't it obvious? I like to eat."

"And I like to cook. We match perfectly."

CHAPTER 19: ANDREW

"Did you check the bathroom?" Nathalie called from the walk-in closet.

Just to make sure, Andrew made another round of opening every drawer and even peeked into the shower to make sure he'd collected Nathalie's shampoo and conditioner. "It's clear. I stuffed everything into two Ziploc bags. Where do you want me to put them?"

Between the bags of clothes Nathalie had brought over several trips, and his recently purchased new wardrobe, they ended up with a lot of stuff to take home with them, but no luggage to carry it all in.

"Just put it in one of the shopping bags."

Ziplocs in hand, Andrew crossed the bedroom into the closet. "I think we should ask Syssi to loan us a couple of suitcases. We can bring them back tomorrow."

From her crouching position on the floor, Nathalie pushed up to her feet and examined the array of plastic bags.

"We can manage. Several trips to the car and we will be done. As it is, I feel like we've imposed on your sister and her husband enough."

Andrew pulled her into his arms. "Sweetheart, you still cling to your old ways, when you had no one to rely on other than yourself. This is no longer the case, and you need to internalize that it's okay to ask family for things. They are happy to help. Not only that, you're making them feel uncomfortable by trying to do without. You have a whole clan of relatives now who've got your back. Get used to it."

In response, she lifted her head and offered him her sweet lips for a kiss. Not an offer Andrew could refuse. He kissed her, only a light peck at first, but as her tongue darted out and sneaked between his lips, he was lost to her. Cupping the back of her head, Andrew deepened the kiss, and when she moaned into his mouth, he couldn't help but push his hand under her T-shirt and gently caress her breast through her bra. Her nipples were very sensitive because of the pregnancy, so no pinching or tugging. It would have to wait probably until the baby was born—or even longer if she decided to breastfeed.

For some reason, the image of Nathalie nursing their infant daughter got him horny as hell, not that he wasn't a moment ago, but that was like dousing fire with gasoline. He lifted her shirt and knelt in front of her.

"What are you doing?" She tried to pull him back up.

A moment later, when he pulled her bra cups down and under her breasts then licked around one stiff peak, her question was answered.

"Andrew!" Nathalie whispered loudly. "They are all waiting for us in the living room. You can't do it now. Wait until we get home."

He palmed her wet nipple. "Just a little more. I can't leave the twin bereft; wouldn't be fair." He licked her other nipple, then rearranged the bra cups and pulled her T-shirt down.

A smile on her beautiful face, Nathalie smoothed her palm over his short hair. "I love you, Andrew."

"Because of this talented guy?" He pointed at his tongue and waggled it at her.

She laughed. "Among other things. Now, get up and start hauling bags."

"Yes, ma'am." Andrew pushed to his feet and grabbed a couple of bags in each hand.

"Need help?" Kian asked as Andrew crossed the living room and deposited the bags near the entry door. "I'm good for now. But later I'd appreciate help getting everything into the car."

Kian nodded. "Bridget asked that you come see her before you go home."

"Why? She already gave me the green light to go."

Kian shrugged. "Do you have all the pain meds you need?"

Nope, he only had enough for two more days. "I don't. I'll better go down to the clinic and get a big supply. I hope Bridget has enough on hand and doesn't give me a prescription to fill out. I'm going back to work tomorrow, and God knows what's waiting on my desk. I'll probably have no time to go to a pharmacy."

Kian waved a hand. "Don't worry about it. I'll ask Shai to arrange a delivery for you."

"First, let me see if Bridget has some for now." Andrew turned to Nathalie. "Don't you dare lift any of these bags. I'll be back in a few minutes, and Kian or Okidu can help me down to the car."

By her guilty smile, he'd guessed right, and the stubborn woman had been planning to do just that. He pointed a warning finger at her, then turned to Syssi. "Make sure she doesn't do anything stupid."

As Syssi nodded, her lip quivered a little. At first, he thought she was stifling a laugh, but then he saw a tear sliding down her cheek.

"What's wrong?" He bent his knees so he could look into her eyes.

"I don't want you guys to go. It was so much fun to have you as flat-mates. The breakfasts. The dinners. It's going to be lonely with just Kian and me."

A snort sounded from Kian's direction. "A tiny hint, and you'll have the entire Guardian force descending on us for every meal."

Syssi laughed through her tears. "I know."

Andrew pulled her into a quick hug. "We live twenty minutes away, not on the other side of the globe. We will see plenty of each other."

With a soft sniffle, Syssi wiped at her eyes. "For some reason, I'm getting overly emotional."

"Oh, oh…" Nathalie cast Syssi an appraising look. "Maybe you're pregnant? As soon as I got pregnant, and I'm talking like right the next day, I started crying at the drop of a hat."

Andrew let go of Syssi and gave her a look-over of his own, not that he had a clue what he was looking for.

"I wish," Syssi said in a sad tone. "But no, I'm not pregnant. Is it so hard to believe that I don't want to see you guys go?"

Nathalie wrapped her arm around his sister's

shoulders and walked her over to the sofa. "Come, let's talk wedding plans. It will cheer you up."

It did, and a moment later the two were discussing the color of the dress; whether it should be pure white, off white, or cream-colored.

Andrew couldn't care less, but he was happy to see Syssi smiling again as he left.

Bridget's office door was open, and he rapped his fingers on the jamb before walking in. "Good evening, Doctor. You wanted to see me?"

She lifted her head from her tablet and smiled at him. "Take a seat, Andrew. There are a few things I need to discuss with you."

Full on doctor mode. Good.

Every time Andrew was alone with Bridget, he had an anxious moment, not sure which Bridget he was about to encounter, the doctor or the ex-lover. The thought of her bringing up their brief past together was disturbing.

Andrew planted his butt in the metal chair Bridget tortured her patients with, wondering if she did it on purpose to get them to leave as quickly as possible. "What's up, Doc?"

"I'm not one to beat around the bush, so I'll get straight to it. Nathalie's pregnancy is complicating things. She can't transition while she is carrying a child."

Did she think him an idiot? "I know that."

"I know you do, but did you realize the impact it will have on your marriage?"

Andrew frowned. "What do you mean?"

Bridget looked like she was gathering patience to explain the facts of life to a simpleton. "In a few months, your venom glands will become active, and your fangs will reach their full length. The urge to bite your mate will be overpowering. But you can't. A bite may facilitate Nathalie's transition. Do you see the problem now?"

"I'm not an animal. If I can stop myself during sex, for any reason and at any time, I don't see why I can't do the same with biting. I'm sure it's not going to be easy, but there is no other way. Under no circumstances would I allow anything or anyone, myself included, to do anything that will endanger my girls."

Bridget's smile was sad. "You're a good man, Andrew, and I know you believe that you'll be able to abstain, but I'm telling you that you won't. You're not human anymore. I'm sure it didn't escape your notice that although in some ways your new physiology is far more advanced than your old one; in others, it's more primitive. The instinctive urges will be undeniable. Not only the sexual ones either. You're more aggressive now and easier to provoke. You need to plan ahead and decide what to do when you feel like killing the next driver that cuts you off. It might be counting from one to ten, or taking several deep breaths, or whatever else works for you. You need to be careful and watch out for triggers."

Damn. He'd thought it was temporary and that the insane urges would calm down in a few days. But according to Bridget, he was stuck like that. He'd turned into a predatory animal, and the only thing he could do was to learn to control it.

Andrew rubbed his brows between his thumb and forefinger. "What am I going to do when the time comes? And how long do I have?"

"If you're lucky, it will take your glands six months to become active, so you'll only have to contend with

Nathalie's final trimester. But it can happen sooner. As to what to do, I don't have good news for you. You either use a substitute or ask Kian to put you in stasis until after the baby is born. I don't see any other options."

Fuck it all to hell.

"Even hypothetically, the suggestion of having sex with a substitute is offensive to me."

Bridget raised her palms. "I know, I know. But it's my obligation to put it out there. It's up to you to decide what you do with it."

"I'd rather be put away like the rabid dog I am now."

"I'm sorry. I wish I had better news for you."

Bridget made it sound like it was the end of the world. It wasn't. After all, something wonderful had happened, Nathalie was pregnant with their child. And after suffering through some pain and misery—hers delivering the baby, and his rotting away in stasis—things would get to be wonderful again.

He and Nathalie would become parents.

"We still have time, and maybe some other solution will present itself. What worries me much more than my ability or inability to refrain from biting is that Nathalie must remain human until after the delivery, and in the meantime, she is as fragile and vulnerable as any other mortal."

Bridget smoothed a finger over the tablet's glossy surface. "Nathalie is a healthy young woman. The chances of something going wrong are really minimal. You shouldn't lose any sleep over it."

Easy for Bridget to say, she wasn't in love with a mortal, her entire life didn't depend on that one, perfect mortal's survival.

"Logically, I hear what you're saying, but it doesn't

make it any easier for me, or give me the peace of mind to sleep well at night. I have a feeling that the only time I will relax between now and the delivery will be when Kian puts me in stasis."

CHAPTER 20: ANANDUR

Twenty-eight hours had passed since Lana's call, and Anandur's phone hadn't left his palm the entire time. He'd even slept with it tucked under his pillow.

Damn, he hoped the girls were okay. The surly Russians had grown on him during his short affair with Lana, and he prayed to the merciful fates that Alex hadn't discovered their plot. A guy who sold women into slavery for money would have no problem killing the entire crew if he'd gotten a whiff of their mutiny.

As he walked down the hallway to Kian's office, Anandur wondered what could have possessed Alex to sink so deep into the darkness. He was a relatively young immortal, just a little older than Amanda, which meant that he'd grown up when the clan had already accumulated enough resources to ensure a good life for all of its members.

It hadn't always been like that, and during most of their history, everyone had to work to support their family.

But other than the few who for some reason had gone crazy, like the infamous Vlad, Anandur couldn't remember any of them doing something so vile. There had been quite a few instances of clan members abusing their powers for personal gain, and some internal scuffles when tempers flared and men fought over this or that, but that was about it.

Since the beginning, Annani's teaching had drilled the sanctity of life, human and immortal, into their heads. The other thing she was unrelenting about was the importance of consent.

Alex was violating both in the most despicable way.

"Come in," Kian called when Anandur rapped his knuckles on the glass door. Ever since Syssi had come into his life, the guy was obsessing about everyone having to knock before entering.

"Good evening, gentlemen," Anandur said before taking a seat next to Onegus.

Kian cocked a brow. "Did you hear from them again?"

"No."

"I asked Onegus to join us for this because Andrew has enough on his plate right now. We can either make a plan ourselves or outsource it to Turner."

Anandur scratched his beard. "I vote for Turner, but I want to be there with the rescue team."

"The problem with Turner is that he doesn't work with anyone other than his own people or subcontractors he's thoroughly vetted. We need to apprehend Alex and bring him to trial. Humans can't do it."

Getting his hands on the scumbag was incredibly appealing, but Anandur was more concerned with Lana and the other girls. "My first priority is the crew," he said.

Onegus nodded. "Of course. They come first. But we don't want Alex to slip away and start the same disgusting operation somewhere else."

"Do you have an idea for a plan?" Kian asked.

Usually, Kian was the strategist and Onegus the implementer, but the head Guardian had no doubt learned something from his boss over the many years he'd served under him.

"We need to take the boat at sea. We will cause an international incident if we attack while it's moored in a Mexican harbor. Given enough time and resources, we could've arranged a cooperation with the Mexican authorities, but we have a narrow window of opportunity here, and we can't afford the delay."

Kian pushed up to his feet and began pacing, which he claimed helped him think. "All we need from Lana is the boat's location or that of their next stop. We can launch a drone to follow the yacht, so we know when it's in the optimal position for a takeover."

"We will need a fast boat," Anandur stated the obvious. "And, naturally, we need to get it there."

"Not a problem. You and another Guardian take one of the larger jets and fly to the nearest port city. I'll arrange for a boat to wait for you there. You use the boat to board the yacht, take Alex into custody, and put him under if needed. The crew gets the yacht to the nearest harbor. I'll have a local crew ready to take it back to Marina Del Rey. From there, all of you fly to our airstrip, where someone will take Alex off your hands. You refuel and continue with the girls to Hawaii. Case closed."

"Not a bad plan. One problem, I don't know how to drive a yacht or use its navigation systems. The last time I took a boat out, we were still navigating by the stars."

Kian stopped and glared at Onegus. "Add it to the list of skills your guys need to know. We will have to bring along a civilian. And if we can't find one who knows what he's doing, I'll have to come with you."

"You know how to drive a boat?"

"And I also know how to fly a plane or a helicopter, drive a tank and any other vehicle. And I know how to operate a submarine."

Anandur's caught Onegus smirking down at his boots. So he'd known all along that Mr. Control-freak had learned how to operate all possible vehicles.

"A real life 007, aren't you? What I want to know is when and how did you manage to learn all of this, without Brundar and me knowing about it? You're not supposed to go anywhere without us or another pair of bodyguards at your side."

Some of the arrogance leached out from Kian's expression. "On a simulator."

That was an interesting piece of information. "We have a simulator somewhere in here, and I don't know about it?"

"Not that kind of simulator—just the software without all the bells and whistles of the real thing. William designed it for me."

Anandur had known Kian for almost a millennium, and it had somehow escaped his notice that the guy was certifiable. "And you think that's good enough? Are you nuts?"

"You've flown with me, did you notice anything lacking in my piloting skills?"

By then, Onegus was laughing so hard that his eyes

were tearing up.

Fuck. Anandur slapped his palm on his forehead; he was such an idiot. He'd never given it a second thought. He should've wondered when and where Kian had acquired his pilot license. But the guy always exuded such an air of command and confidence that no one ever thought to question him.

"I'm not flying with you ever again. Not until you get a real license."

Kian shrugged. "Suit yourself."

CHAPTER 21: NATHALIE

"Home, sweet home," Nathalie said as Andrew switched the lights on in the shop.

She'd thought getting back home would feel good; instead, it was depressing. At night, without the hustle and bustle of customers, her shop, her pride and joy, looked dingy, outdated, and small. Especially in comparison to the elegant opulence of Kian and Syssi's penthouse as well as the rest of the clan's keep.

"Where are we?" Fernando asked.

"We are home, Papi."

"Oh. I thought it looked familiar."

Did he? Or was it one of his attempts to hide his confusion?

"Let's go upstairs. I think one of your shows is about to start." Perhaps his room would remind him that this was where he lived. She took her father's elbow and led him to the staircase, then glanced back at Andrew. "You're okay with the shopping bags?"

"Pfft, do you have to ask?" He waved her on. "Get your dad comfortable, and I'll haul everything upstairs."

"Thanks." She cast him a sad smile. The real challenge would be to find a place for all their stuff. She had a feeling most of it would have to stay in the bags because there was no more storage space to be found. For a moment, she considered checking the big commercial freezer in the kitchen. It was never completely full, and maybe she could store some of their things there. Problem was, a health inspector would not find her solution amusing. Not in the least.

Nathalie cringed as she opened the door to her father's room. His old La-Z-Boy armchair was a poor substitute for the luxurious BarcaLounger Okidu had provided for him at Syssi's. The fabric had faded from its original blue to a dirty bluish gray, and the armrests had so many stains on them that they'd turned yellow and brown. The thing was disgusting.

Even Papi thought so. He didn't say a thing, just sighed heavily and trudged over to the chair.

Nathalie picked up the remote from the top of the television and turned it on. After the large flat screen television her father had enjoyed in his room at Kian's, this big square box with its pitifully small screen must've been another letdown.

She flipped the channels until she found the one broadcasting his show—something about truckers in Alaska. She had no idea why he found the subject so fascinating. Maybe it was all that snow.

"Are you comfortable, Papi? Would you like a blanket? A cup of tea?"

"Yes, please." He didn't smile at her as he usually did when she offered to do something nice for him.

"What's wrong, Papi?"

He shrugged. "I liked our vacation. It was nice there."

"Would you like to go back?"

"I wish we could afford to live in a hotel. But it doesn't matter. As long as we have each other, we should thank the Lord we have a roof over our head and food on our table."

Nathalie leaned and kissed his cheek. "I'll get you the blanket."

When she stepped out into the corridor, she had to plaster herself against the wall to let Andrew pass with the loads of bags he was carrying.

"That's the last of it," he said. "Do you want me to start putting it away?"

She shook her head. "Leave it on the floor. I don't think anything will fit in the closet."

"We really need a bigger place."

She rolled her eyes. "Tell me about it. I'm going downstairs to make tea for my father. Would you like some?"

"Sure. And can I bother you for a sandwich? I'm starving."

She slapped his shoulder. "It's no bother, you big goof."

Ever since his transition, Andrew's appetite had become ferocious, and not only for food. But she wasn't complaining. On the contrary, His appetite suited her just fine.

Going through the fridge, she was glad to see that everything was neat and organized. Jackson's friend,

Gordon, was keeping things in the same order she used to, and using her labeled containers. Made life easier when several orders came in at the same time. To stop and read the labels on the packages of cheeses and cold cuts in the fridge would've slowed things down.

As she made the sandwich for Andrew, her hands did the job without engaging her brain. Muscle memory, she supposed. Years of doing the same thing would have this effect. She scooped some potato salad onto the plate, then laid the roast beef on rye bread next to it.

Wondering who prepared the salad and if it was as good as hers, she dropped another scoop on a different plate and grabbed a fork. It was good. Leaning against the counter, she ate it all.

"My sandwich ready?" Andrew poked his head into the kitchen.

"Yeah, I'll bring it out to you." She finished the last forkful of salad and lifted Andrew's plate.

"The potato salad is great. I think it's even better than mine." She put the plate down in front of Andrew. He'd already poured them both tea, but by the steam rising from the mugs, it was still too hot to drink. Too bad since the salad had made her thirsty.

"Do you want me to bring you an ice cube?" Andrew asked.

Such a sweet man. He knew her so well, was so attuned to her. She smiled at him, hoping it expressed her love and gratitude. "Thank you."

Andrew was up and back with the ice in seconds. "Here you go." He dropped two cubes into her tea.

A moment later, it was just the right temperature to drink, and she took several long sips. "I should call Jackson and ask him to come over. I owe him a big, fat check. Besides, he promised to go over the accounting with me. I have no idea where I stand financially."

Andrew swallowed a mouthful of sandwich and wiped a drop of mayo from his chin. "Can't it wait until tomorrow?"

Talking about appetite, Nathalie knew what was on his mind. "I don't need the extra stress. The shop is too busy in the morning for Jackson and me to exchange more than a few words."

"The last thing I want is for you to get stressed over anything. I was just thinking that Jackson might be out on a date or something like that."

She hadn't considered that, but if he was, he would tell her he couldn't come. Jackson wasn't shy or timid. Besides, the promise of a fat check would be too alluring for him to say no to.

Nathalie made the call.

"I'm coming over," he said before she had a chance to mention the check.

Andrew was chewing the last bite of the second sandwich she'd made for him when the back door opened and Jackson walked in.

"Andrew, my man, so good to see you on the other side." He offered Andrew his hand. When Andrew took it, Jackson pulled him up into a bro hug, complete with the backslapping. It sounded painful. Men were such weird creatures, expressing feelings of friendship by hitting each other on the back.

"It's good to be here," Andrew smiled.

"I'll bet. How are you doing, Nathalie?" The boy finally turned his attention to her. She'd forgive his lack of manners this time. After all, there were extenuating circumstances.

"I'm great. Are you hungry? Can I offer you a sandwich?"

Jackson shook his head and planted his butt next to Andrew. "This place is killing my appetite. Being around food all day is tough on the senses."

Andrew nodded in understanding. "The smells get to you, ha?"

"They do."

Now that he was so close, she noticed that Jackson looked a little skinnier, less fit. This job was taking a toll on him.

"So, tell me, Jackson, anything I should know about?"

Jackson leaned back into the Naugahyde upholstered bench. "Everything is going great, as you have seen during your short visits…" He cast her an accusing look. "The place is packed all the time. Your breakfast regulars were asking about you. They were worried that something happened to your dad, but I told them that you were taking him for some special treatment. Feel free to invent what it was. Gordon and Vlad and I have a good system in place, but we all need a break. This place is a slave camp."

Guilt squeezed at Nathalie's heart. It hadn't been fair to the boys, expecting them to shoulder grownup responsibilities basically on their own. She knew exactly how all-consuming and exhausting running the café was.

"I'm so sorry I dumped it all on you guys, and I'm so grateful to you." She pulled out the check she'd prepared for him from her pocket. "Here, a small token of gratitude. I'll write two more for Vlad and Gordon." She handed it to Jackson.

His eyes peeled wide as he unfolded it. "A thousand bucks? Are you nuts? That's too much! I can't take it." He pushed it back to her.

Nathalie put her finger on it and slid it over toward Jackson. "Don't argue, and take it. Did you buy that guitar of yours already?"

He glanced at the check. "I've put down a deposit, and the store owner is holding it for me."

"Including this check, how much more do you need?"

"Just this week's wages."

"Then take another advance and go get your beauty."

That was an offer Jackson couldn't refuse. With a sigh he palmed the check, pulled out his wallet, and carefully slid it inside. "Thank you, Nathalie. You're the best boss ever."

"And you're the best employee anyone could ever hope to find. You're one of a kind."

Andrew cleared his throat. "Are you guys done with that? Because I need to talk to you both."

Nathalie lifted a brow. "About what?"

"Your work schedule from now on. You can't put in twelve-hour workdays anymore, Nathalie. In fact, I don't want you on your feet for more than four."

Jackson's eyes darted from her to Andrew and then back. "Are you sick, Nathalie? What's going on?"

She smiled and patted his hand. "I'm not sick. I'm pregnant."

He gasped. "Get out of here…when did that happen?"

Andrew cleared his throat again. "I want Nathalie to take it easy."

"No problem. The guys will understand why a vacation is out for now."

Guilt assailed her again. "Maybe we should hire

another one of your friends. So you guys can take time off in turns."

"It will have to be a mortal. All my immortal buddies are here."

"Is it a problem?"

He shrugged. "Not really. We need to keep up appearances for the sake of the customers anyway."

"Then it's agreed."

They shook on it.

Jackson pushed up from the bench. "Check your email, Nathalie. I forwarded to you the profit and loss figures for last month. I'm sure you'll be happy to see how well the shop has done."

Once again, the kid was exceeding her expectations. She hadn't known he could do accounting. "Thank you, I will."

The best part about Jackson organizing the numbers ahead of time was that it solved the problem of going over them while Andrew had other plans.

When Jackson left, she smiled sheepishly. "Well, I guess we have time now. I can look at what Jackson emailed me tomorrow."

Andrew leaned and reached for her hand. "Are you looking forward to getting back to work?"

Was she?

"I am. It wasn't exactly a vacation we were on. It was the most stressful time of my life. My old routine, mingling with my regulars, it will give me a sense of normality. I miss it."

"How about being home? Are you happy to be back?"

"Frankly? Not as much as I thought I'd be. We were very comfortable at your sister's penthouse. In comparison, this place feels more cramped and dingy than ever. And the upstairs smells like a bakery. I guess it takes being away for a while to notice it." She shook her head. "Not pleasant, not at all."

In the brief silence that followed, Andrew looked like he was choosing his words carefully, which wasn't like him. Normally, he preferred the direct approach and didn't beat around the bush even when discussing touchy subjects.

"I think we should move into the keep." Evidently, he'd decided to stick to his blunt style.

God, did it sound tempting. "I can't. You know my father needs his familiar environment. We've talked about it before."

Andrew's lips tightened in that determined expression he got when he thought she was unreasonably stubborn. "He seemed perfectly fine to me during his stay at the keep. In fact, I think he was happier there than I've ever seen him here. He had William and occasionally the Guardians to keep him company and occupy him with this and that. He had Okidu serving his every whim. Did he complain about anything?"

Not even once. "He thought we were on vacation."

"So we keep telling him that. Or, if you want, you can take him with you when you go to work, and he can sit around here for a few hours. There are so many advantages to moving there, especially with regard to your father. In the keep, there is always someone who can watch him; if not William, then someone else. Even Okidu, or Onidu, Amanda's butler."

Nathalie pulled her hand out of his and raised her palms. "We can't live with your sister and her husband. It was fun for a little while, but it can't work as a permanent arrangement."

"I'm sure Kian can find an apartment for us; if not in the same building, then in one of the neighboring ones. The clan owns half of the high-rises on the street."

Yeah, and she could just imagine the rent—five thousand dollars minimum. Probably more. Those were luxury apartments for rich business people, not struggling coffee shop owners. True, thanks to Jackson and his crew she wasn't struggling as much as before, but she wasn't wealthy. Not even close.

"We can't afford a place like that." She shushed Andrew when he opened his mouth to protest. She knew what he wanted to say. That he was earning a good income and that combining their resources would be enough to pay for a fancy place like that.

"You're still making mortgage payments on your house, right? Can you afford rent that is probably over five grand a month? I know I can't because I have to make mortgage payments on this place whether I live here or not."

"So I sell my house. You're right, the mortgage is eating a third of my monthly income, and without it I can afford the five thousand dollar rent on my own."

She didn't want Andrew to give up his house. He loved the place, even though he was spending hardly any time there. "Your house represents your biggest asset, and it doesn't make financial sense to sell it. Besides, what if the rent is even more expensive than five grand? Can you afford it then?"

With an indulgent smile, Andrew shook his head. "Sweetheart, listen to yourself. You're looking for all the excuses in the world why it can't work instead of thinking of a way to make it work. Why?"

That was a dumb question. Because she was scared, that's why. This was another big decision, another upheaval in her life that she wasn't ready for. Couldn't he allow her at least a few days to catch her breath?

She crossed her arms over her chest and pushed her chin out. "It's a big decision, and I don't want to rush into it. I'd rather play devil's advocate and flush out all the possible problems."

"You're right. Let me put your mind at ease. Can you listen for a few moments without losing your cool?"

What cool? She'd lost hers a long time ago, when he'd been teetering between life and death, and she hadn't regained it since. But she nodded, letting him speak his mind.

"Instead of selling my house, I can rent it out. And you can rent out the apartment over the shop as well. In fact, I suggest you offer it to Jackson and his friends. Boys their age crave independence. They are going to love it, provided it's cheap of course."

Nathalie wanted to argue, but there was nothing more to argue about. Everything he'd said was true and made perfect sense. Rationally, she knew that moving to the keep was a good decision, one that would improve their lives, even Papi's. And yet, it was an extremely difficult step for her to take.

It meant taking for granted her new family's willingness to help with her father. She found it hard to internalize that help was out there—offered with no strings attached, just from the goodness of people's hearts.

It was true, though. She'd witnessed it herself. Even Bridget, who should've harbored some animosity toward Nathalie for stealing Andrew away from her, had been incredibly helpful and supportive. And William, who hardly knew her at all, was taking care of Papi as if he was actually enjoying it.

Andrew chuckled. "What? No rebuttals?"

Nathalie let her arms drop. "No. You won the argument. Let's do it."

Andrew lifted his arms, palms up. "Hallelujah, praise the Lord."

"Shouldn't it be, praise Nathalie?"

"Indeed it should." Andrew got up and pulled her to her feet. "Let me take you upstairs and praise you until the angels sing. Correction, just one angel. My Nathalie."

CHAPTER 22: ANDREW

Everything was different at work. Andrew felt as if he'd been gone for a decade and not just a few days. The big office space he shared with four other agents looked and smelled different, the agents looked and smelled different, and so did he. Not the smell part, he'd gotten used to his own scent, but everyone noticed that he wasn't the same.

Most of the guys just cast him surreptitious glances or told him that the time off had agreed with him, but at the end of the day his luck ran out. As he stepped out into the corridor and joined several others who were waiting for the elevators, Tim walked over.

"Are you wearing platforms, Spivak? Because I swear that you are taller than you were before your vacation." Tim looked him over with the critical eye of an artist. "And take a look at this skin, baby soft." He pinched Andrew's cheek.

Andrew slapped the guy's hand away. "If you value your fingers, buddy, keep your hands to yourself."

The threat had been effective, and Tim stuck his hands in his pockets. As an artist, he needed his hands in good working condition and was obsessed with protecting them from harm.

"Have you gone to some rejuvenation spa? Because if you did, I want the name."

That worked with the story Andrew had prepared in case anyone inquired about the changes he'd undergone. "Yeah, exactly. It was a gift from my fiancée. Massages all day long, and spinal realignment. Apparently, my poor posture made me look shorter than I actually was."

Tim's eyes narrowed into slits. "What are you talking about? You always had fantastic posture, Spivak."

Damn Tim and his sharp observation skills.

"I kept my shoulders squared, an old habit from my time as a Marine, but according to the chiropractor, the vertebrae in my lower back were compressed."

That bull-crap answer seemed to satisfy Tim. "I want the name and phone number of that spa. That's my destination for my next vacation. If they can make me look taller, I don't care how much it costs."

"I'll have to ask Nathalie. It was some weird French name I can't even pronounce."

"Thanks."

"See you later, Tim."

As soon as Tim walked away, Andrew released a breath. The problem with lies was that they usually meant more lies. Now he'd have to come up with a story about the nonexistent spa burning down to the ground or some other shit like that.

The elevator door opened and he stepped in, pressed the button for his parking level, and leaned against the mirrored back wall. The car made its way down, stopping at nearly every floor. People were going home. Most he knew in passing, a few he nodded hello to. Then as the doors opened at the gym level, he saw someone he actually wanted to talk to.

Roni, the hacker, was outside in the hallway, waiting for the elevator going up.

Andrew stepped out. "Hey, Roni, how are things going for you? You look good, kid."

He wasn't lying. Since Andrew had last seen him, Roni must've been working out vigorously. His arms looked a little less scrawny, and he was standing tall instead of hunching over.

The kid grinned. "I asked for a personal trainer, and the boss assigned me one. The guy tortures me every day, but if I look good, then it's worth it."

"You do. And I'm not saying it just because I need another favor."

"What is it?"

"Just one more check up on the same thing. I need to know when was the last time she made a withdrawal. My friend is heading out there, and it will make his life easier if he knows when to stake out that bank."

"No problem. I'm glad to help." Roni transferred his gym bag to his other hand.

That had been too easy. Roni wasn't the type to offer something for nothing.

"I need a favor too," Roni murmured while looking down at his sneakers.

Here it goes. "What is it?"

"Can you hook me up with Sylvia again?"

Right.

Andrew leaned and whispered in Roni's ear, "That was a one-time deal. I'm not a pimp."

"No, not like that. I mean, only if she wants to. I don't have her number, and she doesn't have mine. So maybe there is a chance she would like to see me again? Like for coffee or something?"

There was so much hope in the kid's voice that Andrew hated to disappoint him. There was probably no chance in hell Sylvia wanted to have another go at the geeky kid with an attitude. It would be futile and embarrassing, but he was going ask.

"Are you allowed to leave? Or are you still confined to this building?"

"I can meet her for dinner or a coffee shop. My handler will have to be there, of course, but he'll give me space if I'm with a girl. He's a decent dude."

Andrew clapped Roni on the shoulder. "I'll see what I can do. I'll call her tonight, and if she is agreeable, I'll set up a time and a place for you to meet the following day. Good?"

Roni looked as if he'd just won the lottery. "It's better than good. Thank you. And I'll check on your lady friend and her visits to the bank."

"Good deal." They shook on it, parting when Roni stepped into the cab going up.

Andrew called Sylvia as soon as he cleared the parking garage and got reception.

She shocked him. "Sure, I will be happy to see Roni. I was wondering why he didn't ask for me. The poor kid desperately needs a friend. I'll text you the details of a place I like."

Sylvia was genuinely interested in meeting freaking Roni again, so much so that even over the phone Andrew had no doubt she was truthful.

"You're awesome. Text me the time too."

"I will. Thank you, Andrew. It was a nice thing to do."

Not really, but whatever. He would let her think he had done it out of the goodness of his heart.

As Sylvia terminated the call, another one came in. Andrew smiled at the gorgeous face staring at him from the screen and accepted it. "Hello, sweetheart, I'm on my way home."

"That's great because we need to be at Dalhu's in less than an hour."

Fuck, he'd forgotten all about it. "Do I have to dress up?"

"Of course, you do. I want us looking our best."

"We didn't buy a new suit."

Nathalie sighed. "I know you're going to hate it, but we need to borrow one from Kian. There is no time to go shopping, and your old one doesn't fit. I'm going to call Syssi right now, and have her bring one to Amanda and Dalhu's place."

"Fine." Andrew really hated borrowing clothes from his brother-in-law.

When he got home, Andrew grabbed a quick shower and even let Nathalie gel his hair into place. "I look like a gangster from the thirties," he said once she was done fussing with it. "And I'm packing too." He glanced down at the bulge in his pants.

Nathalie had showered before him, and the only items of clothing she had on while playing with his hair were a tiny pair of see-through panties and a matching bra.

She kissed his forehead, which brought her breasts so close to his nose he could feel the vapor coming off her damp skin. Unable to help himself, he reached with his hands and cupped both.

"They are getting bigger every day," he murmured before planting a gentle kiss above one swell and then the other.

"I know, right? That's the best side effect of the pregnancy. I feel buxom, sexy." She waggled her breasts in front of his face.

Andrew circled her tiny waist with one arm and delivered a hard smack to her butt cheek with his hand.

"Ouch! What was that for?"

"You are always sexy, and I love this butt." He palmed both cheeks and gave them a squeeze. "You don't need larger breasts. Everything about you is perfect the way it is."

She slapped his cheek playfully. "You're such a sweet-talker. But we don't have time for any hanky-panky. Let me get dressed." She removed his arm from her waist and turned around.

Her panties were the almost thong type, a narrow strip of fabric in the back leaving most of her beautiful ass exposed. His smack had left a very faint imprint on her left butt cheek. Sexy as hell. He wanted to adorn her right cheek in a similar way, but was afraid she wouldn't react favorably.

Maybe some other time.

He almost came in his pants when she bent at the waist to pull out her new, red dress from the plastic bag on the floor.

"What are you doing to me, woman?" he croaked, shifting his position to try and relieve the pressure on the club in his pants.

Turning her head with a wicked smirk on her beautiful face, she winked. "Payback, sweetheart."

The woman was a witch. With her gorgeous ass high in the air and her long, luxurious hair hanging down to the floor on one side of her head, she was sin and temptation personified.

"Ooh, you just earned yourself another smack." He was up and delivering a loud slap to the other cheek before she had the chance to cover what she was so carelessly flaunting.

"Stop it! Andrew! What has gotten into you? Are you suddenly into spanking?" She tried to sound upset, but he could tell she was having as much fun with it as he was.

Cupping both cheeks in his hands, he massaged them gently and kissed her neck. "You call this a spanking? Those were love taps."

"Aha. Whatever. Now leave my ass alone so I can get dressed. And put your shoes on. We need to get going."

With a sigh, he let go.

Half an hour later they were standing in the vestibule in front of Amanda's penthouse doors.

"How do I look?" Nathalie asked.

"I would rather show you than tell you, but then I'll mess up your makeup and hair, and you'll get mad at me. You're stunning, baby. And I'm the luckiest guy in the universe to have you. I can't believe some other schmuck didn't snap you up a long time ago."

She grinned, her red-painted lips forming the most beautiful shape. "That's because I was waiting for you."

"Damn right you were." He lifted her hand and kissed her knuckles.

The door opened to reveal Amanda and her mocking

smirk. She braced one hand against the doorjamb and put the other on her hip. "Are you going to come in anytime soon? Or should I close the door and keep listening to you lovebirds sing each other's praises?"

Nathalie blushed and Andrew knew why. Just as he'd promised, last night he'd *praised* her into several screaming orgasms. Muffled by a pillow, naturally. Damn, they really needed to move. He loved that his woman was a screamer, and he hated that she wasn't free to do so.

Dalhu's tall frame appeared behind Amanda, and he pulled her aside, tucking her under his arm as if she was a dainty little thing and not a six-foot-tall woman. "Come in, guys."

"Thank you."

"Follow me," he said as he strolled down the hallway to one of the bedrooms.

"Wait," Amanda called. "Do you guys want something to drink?"

Nathalie turned around. "Not yet. I don't want to smear my lipstick."

"Give me a holler when you do."

"Nice," Andrew said as they entered Dalhu's new studio. It seemed that Amanda had had a wall knocked down between two bedrooms, combining them into one big, open space. There was a staging area with an armchair and some soft velvety fabric draped on a wooden contraption behind it. Several lamps were aimed at the chair, but they were turned off. Hopefully, Dalhu didn't intend on turning them all on. If he did, they would be baking from the heat.

"The suit Syssi brought is hanging on the hook in the bathroom. You can change in there." Dalhu pointed to a door.

When he was done, Andrew stepped out of the bathroom and looked at himself in the tall mirror Dalhu had put up on one of the walls. "I look damn good in a designer suit." The fit wasn't perfect, but it was better than any other suit Andrew had ever worn—including the tuxedo custom-made for him for Syssi's wedding. He just filled the thing better now.

"Stop admiring yourself and get over here." Dalhu waved a hand toward the chair Nathalie was sitting in."

"How do you want to do it? With me standing behind the chair, looking regal? Or should I take the chair and have Nathalie sit on my lap."

Dalhu shrugged. "It's your portrait, you guys decide."

There was only one person here who was going to make any decisions, and it sure wasn't Andrew. Even an old bachelor like him knew that it was the lady's call.

"Nathalie? What would you like?"

She pushed up to her high-heel clad feet and tugged on his hand. "I want to sit in your lap. I want our kids to look at this portrait and know how deeply in love their parents were from the very beginning."

Andrew heard Amanda sigh in the living room and murmur, "That's so romantic."

He had to agree.

CHAPTER 23: NATHALIE

Nathalie's face was getting numb from holding the same expression for the past hour or so. The rest of her wasn't doing so great either. Andrew hadn't voiced any complaints yet, but his arm, the one holding her, must've gone numb. Her macho guy was probably waiting for her to say something first.

Andrew would let that arm fall off before admitting that his pregnant, mortal fiancée was tougher than him.

Fortunately, women didn't suffer from that particular mental affliction, and she was definitely done for today.

Nathalie let her face relax. "Can you give me a push up, Andrew?" she asked.

"Certainly, my love."

She stifled a snort at his relieved tone and pushed all the way up to her feet. "We are done for today, Dalhu. I was getting numb all over." Lifting her arms over her head, she did a couple of side stretches, remembering too late that her dress wasn't long enough for such a maneuver. Her arms dropped, and she put her hands on her hips for a couple more.

"Do you want to see how the portrait is coming out?" Dalhu asked with a shy smile.

Cute.

A guy who would've terrified her if she bumped into him on the street, a huge ex-mercenary, was acting like a little boy showing his mom a drawing he'd made and hoping for her approval.

"Sure, if you don't mind. Some artists don't like showing their work in progress. Only when it's done."

"Then it's good I don't consider myself an artist."

Yeah, right. Of course, he was. Like most people, Dalhu was shielding his ego by pretending he didn't put any stock in his talent.

He stepped aside as Nathalie walked around the easel and took her first look at his work.

"It's beautiful, Dalhu." In the hour or so they'd been posing for him, Dalhu had finished sketching their outline and started adding detail to their faces. She wondered if Dalhu had captured Andrew's real expression or had allowed himself artistic license. The love and pride radiated from the canvas. This was exactly how she wanted their future children to see them.

"Let me see." Andrew came around, but she grabbed him for a fierce kiss before he had a chance to see anything.

"What was that for?" he asked when she let go of him.

"For the way you look at me." Nathalie pointed at the picture.

As he glanced at the portrait, Andrew's eyes skimmed over his own outline without really looking and focused on hers. He frowned as if he didn't approve.

"What? You don't like how Dalhu drew me?"

"Oh, I like the way you look, what I don't like is how he sees you."

"What do you mean?" She cast a worried glance at Dalhu. By the amused look on his face, the guy seemed to know what Andrew was talking about.

Andrew pointed at the drawing, first at the swell of her breast and then at the curve of her hip.

"I think I look sexy."

"Exactly."

"Relax, Andrew. I view Nathalie with an artist's eye. There is only one woman for me, and you know it."

"In here, I do." Andrew pointed to his head. "But in here, I don't." He pointed to his chest.

Dalhu chuckled. "You want to talk about it? I'm avoiding visiting Amanda at work even though I'm not under house arrest anymore. I know I'll go postal seeing all the ogling looks I'm sure she's getting from her horny students. And the funny thing is that I'm not even the jealous type. I trust Amanda completely. I just hate thinking about what goes on in those little punks' dirty minds."

"Fuck, I hadn't considered the ogling customers my Nathalie will have to deal with again." He turned to her. "You can't work at the coffee shop anymore."

She patted his arm. "Down, Andrew. You're talking nonsense. I'm thirsty, and I'm going to take Amanda up on her offer."

Amanda wasn't in the living room when they got there, and Dalhu played host, pouring some carbonated water for her and scotch for Andrew.

"She is probably in her office. I'll go get her." He left

them sitting at the counter.

Andrew took a sip then put his drink down. "Sorry for before. I didn't mean it. These immortal hormones are difficult to control."

Poor guy. He was having a hard time adjusting to his new physique. It was good Andrew had such a strong personality, otherwise the change would have affected more than his body. He would've become a different man. Funny how people didn't realize that their personalities were influenced by their body's chemistry, and not controlled solely by the command center up in their brains.

"I know, baby. I'm not mad, just amused."

Andrew opened his mouth to say something when they heard someone knocking on the door. He leaned back and glanced at the corridor. "Should we answer it, or give Dalhu a holler?"

"Both. I'll open the door, and you get them. On second thoughts, a holler is a better idea. God knows what they are doing in there."

"You're right. He should've been back already."

There was another knock, and then the door opened, saving Nathalie the effort.

Kian strode in as if he owned the place, which in a way he did, and Syssi was right behind him with a frown on her face. "You should wait to be invited. You hate when people barge into our place, and yet you're doing the same thing."

"I knocked." He walked over to the counter. "You guys look fancy." He gave Andrew a look-over. "Nice suit."

Not for the first time, she'd noticed that Kian was barely looking at her, and he didn't offer his hand for a shake either. At first, she'd assumed he was indifferent to her, but now she was starting to suspect it was the standard protocol between immortal males. Giving too much attention to another man's mate was apparently considered rude.

"It sure is. It's yours." Andrew offered his hand, and Kian shook it.

"You look gorgeous, Nathalie." Syssi leaned and kissed her cheek. "You should always wear red."

"That's what Andrew says. But I think it's too flashy for everyday wear."

Syssi shook her head. "It's not. But we all have our little quirks and habits. For me, it's skirts and dresses. I feel weird if I wear anything other than pants to work."

"Hey, guys." Amanda finally decided to show up. "Let's move to the living room so everyone can sit." She shooed them away from the counter.

"Onidu! We have guests."

Her butler rushed out of his room, buttoning his jacket on the go. "Yes, mistress. Should I serve hors d'oeuvres?"

"That would be lovely." She turned to her guests with a dazzling smile that a few weeks ago would've made Nathalie's gut clench with envy. "Who wants a drink?"

"I want one, but I can't have it." Nathalie pouted.

Amanda tapped a finger on her red lips, and Nathalie wondered if she was always wearing lipstick, even at home. "I can make you a non-alcoholic cocktail."

"No, thank you. I'm fine with the sparkling water. I don't need the empty calories."

"As you wish. Andrew, I see you have your poison. How about you, Kian?"

"A beer."

"I'd like one too," Syssi said.

"I'll get it," Dalhu offered.

A moment later he returned with four bottles and handed one to Kian and one to Syssi, then put the third one in front of Andrew. "For later."

"So tell me, how is it to be back home?" Syssi asked. "Miss us already? We certainly miss you. The penthouse feels empty without you."

With a grimace, Nathalie cast Andrew a pointed look. She didn't want to bring the subject of an apartment in the keep.

"We need a larger place," Andrew said without preamble. "I was wondering if we could rent an apartment here or in one of the neighboring buildings. We didn't consider a move before because of Fernando's condition, but he surprised us with how well he adjusted here. We could use help with him. Someone to keep an eye on him so Nathalie and I can have a breather."

Nathalie's cheeks warmed. This was exactly what they'd discussed the day before, but asking for help taking care of her father was embarrassing as hell. He was her responsibility.

"You can't rent an apartment in the keep," Kian said.

Nathalie's cheeks blazed hotter. She hadn't expected a refusal.

With a smile tugging at her lips, Syssi punched her husband's arm—not gently, given his wince. "He is joking, you guys. What he means is that you can have an apartment here. No rent required."

They were offering Andrew and her charity. As if asking for their help with her father hadn't been humiliating enough. "Andrew and I can afford to pay rent. We are not rich, but we are not destitute either. Don't treat us as a charity case."

Nathalie was itching to get up and walk out the door. She wouldn't, of course; she wasn't ungrateful and rude. But Andrew's relatives were making her very uncomfortable.

Amanda snorted. "I don't pay rent. No member of the family does. Kian built this building as a safe haven for all the clan members he is responsible for. If they choose to live elsewhere, they have to pay for their lodging, but not here. Don't forget that he used clan resources to build this, not his own money. The building belongs to the clan."

Great, she'd gotten pissed off for nothing.

Andrew rubbed a hand over his jaw. "Define clan members for me. Because I don't think I am. Only Annani's descendants and their spouses can claim that honor."

"Let me answer that." Kian stopped Amanda. "First of all, as Syssi's brother and an immortal, you are part of the family. But you're right; we didn't adjust the law to cover your situation yet. We will, though. I don't want any ambiguity. I'll talk to Edna and have her prepare a draft. The thing is, even if your status is not a hundred percent clear, Andrew, yours, Nathalie, is. You are Bhathian's daughter, and therefore Annani's descendent. In fact, it was a gross oversight on my part, as well as your father's, not to realize that you should receive a share of the clan's profit like every other clan member who turned twenty-five. We owe you five years of unpaid dividends."

Talk about speechless. "But you didn't know I existed! You didn't account for an extra person, whatever money was earned during those years was already divided between whoever was on the books."

"Let me worry about the accounting, Nathalie."

Damn, when Kian used that tone, it was impossible to argue with him. Nathalie glanced at Syssi, wondering if he had the same effect on his wife.

He had an effect on her all right, but of a different kind. Syssi's eyes were glazed with passion, and her cheeks were flushed. Kian's commanding tone was a major turn-on for his wife.

They were such a cute couple. Well, maybe cute wasn't the right term. Nothing about Kian was cute. Problem was, a well-matched couple sounded too clinical. A passionate couple? A loving couple?

Andrew nudged her. "Penny for your thoughts?"

"What? Oh, nothing really. Thank you, Kian, Syssi, Amanda, Dalhu, you are all so wonderfully generous."

Dalhu raised his bottle. "I'm not. I'm still charging you for the portrait, and I regret giving you a discount. You can afford the full price now."

Nathalie wasn't sure if he was joking or not.

"*Mesdames et messieurs*, the hors d'oeuvres are ready." Onidu put a large oval platter on the coffee table. A moment later he returned with six small plates and six tiny forks. "*Bon appetit.*" He bowed and retreated.

"So how is it going to work?" Amanda asked. "You're going to commute to your coffee shop every day?"

"Yes. Jackson and his buddies are going to run it, and I'm going to come in only for a few hours a day. Andrew doesn't want me to exert myself."

Syssi nodded with approval. "He is right. Especially when that belly grows larger."

Andrew rubbed his neck the way he did when he was uncomfortable saying something. "Maybe you should stop working altogether. Financially, you no longer need to. Only if you enjoy it."

Nathalie shook her head. "I wouldn't know what to do

I.T. LUCAS

with myself all day long. I love baking, and I love interacting with customers. What I hated was the grueling routine. I had no life to speak of. I was waking up at four in the morning and collapsing at nine. That's no longer the case. Thanks to Jackson and his crew, I can take it easy and enjoy myself."

Andrew nodded and pulled her closer, kissing the top of her head. "Is she the best, or what?"

Nathalie rolled her eyes. It was nice to have an adoring guy gushing about every little thing you did and said, but it was kind of embarrassing in company. "Stop it, Andrew, you're making me blush," she whispered, forgetting it was futile. The freaking immortals could hear a butterfly flap its wings in the other room.

Braving a glance at her new family, she was relieved that most of the indulgent looks were directed at Andrew and not at her. A man in love was allowed to make a fool of himself over his woman.

The only one who wasn't smiling was Kian. He appeared deep in thought. "I'll give you Ingrid's phone number." He pulled out his phone from his pocket. "You should call her and schedule an appointment. She can show you all the available apartments to choose from. Andrew, I'm sending you the contact."

Andrew's phone pinged. "Got it."

Kian put his phone back in his pocket and lifted the mostly full beer bottle to his lips, took a short swig, and lowered it back to the table. "I have an idea I want to run by you, Nathalie," he said, training his intense gaze on her.

She was getting used to the immortals' strange eyes, but the intensity that was unique to Kian still managed to unnerve her. "Yes?"

"What if we open a coffee shop like yours right here

168

in the building? Most of the lobby is a wasted, empty space. We can section off part of it and build you a trendy and elegant place."

Wow, that was one hell of an offer. One she unfortunately couldn't accept. Not unless her five years of back dividends amounted to a small fortune. Because that was what building a fancy coffee shop in a high-end building like this would cost.

She shook her head. "I have no idea how much I'm getting in those dividends you've mentioned, but I'm sure it's not enough to cover the cost of something like this. Besides, I don't know if it's a financially viable idea. Spending so much money could only be justified by very favorable profit projections."

Was she imagining it, or was Kian looking at her with newfound respect?

He grinned. "It's a pleasure to talk business with someone who actually understands it. The thing is, I'm not thinking profits here. I'm thinking about a nice place for our people to hang out at, where they can grab a quick bite, or sit down with a cup of coffee and shoot the breeze. We have nothing like that, and I think it would improve the quality of life here. I'm willing to finance the entire building project, and you can collect the profits from whatever you sell."

When she tried to object, he raised his palm to shush her. "If it makes you feel better, you can pay the clan a symbolic rent."

Tempting, it was very, very tempting.

"What am I going to do with my other location?"

He shrugged. "Either close it or give it to Jackson and collect a share of the profits. From what I hear, he can run the place with minimal input from you."

"I'll have to talk to him. I think he would love to have the old place to run as he pleases, but I'll probably need his help with the new one."

"Well, you have plenty of time to figure it out. It would take a month or so to build the place."

"A month? I thought something like that would take much longer."

"Not really. We are not even going to build walls to enclose it because the ceiling is too high. It's not a complicated project."

"What about the kitchen?"

"We can use the commercial one in the basement for the baking, and have only a prep area upstairs."

Nathalie had no more objections. Apparently, Kian hadn't lied when he'd said a coffee shop at the keep was something he'd spent some time thinking about. Either that or he had a very quick mind.

"Well, what do you think, sweetheart?" Andrew asked.

"I love it."

CHAPTER 24: ANANDUR

"Lana." Anandur accepted the collect call. Ever since she'd called him from Mexico that first time, he'd been jumping every time his phone rang. It was good his immortal body was immune to coronary disease or he would've dropped dead from the stress by now.

Why the hell did he care so much?

He didn't love Lana, and the rest of her crew were barely tolerable, but he felt responsible—especially for Lana. If anything happened to her, it would be on him.

"We have a problem," she said.

He gripped the phone tighter, the metal casing groaning from the pressure. "What's going on?"

"We have cargo. Four."

They weren't on a private line, and she was right to be cautious, choosing her words carefully.

"The same as always?"

"Yes, but this time also customers on board."

Fuck and double fuck. That complicated things. "How many?"

"Also four, each purchased one for himself, and they be here until next stop."

"They are getting off at the next port?"

"Yes."

"Good. We can wait."

"No. They take cargo with them."

Anandur raked his fingers through his bushy curls, pulling out hairs and welcoming the pain. Maybe it would help sharpen his focus. "What's the next port?"

"Acapulco."

"How long will it take for you to get there?"

"We go slow. Three days, maybe a little more."

"We'll be there before."

She sucked in a breath. "Anything we should do?"

"Absolutely nothing. Business as usual."

"Okay."

"Be well, Lana."

"You too."

As soon as he disconnected the call, Anandur speed-dialed Kian. "I need to see you right away. Lana just called."

"I'm in my office."

Three minutes later, Anandur pushed the door open, strode into the office, and took a seat in front of Kian's desk.

"Do you want me to come back later?" Shai asked Kian.

"No, stay. Take the files to the conference table. You can work there until we are done."

Shai nodded and lifted the stack of files from Kian's desk. Tucking them under his arm, he grabbed a notepad and a pen in his other hand and walked over to the oblong conference table.

"Shoot," Kian said.

"They have cargo."

"Damn."

"And customers on board."

Kian banged his palm on his desk. "What the hell is he doing? Running a bordello aboard his yacht?"

"I think the customers wanted a taste before finalizing the deal. Lana said that they would be taking the girls with them when they disembark in Acapulco in three days. That's our window of opportunity. We have to move fast."

Kian ran his fingers through his hair. "I need to call Turner. We need a human crew to handle the customers."

Anandur narrowed his eyes at Kian. "What do you mean by handle?" Kian was a bloodthirsty bastard, but he usually managed to control those urges.

Kian chuckled. "I wish there was a market for male sex slaves. It would've been the perfect payback. But I guess throwing them in jail will get similar results. Even hardened criminals don't tolerate pedophiles and slavers. They'll get what's coming to them."

Anandur nodded. "Are you going to make the call now? Time is of the essence."

"Yeah, but knowing Turner, he will take his sweet time answering. I'm not sure if he's really a sociopath with no emotions whatsoever or just a great actor. As far as he is concerned, nothing is ever urgent. Things get done at the pace he thinks they should be done and that's it."

"That's good. He keeps a cool head under pressure."

"Yeah, that's true. But I have a problem with purely analytical people who keep emotions out of the equation. The mind can come up with pretty convoluted stuff if it isn't guided by at least some feelings."

"Way over my head, Kian. I'm not one for deep thinking and philosophizing. This is a conversation you should have with someone smart, like Edna, not me."

Kian waved a dismissive hand. "You don't fool me for a moment with that dumb act. I know you have a good brain under all that red hair."

Anandur dipped his head. "Thank you."

Wow, a compliment from Kian was as rare as a smile from Bhathian. Perhaps he should look for the guy and see if he could get a smile out of him. Two positive outcomes increased the possibility of the third one being positive as well.

Damn, it seemed Dalhu's stupid superstitions had managed to infect him as well.

CHAPTER 25: ANDREW

"What do you think, Papi?" Nathalie opened the door to his new room.

"Is this the same hotel room we stayed in before?" He asked while trudging to the BarcaLounger Okidu had been kind enough to schlep from Syssi's penthouse down to their new apartment.

"Not the same room, but the same building."

He lowered himself carefully, bracing his weight on his hands to help his weak leg muscles and achy knees on his way down. He sighed when he sank into the soft comfort of the chair. "This is such a good easy chair. I wish I had one like that at home."

"We will be staying here for a while, and you can enjoy it to your heart's content." She was expecting a rebuttal, but her father found the remote and got busy flipping channels on the big flat screen hanging on the wall.

"Do you want your door closed or opened?" Nathalie

asked as she stepped out.

"Closed, thank you," he said without sparing her a glance.

That went way easier than she'd thought it would, which meant that the shit storm was still waiting to happen. She wasn't that lucky. Instinctively, she rubbed her hand over her belly, a mini panic attack stealing her breath away.

Whatever it was, it had better not touch her baby.

Nathalie closed her eyes and willed herself to calm down. Stress was bad for the baby. She was silly and superstitious. Of course, she was lucky. She was blessed beyond belief.

She was getting married to a man who was better than any dream she'd ever had, was expecting a beautiful and healthy baby, was opening a new business, and she was about to live like royalty in a most gorgeous apartment.

Ingrid had shown them several of the already furnished ones that had originally belonged to the timeshare portion of the building. She'd explained that most of the apartments she was readying for incoming clan members were smaller, with only one or two bedrooms. After all, with very few exceptions, most lived alone.

That entire floor was getting annexed for what comprised the clan's living quarters, and as Andrew and Nathalie had walked from one apartment to the next, a bunch of technicians had been rewiring cameras in the wide corridor.

The layouts and furnishings of the apartments on this level were almost identical, but this one had the best view. A living room and a dining room shared one big space, with a bank of windows overlooking the city. In addition, there were three bedrooms and three bathrooms, a laundry room, and a kitchen with a walk-in pantry—a true luxury.

The only things she'd brought from her old home were a few pictures, pillows, Papi's favorite throw, and clothes.

There were walk-in closets in all three bedrooms, and the master's was as big as her entire bedroom in the old house. The best part, however, other than having a room in between the master and her father's, was the master bathroom. It had a bathtub big enough for two and a shower big enough for four. Not that she was planning on inviting anyone other than Andrew into that shower.

Nathalie sat on the king-sized bed and flopped back. So soft. She spread her arms over the coverlet and closed her eyes, letting her other senses take over. Everything smelled new and clean.

Lovely, but it didn't smell like home.

She was so used to the slightly moldy scent of the old building's walls, to the food smells clinging to the furniture, to the odor of rotting trash wafting from the overturned trash cans in the back alley, and illogically, she missed them. They represented something that was hers.

Theoretically.

Practically, the bank owned most of it. Her equity in the place was less than a third. Still, it was more hers than this beautiful apartment in this brand new building.

Syssi tried to convince her that it belonged to her and Andrew, but it didn't. Even if she accepted that in some small way she owned a share in the clan's net profits and its assets, she had a hard time with this communal ownership thing. The building supposedly belonged to the clan, and as such, each member was entitled to an apartment. Logically, she understood what it meant, but in her heart she didn't feel like it was hers. She hadn't earned it; she didn't work for it; so how could it be hers?

"Are you taking a nap, sweetheart?" Andrew walked in with a bunch of trash bags overstuffed with clothing and shoes.

She sat up. "No, just checking out the bed."

He dropped his load inside the closet and stepped out. "And what's the verdict? Is it fit for my queen?"

"Come and check for yourself." She patted the spot next to her.

Andrew glanced her way longingly but shook his head. "I'd better not. You know what would happen if I get in bed with you."

"You'll fall asleep?" she teased.

"No. Your father is going to schlep the rest of the stuff up and walk in on us."

For a moment she thought he'd meant Papi and got confused. "We shouldn't refer to Bhathian as my father with Papi around. He might overhear and get upset."

"You're right." Andrew bent at the waist and planted a kiss on her lips. "Just a little advance on what I plan to deliver later."

Sweet Andrew, always hungry for her. She was indeed lucky. Hopefully, he would still find her sexy and desirable when she was big as a whale. A little snort escaped her throat. She shouldn't worry about that. Andrew had been a walking hormone before his transition; now he was a squadron of hormones folded into one. He would want her no matter what she looked like.

Or not.

What if he started lusting after other women?

Stop it! Andrew loves you, and he will never look at

another woman the way he looks at you.

Again, logic was saying one thing, while the jealous Godzilla living inside her was whispering hateful things in her ear.

Nathalie shook her head. The Godzilla was imaginary and easy to banish, and luckily no real ghosts had paid her a visit in a long time. She wouldn't have minded a chat with Mark, she kind of missed him, but it was nice to have silence in her head, to be alone with her thoughts.

Maybe it was the pregnancy.

Who knew what a baby was aware of?

Perhaps pregnant women were off limits for ghosts, and she was looking into nine months of reprieve.

Yay!

Energized, Nathalie got up and headed to the closet. Their stuff wasn't going to jump out of the bags and magically arrange itself on the shelves.

She was done with one bag when Andrew came over with a new load. "These are your dad's things. Where do you want me to put them?"

She pointed to the far corner of the closet. "Put them there. I'll sort them away after I'm done with ours."

He offered his hand and helped her up, then pulled her in for a gentle hug. "Take it easy, Nathalie. It doesn't need to be all done today. You need to pace yourself." He placed a warm palm on her tummy. "You need to be mindful of the little one in here."

Silly man. She was just at the beginning stages of the pregnancy, and the little one was probably invisible without a microscope. She was perfectly fine working the same as she'd done before. But unless she wanted a long lecture, she'd better humor him. "I will."

He lifted a brow. "Promise?"

Damn, he knew her too well. "I promise. The moment I feel tired, I'll stop."

"I guess that's the best I'm going to get from you, so fine. I'm going to the house to pick up more clothes. Do you want anything from there?"

In fact, she did, and for some reason had felt shy to ask. But now that he brought it up... "Your grandma's china. It's so beautiful, and it would be a shame to leave it there to collect dust, or worse, for your tenants to break it."

Andrew smiled. "Consider it done. And it's our tenants, not mine. My home is your home."

"We are not married yet."

He grabbed her chin between his thumb and forefinger and gave it a little shake. "In everything that matters we are. A pagan ceremony performed by a superior being who isn't really a goddess is not what will define our commitment to each other."

"You're right. We should get married in a civil court."

Andrew rolled his eyes. "Stubborn woman. Do you really want to?"

"Of course. I want to be legally married. We are having a child. She would want her parents to be married for real."

"As you wish."

Smart man. She wasn't going to budge on that even though the idea of a civil marriage had just occurred to her.

"Well, that's the last of it," Bhathian said as he walked in with more trash bags. By the shape of them, they contained pillows and blankets and other bedding, which she now realized wouldn't fit her new, king-sized bed. She should take it back and let Jackson use it.

The boys had been ecstatic about having the place for

themselves, especially since she'd offered it to them as a bonus and wasn't going to charge them rent.

"You can leave those in the hallway," she told him. "You guys are probably thirsty after all this schlepping back and forth. Let's get something to drink." She motioned for them to follow her to the kitchen.

"Do we have anything?" Andrew asked.

She turned her head around and smiled. "A full fridge thanks to your sister and her trusty butler. "

Syssi had thought of everything, making sure they didn't need to go grocery shopping for at least a week.

Nathalie opened the fridge and pulled out two beers for Andrew and Bhathian and a Perrier for herself. She handed the beers to the guys, then watched with envy as they gulped them down. A cold beer would've been wonderful. She unscrewed the top of her soda and took a long sip. Not as good, but good enough.

"Can immortal females drink beer while pregnant?" she asked Bhathian.

"I don't know. You'll have to ask Bridget." He emptied the bottle and threw it into the recycling bin.

"Well, I'd better say my goodbyes now. I'm flying out to Rio tonight."

Nathalie pulled him down to her and kissed his cheek. "Good luck."

Andrew clapped him on the back. "Roni said that he'd done something so he would get a notification whenever there is activity in Eva's account. Don't ask me to explain what or how because I didn't understand most of it. But in any case, he is going to call me as soon as there is any activity in that account, and I'm going to call you."

"Good deal." They clasped hands.

"Are you going to make it to the wedding?" Nathalie asked just to make sure. He'd said he would, but it couldn't hurt to ask again.

"I wouldn't miss it for anything. If we are lucky, I'll have your mother with me, If we are not, I'll resume the search after the wedding."

Nathalie nodded. "Don't feel bad if you can't find her."

He nodded in agreement, but his expression told another story. "Take care of my baby, Andrew."

"Naturally." Andrew wrapped an arm around her shoulders and pulled her close.

Bhathian smiled, which was almost shocking because he practically never did. "I'm happy for you. You look good together." He rubbed his hand over his jaw as if not sure what to do or say next. "Well, I'll see you at the wedding." He turned around and walked out.

"I'm going to miss him," Nathalie whispered, suddenly sad to see him go.

She should be glad. Bhathian was going to find her mother, something she'd been praying for ever since Eva had disappeared.

She couldn't help feeling anxious, though.

What if something happened to Bhathian? What if she never saw him again? What if he disappeared from her life the same way her mother had?

Her fear was irrational, she knew it, and yet she couldn't help it.

Andrew hugged her even closer, then kissed the top of her head. "He is going to be okay, baby. Bhathian is a powerful immortal, one of the strongest, deadliest creatures on earth. You have nothing to worry about."

CHAPTER 26: KIAN

"When are you going to be done?" Syssi poked her head into Kian's home office.

"When I decide I'm done. It's not like this shit ever ends." He pointed to the stack of files he'd brought with him from his underground office. He was still working the same insane hours as before, but for some reason dividing his time between the basement and his home office made a difference. At home, he could work barefoot, in a pair of old jeans that were softened by endless wash cycles. He could also take breaks and have a snack in the kitchen with Syssi, or just have Syssi.

Life was good.

Andrew and Nathalie moving into the keep was another source of satisfaction. He liked having his family near him. Not necessarily interacting with them—who had the time or the patience—but knowing they were within reach and safe, gave him much-needed peace of mind.

"Please decide soon. I want to bring Andrew and Nathalie a housewarming present."

"Can't you do it without me?"

She shook her head. "You're coming with me. It would be rude not to."

"What did you get them?"

She smirked. "What do you think? A cappuccino maker."

Naturally. His wife's new hobby, or rather obsession. "Good choice."

"Right? I thought so too. By the way, did you call Sari?"

"About what?"

"The wedding, silly. Don't tell me you forgot."

Fuck. He did. Alex and the Russians had taken over his cognitive ram. Between talking with Turner and planning a coordinated extraction involving several units working together on foreign soil, a nice little thing like his brother-in-law's wedding had been shoved to the to-do-later file of his brain and then forgotten.

"You should have reminded me. I'll call her right now." He glanced at his watch. It was early morning in Scotland, but Sari should be up already.

"Blame the wife, why not?" Syssi murmured as she turned to go.

"Wait! Don't you want to be here when I talk to her? Discuss details?" What did he know about weddings?

"No. Just see if she is willing to do it and close on a specific date. I'll call her later with the details. There is no point in discussing the particulars before she agrees. What if she says no?"

He frowned. "Why the hell would she refuse?"

Syssi shrugged. "Maybe they are in the middle of remodeling the ballroom? You've said they are renovating the castle. Or maybe she has a vacation scheduled? You shouldn't take a yes for granted."

"Fine."

She blew him a kiss and sauntered away, her pert little ass swaying enticingly from side to side. He was tempted to drop everything and chase after her, get his hands on that beautiful ass.

Damn, she would shoo him away if he didn't make the call first. He picked up the receiver and dialed Sari's private line.

"Kian, what's wrong?"

He grimaced. Sari assumed something had happened because he only called when disaster struck or there was some kind of emergency, and he needed her help.

"Nothing, everything is fine. For a change, I'm calling with some joyous news."

He heard her puff out a breath. "That's a relief. I could use some good news for a change."

"Remember Nathalie? Bhathian's daughter?"

"Of course."

"She is marrying Andrew, Syssi's brother."

"Congratulations! Am I invited to another wedding?"

"Actually, I'm calling to see if you could host it. I don't feel it's safe bringing everyone over here again."

"Sure! I'll be happy to. When?"

"Six weeks, less if you can manage it. I was supposed to call you about it a few days ago, but I got distracted by other things."

"What's the rush? Don't get me wrong, I can do it, but a little more time could've been nice."

"Nathalie is pregnant, and she doesn't want it to be obvious when she walks down the aisle. You know how women are, she wants the dress to look good."

"I understand. Any specific instructions? Or am I free to do as I please?"

"Syssi will call you later with Nathalie's wish list. I don't think it will be anything grandiose, she is a very down to earth kind of girl. Nathalie, I mean. Syssi too."

He felt bad about dropping the task in Sari's lap. If she was as busy as he was, and he had no reason to think she wasn't, planning a wedding was the last thing she needed to be added to her load.

"I'm sorry I'm burdening you with this, but I see no other choice. Not if we want the entire clan to attend."

"Don't worry about it. I'll have my assistant take care of all the arrangements, and if she needs help, she knows where to get it."

"That's good. Makes me feel less guilty."

Sari chuckled. "Not so fast. You're still guilty of not calling more often."

"Ditto, sister mine. You can pick up the phone as well."

Sari laughed before disconnecting the call. They were so alike, Sari and he; workaholics, obsessive, driven. Syssi was his balance, the antidote, the one who forced him to slow down and enjoy life. He wished Sari would find someone like that too.

With a sigh, he pushed his chair back and got up. It was time to end his workday and go socializing.

What a concept…

"Oh, good, help me out." Syssi thrust the big box into his arms. "Hold it while I tie the ribbon around it."

She'd wrapped the box in some shimmery paper, not an easy feat given the size of it, and was now arranging an elaborate bow with the gold ribbon she'd used to hold it all together. A complete waste of time since it would get torn and thrown away in a few minutes.

"Why are you fussing with this so much?"

She lifted a brow, giving him that look women use when their men question something they consider self-explanatory. "You can't bring a gift unwrapped."

"Why not?"

"Because wrapping it nicely means you care. And that's even more important than the gift itself." She finished the bow and took a step back to admire her work.

He shrugged. "If you say so. Ready to go?"

"Aren't you going to change into something that's a little less worn out?"

"Nope."

Syssi put her hands on her hips and tapped her foot on the floor—Amanda's style. "How about shoes?"

"We are just going across the hall."

The tapping got a little faster. "Humor me. It's not polite."

The exchange reminded him of another conversation during which he'd admonished Amanda for walking into his home office barefoot and wearing a nightshirt.

Damn, he would look like a hypocrite. "Fine. If it will make you happy." Kian put the box on the kitchen counter. "I'll be back in a minute."

CHAPTER 27: ROBERT

Robert collected his tools and handed them to the shift supervisor.

The guy put them in the lockbox. "I'll see you tomorrow, Robert. Enjoy your evening."

"You too." Robert wiped the sweat off his brow with a handkerchief, then returned it to his back pocket. If he intended to keep the job, he would need more work clothes.

Not that he had a better alternative.

Carol's talk with whoever was in charge back home hadn't gone as well as she'd hoped for. What they were offering was a comfortable cage. He could live with Carol in an apartment in some secure building, but he wouldn't be allowed to leave. They promised they would find him something to do, but they didn't specify what.

Thanks, but no thanks.

He liked his newfound freedom too much to give it up so soon.

188

Frankly, he'd expected as much. Carol was naive and an airhead. What had she been thinking? That her people would accept him with open arms and give him full privileges because he'd saved her?

He knew they would suspect it was all a trick to infiltrate their stronghold. Hell, in their shoes he would have thought the same. But the fact remained that there was nothing for him there.

His only option was to stick to his original plan and convince Carol to marry him.

To achieve that goal, though, he would need to make an effort to appear more exciting. During lunch he'd talked with some of the guys he worked with, sharing his troubles, or rather a modified version that he hoped would fit a normal human couple. Chatting casually about personal stuff with other men had felt surprisingly good, making him feel less alone in the world.

Doomers didn't share much. They talked about battles and who killed the most, or which hookers were the best. No one ever talked about what bothered him on a personal level; like how to win a woman's heart.

The guys had told him he should take Carol out to nice places. Wine her and dine her and buy her presents. Apparently, that strategy worked with their wives and girlfriends. The thing was, these guys were the providers in the relationship and not the other way around. His so-called girlfriend would have to foot the bill. His next paycheck wasn't until Friday.

Still, it wouldn't hurt to try their suggestions. If it worked fine, if not, then not. The worst that could happen was spending too much of Carol's money in a fancy restaurant.

Later, when he got back, Carol wasn't in their room. She'd left a note; something about going out to buy new periodicals to read.

Robert glanced around at the messy room. There were fashion and gossip magazines strewed about every surface, and he knew there were more in the bathroom.

It was obvious that Carol was bored and needed to find something to do. Robert flinched. The problem was that her idea of keeping herself busy was doing someone, not something.

She got back when he was getting out of the shower. "Hello, handsome," she purred, her eyes roving over his nude body.

At least there was that. She liked the way he looked.

"Hello to you too...gorgeous," he tacked on at the end.

According to the guys, complimenting your girlfriend as much as possible was the best way to win her over. Jorge had said it was even better than giving her presents.

Given Carol's broad grin, the guy knew what he was talking about. Jorge's other pearl of wisdom was that nothing trumped great sex, and as a tutorial he'd suggested Robert watched a couple of his favorite porn flicks.

As if an immortal male Robert's age needed tutoring. But just to cover his bases, he'd watched them on the bus on his way to the hotel.

She sauntered to the bed and sat down, patting a spot next to her. "Come here."

A perfect opportunity to practice what he'd learned.

Instead of sitting where she told him to, he walked over and pushed her back on the bed, then covered her with his body.

190

Her eyes sparkled. "Did you miss me, big boy?"

"I did, desperately." He smashed his mouth over hers and kissed her until she couldn't breathe.

It started as an act, repeating a line from one of the clips, but he was getting into it. His shaft was bursting with the need to be inside her. But maybe it wasn't his acting that was arousing him so, but her response to it. He hadn't seen such an expression of joy on her face since, well, ever.

If it made her that happy, he could keep acting. "You're so beautiful, I can't keep my hands off of you." He touched her everywhere, stroking, kneading, pinching. She watched him with hooded eyes, breathless, as he pulled her T-shirt off and roughly pushed her shorts down. His fingers found her liquid center, and he slid two inside her, then three on the next thrust.

Carol gasped. She wasn't used to such rough treatment from him, her tight channel squeezing forcefully around his three thick digits. Was he hurting her? Or was she enjoying the rough play? He'd better find out.

"Do you like it?" he whispered in her ear, then nipped it.

"Yes," she breathed.

Mindful of her suffering at Sebastian's hands, Robert had been treating her with extra care, but it seemed she was ready for things to get a little rougher, more intense. Perhaps it was a good sign. Maybe it meant that she was over her ordeal.

Without pause, he pulled his fingers out and speared her with his cock, shoving all the way in while still holding her down.

She orgasmed on the spot.

Holy Mortdh.

Robert had never been so rough with a female before, would have been appalled witnessing such a thing. But then he'd been dealing with mortal females. Fragile, breakable.

Carol only looked like a china doll, but she didn't like being treated like one. On the inside, the female was diamond tough.

For once, Robert didn't hold back. He fucked Carol with such gusto that the mattress slid off the box springs, landing partially on the floor while the box spring remained in place. He didn't stop. If she wanted a rough fuck, he was going to give her one to remember.

The whole thing lasted less than ten minutes, and when he sank his fangs into her neck, he didn't try to be gentle either. Not one of his best performances, but Carol wasn't complaining, and that was all that mattered according to Jorge.

"Listen to your woman, bro," he'd said. "Watch her body and find out what she likes, then do it even if you're not sure about it. If she loves it, so will you."

Smart guy.

Several long moments later, Carol opened her eyes with a blissed-out expression on her face. "Wow, Robert, is it really you?" She patted his back as if checking to make sure. "You're not some doppelgänger?"

What or who the hell was a doppelgänger?

"No. It's still me." He pulled out on a gush of liquid. Damn, he must've emptied one hell of a load into her. "Get showered and dressed. I made a reservation at the Wynn hotel's steakhouse for seven."

She narrowed her eyes and slapped his bicep. "Now I know for sure you're a doppelgänger. What have you done with my Robert?"

Her Robert?

It had a nice sound to it.

"Come on, silly woman. There is no time for games. Unless you want to forget about the reservation and save the money for something more important."

She smirked. "Okay, now you've proved that you are still you."

An hour later, they exited the taxi and walked into the fancy lobby of the Wynn.

Carol took his hand and tugged. "Come on, I'll show you the high rollers' tables. The really big money is behind closed doors, naturally, but it's interesting to watch the guys in the enclaves too. For some reason, there are very few women who gamble at the tables. By the way, do you happen to have some precognition talent? Because if you do, you can make a killing here."

He shook his head, not understanding what she was talking about. The noise level in the casino was deafening, and the gamblers emitted a nasty smell he wasn't familiar with—a mix of anxiety and excitement with a hefty dose of greed.

Carol tugged on his hand again, pulling him down to her. "Look over there." She pointed. "That's a high roller for sure. Four bodyguards. I've never seen one with so many."

The man she was pointing to was indeed surrounded by four burly guys. About a hundred feet or so ahead, the five were walking in the same direction he and Carol were heading. Perhaps the high roller was on his way to the steakhouse as well.

The bodyguards dwarfed the guy they were protecting, and yet there was an unmistakable air of power around him. Of medium height and build, his posture relaxed, the man walked with the fluid gait of a gymnast or a dancer—his arms swinging slightly as if he was listening to some catchy tune and moving them in sync to the music.

There was something familiar about the man. Robert had seen that exact kind of walk before...

He grabbed Carol's elbow, turning her around, and whispered while propelling her forward, "Don't say anything and don't look behind you. Walk a normal walk."

"What's going on?" she whispered back.

"Not now, later." He gripped her arm even tighter.

"You're hurting me," she hissed.

He eased his grip, but only a little. Once they cleared the entry doors, he kept walking, Carol's high heels clicking on the sidewalk as she tried to walk as fast as he did.

When they were about a thousand feet away from the Wynn, he dared to look behind him. A relieved breath whooshed out of his lungs. They hadn't been followed.

"Can you talk now?" Carol's voice shook.

"Keep walking. We'll catch a taxi at the mall."

After another few minutes, he glanced behind him again and finally relaxed. "The guy you saw. I think I know him."

"Who is he?"

"If he's who I think he is, that's Sharim's father."

She glanced up at him with questioning eyes. "Who's Sharim?"

"Sebastian. That's his real name."

A violent shiver went through Carol, and she listed to the side. She would have fallen if he hadn't caught her. For a moment, he considered lifting her into his arms and carrying her the rest of the way, but that would've attracted too much attention.

Instead, he tucked her under his arm, propping her against his side. "You have nothing to worry about. He is not a sadist like his son. I heard that he is an even-tempered guy. But that doesn't mean that he won't kill me on the spot if he recognizes me, and then thrall all the humans around to forget it. He's one of Navuh's own sons, and they're very powerful immortals with abilities the rest of us could only dream of."

Carol shivered again, her slight body trembling all over. For a split second, Robert entertained the notion that she was worried about him, but then dismissed it. More likely, she feared recapture. They were both in danger, and it was best to get out of there as soon as possible.

The line for the taxi at the mall was no shorter than the one at the Wynn, but at least they were a safe distance away.

Hopefully.

Fifteen minutes later, they were sitting in a yellow cab and heading back to the MGM.

"Do you think he is looking for me? For us?" Carol whispered. She was clinging to his arm like a frightened kitten, her sharp nails digging into his flesh. He'd been wrong to assume she was over her ordeal.

Not even close.

"Not likely. He's too important for a retrieval mission. I'm surprised he was allowed to leave the island. The other sons, the generals, only leave for short military excursions and only when accompanied by a battalion of soldiers."

Carol tightened her grip on his arm. "I know why he is here; revenge."

She was trembling so hard Robert wished he had a blanket to wrap her in. "I don't think so. We are not important enough. But one thing is certain; with him here, we need to get out of town. It's too risky to stay."

Carol nodded her agreement.

The random encounter with Losham had put things in perspective for Robert. He'd been deluding himself thinking he could strike out on his own and make a home with Carol away from all other immortals. If he could accidentally bump into Navuh's son and top adviser in Las Vegas, he wasn't safe anywhere. And what's more, he couldn't guarantee Carol's safety either.

"Do we rent a car or steal one?" he asked as they exited the taxi.

"Rent. The monster never learned my last name, and Carol is a common given name."

"Let's stop by the front desk and see if they can get us a car."

She nodded. "Where are we going?"

To the only place that was safe. "You're going home. I'm accepting the deal your people are offering me."

CHAPTER 28: ANANDUR

Anandur cast Onegus a sideways glance. "I have to hand it to Kian; the guy knows how to get things done in record time."

The chief Guardian tapped his fingers on the car's armrest. "Money is a great expeditor."

They didn't have all the details yet and would get another briefing once they met up with Turner's crew, but at least the major logistics of arranging the various modes of transportation had been solved.

It was early afternoon, and the drive to the clan's airstrip was pleasant—after they had cleared the goddamned city traffic, that is.

Onegus snorted and crossed his arms over his chest. "Turner was no doubt invaluable to that effort and cost accordingly. The bastard knows people turn to him only when things get too complicated for anyone else to handle, and his pricing reflects that."

"Yeah, the dude holds a monopoly on mission

impossible. Imagine the movie scripts he can write."

Onegus shrugged. "Turner doesn't strike me as the creative type. Dry toast has more personality."

"I don't know about that. You have to think creatively to plan impossible missions."

As Anandur parked the car near the clan's airstrip, the jet they were going to use was already out of the hangar, ready and waiting for them.

It was such a waste of time to drive all the way out there. If not for Kian's paranoia, they could've used a chopper and gotten picked up from the keep's rooftop. The boss had gotten it into his head that there might be more criminals and traitors among his clansmen and that Alex might not have been working alone. A chopper would have raised questions; like who had arrived or who was departing and why. Kian preferred to keep their mission low key, with as few people involved as possible.

Total crap, but it was a blessing in disguise.

To keep things hush-hush, Kian wasn't joining them, which Anandur was grateful for. A civilian pilot, one with a real license, was going to fly the jet to Mexico. With all due respect to their regent's capabilities, no one who learned to fly with the help of a computer game should be allowed to pilot a real craft.

Not with passengers, that's for sure.

They got out of the car, and Anandur locked his baby up, then tossed the keys to Jeff, the hangar supervisor. "Take good care of her."

"Don't worry, I won't take her out on a joy ride... more than once a day."

Anandur pointed a finger at him. "I find a scratch on her, and your baby gets double."

Jeff had a love affair with his Cessna and treated her with as much care as Anandur his Thunderbird. The dude flipped him off, and as he walked away, he tossed Anandur's keys in the air then caught them mid-flight.

"Don't say I didn't warn you," Anandur called after Jeff, then slung his duffle bag over his shoulder and followed Onegus to the waiting jet.

A few moments later, their pilot revved the engines and they were off. The jet was one of the smaller ones and could seat five in addition to the pilot. The transport that would take the yacht's crew together with the scumbag, Onegus, and Anandur back to Los Angeles had been chartered from a private Mexican airline, and it would be waiting for them at the Acapulco airport.

Once they were up in the air, Anandur pulled a couple of beers from the mini fridge and handed one to Onegus.

"Thanks." He flicked the top off and lifted his bottle in a salute. "To a successful mission."

They clinked bottles and for a couple of moments drank in silence.

A frown furrowing his brow, Onegus put his beer down on the pullout table. "Doesn't it strike you odd that Alex is departing from his usual routine? Did Lana mention prior incidents of customers on board?"

Anandur shook his head. "No. From what Lana said, and also Amanda, I got the impression that he never invited men."

"That's what I thought. What do you think made him change his tactics?"

Anandur shrugged. "More money would be my guess. Maybe the buyers offered to pay more if they got to sample the merchandise before taking it off his hands."

"That would mean that the girls aren't thralled unconscious this time."

Anandur scratched his beard. "I wonder if they are thralled at all. He might have told them that it was a yacht party, with some rich dudes who would wine them and dine them and buy them presents once they arrived at Acapulco."

Onegus cast him a doubtful look. "You think this was enough to convince a bunch of girls to spread their legs for strangers?"

Anandur chuckled. "Onegus, my man, they do it for much less. Have you ever had to work at getting a girl at a club? They practically throw themselves at us."

Onegus flashed him his movie-star smile. "That's because we are so handsome."

"Maybe. But I've seen dudes who were below average in that department succeeding with not much more than nice clothes and a thick wallet. That and buying a girl a few drinks was enough."

"We'd better communicate this to Turner's men. In addition to being mindful of the female crew, who know what's going on and will take cover, we will now have a bunch of untrained civilians that can and will get in the line of fire."

Onegus raked his fingers through his hair. "I didn't want to even consider it, but I think we will need to use a chemical incapacitating agent."

Bad idea. The thing worked like a charm, silent and efficient, but also potentially deadly. Not as in a remote chance of one in a thousand deadly, but in a staggering ten to twenty percent. Unacceptable, unless all other methods of rescue were estimated to yield even more casualties.

In the somber silence that followed, Anandur tried to

come up with better solutions. Trouble was, he had a hard time estimating their success. They had no way of knowing what the situation on board the *Anna* was. They might be all hanging around the grand salon, or sunbathing on the top deck, or lingering in their bedrooms, each guest entertained by a girl. The most likely scenario was a combination of all three.

A tactical nightmare.

"I'm calling Kian. I don't know if he and Turner considered the possibility that the girls are up and around, intermingling with the men." Anandur pulled out his phone.

Onegus shook his head. "I'm sure they did. Neither is the type to overlook such an obvious possibility."

One never knew.

Everything had been rushed, and plans had been hastily drawn. No one was infallible. Not even the infamous Turner. Besides, Anandur doubted Turner cared about casualties. To him, it was a question of numbers and probabilities, not individual lives. "I'd rather call and make sure." He dialed Kian's number.

Kian listened patiently for about thirty seconds then cut him off. "We are taking it for granted that the girls are with the men. The details are not ironed out yet. I'll call you when we finalize the plan."

"We don't have time."

"Yes, we do. We flew a drone out from Acapulco, and it caught up with the *Anna*. At her current speed, she is still a day away from reaching the port. Alex and his guests are evidently in no rush."

"We have drones in Mexico? I wasn't aware of that."

"A few months back we sold a couple to a local customer. I called and asked for a favor in exchange for a substantial discount on future orders."

"Good. So does it mean Onegus and I have the night off?"

"You wish. You are to rendezvous with Turner's team and go over the plan."

CHAPTER 29: LOSHAM

For no apparent reason, Losham felt a peculiar prickling at the back of his head and turned around. Scanning the crowded Wynn casino, he spotted a tall, dark-haired guy holding a small, curvy blond by the elbow and rushing her out.

There was something familiar about the guy. Losham closed his eyes for a moment, letting his brain scan rapidly over every male he'd ever met. With his eidetic memory, nothing and no one was ever forgotten, but it usually took a second or two to retrieve the information. The other problem was that he didn't see the man's face. From the back, though, he looked a lot like Sharim's second in command, whatever his name was.

It must've been someone with a similar build.

It couldn't have been his son's second.

Sharim and everyone else at that compound were dead.

Burned to ashes.

Losham turned his head back and resumed walking in the direction of the restaurant he'd been heading to, but then he stopped and looked again.

The guy had also moved the same way Sharim's second had. Ungraceful for an immortal. His strides were heavy and his posture stiff, not fluid like that of most immortal males.

On the other hand, it was fairly common for a large human male. *Pathetic creatures, these humans.*

Losham shook his head. Grief was playing tricks on his otherwise infallible brain. Logic dictated that Sharim's second was dead, like the rest of his son's men, and not gambling in a casino in Vegas.

"Is there a problem, sir?" one of his bodyguards asked.

"No. I thought I saw someone familiar. Let's proceed."

Immortals were a superior breed, even such dumb meatheads as the males comprising his guard. They should be masters of this world, not fugitives living in secret, manipulating affairs from behind a smokescreen.

One day they would be.

He'd been working tirelessly toward that goal, but it was difficult. Not because humans were as numerous as ants while immortals were an endangered species. That was just one side of the equation.

The other was Navuh: a stubborn son-of-a-bitch who thought himself a god.

His father was charismatic, Losham had to concede, but as far as intelligence and cunning went, he couldn't hold a candle to Losham.

He let out a quiet sigh. Unfortunately, Navuh was indispensable. You couldn't lead people with smarts alone. Same as their inferior counterparts the humans, immortals needed a leader who could whip them into a mindless frenzy and unite them around a common goal, no matter how idiotic. A leader was the glue that held them together.

Without a charismatic central figure, their camp would dissolve into several militias, each headed by one of Navuh's power-hungry sons. In no time, the infighting would decimate their numbers.

As much as Losham despised the pompous despot, Navuh had to stay. That elusive magnetic quality, the dramatic instincts that made his father the perfect central figure, were not something that could be learned or imitated; they were innate, and they were extremely rare. There had been only a few such leaders throughout human history. Their power over the masses had been astonishing. Not even the gods could've managed to sway millions using only the power of their personality and a few motivational speeches.

Losham would have to keep dancing circles around Navuh, seeding ideas in his head and making him believe that he came up with them on his own.

From the corner of his eyes, Losham caught a shimmer of a dress, covering something delightfully curvy, and when he glanced her way, she cast him the unmistakable come-hither look.

A hooker.

Sin city was full of them. This one was working the casino floor, a cheapie—good enough for the goons protecting him, but Losham had more refined tastes. A high-end service was delivering a first class trio to his suite tonight.

As much as he sneered at human males, Losham had no problem with the females. Very pleasing when well paid.

Useful.

A beginning of an idea began germinating in his brain. Sharim and his predecessor's method of attempting to capture immortal males had its merits, but they had gone about it all wrong.

Endless patrolling of night clubs and bars in the hopes of finding an immortal male was like looking for a needle in a haystack with a table fork. Instead, the smart thing was to lure those males into a trap.

As with his people, most of these males weren't young. They had been frequenting whorehouses for centuries. But those establishments were not as prevalent and accessible as they used to be.

If he built them a quality one, they would come.

Not one, a chain.

A high-class chain of brothels run by humans who were enthralled to follow Losham's instructions. He remembered Sharim telling him about a special sex club he'd been a member of—a place that catered to his deviant needs. It seemed there was a demand for places like that, and both those who wanted to inflict pain and those who wanted pain inflicted upon them paid hefty membership fees.

A sweet deal, and a perfect cover-up.

Who said that only deviant sex had to be practiced in a club like that? He could create clubs that catered to everyone. The vanilla crowd as well as the spicy crowd, or whatever the deviants called themselves.

And everyone would pay membership.

Naturally, he would keep a supply of beautiful hookers on hand, and let the men believe they were members just like them. The membership the others would pay would be steep enough to cover the expense.

Losham grinned. He liked this plan. Loved it, in fact. And selling the idea to Navuh would be a piece of cake. His greedy father would love a new profitable business that doubled as a trap for immortal males.

The idea was solid. The only missing part was a detection method that didn't involve Doomers circling the premises. Perhaps hidden cameras would be enough. Extremely well-hidden. After all, if a male flashed a pair of fangs and it was caught on camera, there was no need for any other type of detection.

There was another benefit to the membership club formula. It might be far-fetched, but what if it lured immortal females as well? Logic dictated that immortal females' sexual appetites matched those of the males, and therefore they also had to satisfy their needs with random mortals.

The thing was, their detection was even trickier than that of the males. As far as he knew, their fangs were tiny and didn't elongate, and he had no idea if they liked to bite or not. The only sure telltale sign was their superior strength. But again, it wasn't as if they flaunted it indiscriminately.

Still, a remote chance of snaring a coveted immortal female was better than none.

CHAPTER 30: DALHU

Crouching, Dalhu snapped several pictures in quick succession, concentrating on Nathalie's dress. He didn't need Andrew and his lovely bride to pose for endless hours if he could capture their clothing on camera. As it was, they were getting impatient. "Just a few more," he said.

"I think you have enough." Andrew lifted Nathalie an inch and repositioned her on his lap.

Dalhu let his camera arm drop by his side. "Now why did you have to do that? You messed up the folds in her dress. They are not the same as before."

"My leg is getting numb."

Lifting the camera back up, Dalhu pinned Andrew with a hard stare. "No, it's not, you are an immortal. Be a man and sit still for a few more minutes."

He'd made good progress with their portrait, but he was leaving for Hawaii later that evening and wanted to continue the work there. At this stage, with Nathalie's face and hair done, and Andrew's almost there, he could complete the rest using photographs instead of live modeling. Capturing the exact shade of their clothing wasn't as important.

"You really shouldn't take work with you on your vacation," Nathalie said for the tenth time. "You should enjoy your time off with Amanda."

Dalhu still couldn't believe Kian had agreed to let him go. All he had to do was ask. It seemed he was indeed a fully-fledged member of the clan now. Except for one thing—no share in the profits. He still needed to earn his keep. But it didn't bother him. He wasn't a member by birthright and therefore didn't deserve a share of the clan's extensive fortune. He had all the riches he could have ever dreamt of. A female to love and who loved him back, a place to call home, and an occupation to help heal his soul and push the darkness away.

He snapped another picture. "Amanda is going to be busy getting the rescued females settled. I'm sure I'll have plenty of free time on my hands."

"Are you done?" Andrew grumbled.

"Yes. You can get up." Dalhu took the camera, a fancy piece of equipment Amanda had surprised him with, and hooked it up to his laptop to upload the pictures.

Gently, as if she was a delicate flower, Andrew lifted Nathalie off his lap and helped her stand. Once he was sure she was steady, he stretched.

The girl looked tired. While snapping pictures, Dalhu had noticed the dark circles under her big, brown eyes. He supposed it was to be expected in her condition. Not that he had any reference to judge by, but it made sense. Her body was working double duty now, doing everything it had always done while also building a new life.

Quite miraculous.

He glanced at Amanda who passed by the studio's open door with another suitcase in hand, wondering how he would feel if she was with child.

Crazy with worry, that's how.

From the little he'd learned while listening to Bridget talk about immortal pregnancies, he'd surmised that there was no risk to the mothers. If anything went wrong, their bodies' rapid healing took care of it. But miscarriages were common, which was especially devastating given the low conception rate.

Amanda had already lost a child and had barely survived the tragedy. Losing another would shatter her to pieces.

If contraception were an option for immortals, he would have used it. Not that he didn't want to have children, he would have loved nothing more, but risking Amanda's mental health wasn't worth it. Not to him.

"Darlings," she called while passing by again. "I hate to rush you, but Dalhu hasn't packed yet. We need to go."

Andrew pulled Dalhu into a quick embrace and clapped him on his back. "Enjoy your vacation, Dalhu. See you in a few days."

Nathalie smiled. "Have fun," she said, patting Dalhu's arm on her way out.

He cast a worried glance at Andrew, but apparently, the guy didn't mind the small token of affection his fiancée had shown Dalhu. Kian was so much worse. He got angry if anyone's eyes lingered on his wife for too long—and what he considered too long was about a half a second.

Dalhu frowned. It was strange that he'd never experienced jealousy or possessiveness toward Amanda. It seemed he was the odd immortal in that regard. The only thing that bothered him about other males leering after her was that they didn't deserve to even think about her, let alone have the nasty thoughts he knew they had. It was akin to sacrilege. Mortals shouldn't have these kinds of thoughts about a goddess.

Amanda wasn't as openly affectionate toward him as Syssi and Nathalie were toward their mates. And yet he had never doubted her, or her love for him. He was as sure of it as he was of his own. She'd never mentioned a wedding either, and it was fine by him. The last thing he needed was to be the center of attention with several hundred clan members eyeing him with suspicion. He wasn't naive; not everyone had accepted him wholeheartedly.

"Dalhu!" she called from their walk-in closet. "Don't just stand there, get moving! Do you want me to pack for you?"

Not a bad idea. "Would you, please?"

She marched into the studio and put her hands on her hips. "When I offered to do so this morning, you said you'd do it. I could've been done with it hours ago."

Amanda looked magnificent when she was angry, and Dalhu couldn't help himself. He pulled her against his body and kissed her until her body went soft in his arms. "I'm sorry. I got carried away with the portrait, which I still need to pack carefully because the paint is wet. And then there are the rest of my supplies."

When she lifted her eyes to him, there was only love in those twin blue lakes. "Why are you taking so much stuff with you? We are only going for a few days."

"As I told you, I want to paint a Hawaiian sunset and sunrise because they are magnificent. Besides, it may take longer. You said so yourself."

She lifted her chin and kissed him lightly. "Okay. But

when I say stop, you drop everything, and we go out to have fun."

A chuckle bubbled up from deep in his belly. "Was there a time when I didn't? I always do what you want."

Her cheeks pinked and she rolled her eyes. "I wish. You never say no, but you use all kinds of delaying tactics."

"Oh, yeah? Give me one example."

She waved her hand at the room. "You were supposed to be done hours ago, and everything should have been packed already."

She had a point.

He kissed her forehead. "I need to retain some male dignity, woman. Besides, what's the rush? The plane isn't going to leave without us."

They were taking the largest of the clan's jets, and he was looking forward to experiencing the luxurious mode of transportation. Regrettably, they would be sharing the ride with the rescued females, and he would be exiled to the cockpit, out of their way. After what they'd been through, a male his size might look too intimidating to them.

A pity. He would've loved to join the mile-high club.

"I know, but I don't want a group of twenty-four women waiting for us."

He sighed. "I wish we were flying by ourselves."

Her eyes sparkled as she asked, "Why? Did you have some naughty ideas?"

"Aha."

"Don't worry, darling." She winked. "Leave it to Amanda. I'll find a way."

His woman was the best. "I love you," he said.

"I love you too. Now hurry up and pack your supplies. I really don't want to be late."

CHAPTER 31: NATHALIE

"How is Tiffany doing?" Andrew asked when Nathalie came back from saying goodbye to the girl, as well as to the rest of the women who were leaving for Hawaii.

She sat next to him on the couch, kicked off her shoes, and tucked her feet under her. "Excited, a little anxious. This is going to be her first plane ride."

Andrew wrapped his arm around her, and she rested her head on his bicep. "What did Vanessa tell them about the trip? Were they already thralled?"

"No, not yet. Amanda told them about this great job opportunity in a luxurious new hotel, with lodging and training included. She then asked each one of the girls if she was interested. Vanessa wanted to make sure they were told about it without influence to gauge their responses."

"And?"

"Unanimous excitement. Come on, who wouldn't want to move to Hawaii with a guaranteed, well-paying job?"

"Not me."

"Why not?"

"Because I love it here. Just look at this apartment. And most of the people we love are within an elevator ride."

Nathalie snuggled up to Andrew and pushed her hand under his T-shirt, resting it on his warm skin. "Yeah, I don't want to go anywhere either. Syssi showed me the movie theater in the basement, we should try it out."

Andrew kissed her forehead. "You know what we haven't done yet?"

Stifling a chuckle, Nathalie sighed dramatically and asked, "What?" Knowing Andrew, whatever it was, it surely had something to do with sex.

He leaned and whispered, his hot breath tickling her ear. "We didn't try sex in the tub yet."

"Nor did we try the kitchen counter..." she added.

"Or the lounge chair on the balcony outside our room."

"Pervert."

Andrew released an offended puff. "Get your head out of the gutter, woman, I was talking about sunbathing."

Yeah, right.

She looked up at his smirking face and arched a brow. "Really?"

"No, not really."

Andrew was so predictable, but in a good way. She wouldn't want him to change a bit.

"We have to wait until my father is asleep."

"I think he already is. I hear snoring from his room."

Nathalie sighed. With his new and improved hearing, there was no doubt that what he heard was true. "He must've fallen asleep in the BarcaLounger. I'll better check up on him."

"While you do that, I'll fill the tub."

"Sounds good."

As she'd suspected, she found Papi asleep in his chair. He'd reclined it fully, so it was almost flat. The television was still droning in the background, but she didn't turn it off. Papi slept like a baby with the television on but woke up the moment it was turned off.

Instead, she picked up the blanket that had slid down to the floor and covered him, then snatched a pillow from the bed and tucked it under his head. Satisfied that he was comfortable, she tiptoed out and closed the door quietly behind her.

Once again, as she walked the twenty feet or so from his room to the master bedroom, Nathalie felt like skipping with joy. Finally, they had some privacy.

Her grin grew wider when she found Andrew lying in the rapidly filling bathtub, his magnificent nude body a vision to behold. For a moment she just gazed at him, getting her fill of his masculine yumminess.

"Are you going to just stand there? Or are you going to join me?"

Damn his hearing. He'd known she was there, ogling him. As if the guy needed any more fodder for his ego.

She made quick work of shedding her clothes and walked over to the tub. "Is the water hot?"

She lifted a foot over the rim and dipped her toes. It was slightly too warm for her liking. She remembered reading somewhere that it wasn't good for the baby.

"Could you add a little more cold water, please?"

Andrew made a face but did as she asked.

She waited a few moments for the water to chill and lifted her other foot over the rim. "That's more like it."

Nathalie lowered herself into the water and sat across

from Andrew. The tub was so wide that they could lie side by side without touching, but what was the fun in that?

Andrew was of the same opinion. "What are you doing over there, love, come here," he said tapping his muscular chest.

"Much better," he said as she laid her back against his chest, her head resting comfortably on his hard muscles.

"How are your breasts? Still tender?" Andrew cupped them gently.

Nathalie loved her new larger boobs, they looked great, but she missed the sensation of Andrew's fingers, tugging her tight buds. He was always gentle, but now even the slightest touch hurt too much to be pleasurable.

"Unfortunately, yes."

"Poor baby." Andrew circled his thumbs over her areoles, avoiding her stiff nipples. "How about my tongue? If I lick very gently?"

His cock twitched against her backside. The idea of licking her nipples was apparently turning him on.

She sighed. "I like lying like this. I don't want to turn around. Maybe a little later." She wiggled her butt, giving his hard length a rub.

"I like it too," he whispered and leaned to kiss her neck in the spot where it met her shoulder, then nipped a little, letting his new fangs scrape against her skin. She was getting used to them, and fear was the furthest thing from her mind when she felt them press against her skin. In fact, she was kind of craving a bite. Not that she was going to admit it to Andrew, not yet.

One of his large hands abandoned her breast and slipped lower to cup her center, his middle finger parting her folds. She was wet for him; his hands on her breasts had been enough to turn her on.

The moan she let out was unrestrained, and it felt damn good not worry about making noise.

"You like that, baby?"

"Yes, please, more."

His finger slipped into her, then was joined by another while his thumb pressed against her clit.

"Yes, just like that." She rubbed her butt against his cock.

Andrew hissed into her ear and caught her chin, twisting her head around and taking her mouth in a hungry kiss.

The sound of water splashing out of the tub made her turn back. "Oh, my God, we are causing a flood." She leaped to turn the faucet off, while Andrew opened the drain.

Nathalie looked at the big puddle on the floor. "Our second week at the keep, and we are already causing destruction. They are going to kick us out."

"It's nothing." Andrew stepped out of the tub and grabbed a towel. He dropped it on the floor and let it absorb the water, then used another one to mop up the rest. In a few moments, he had the situation under control and was ready to get back inside.

She grimaced. "Sorry, it kind of spoiled the mood for me to keep fooling around in the bathtub. How about we dry off and continue in our nice king-sized bed?"

Andrew grabbed a fresh towel and spread it out for her to step into. "Your wish is my command, my lady. I'm your humble servant."

"Humble my foot." She snorted as she stepped into the large bath sheet he was holding up. Andrew wrapped her in it, and then lifted her into his arms.

CHAPTER 32: ANDREW

As he lowered Nathalie to the bed, Andrew waited for her to climb under the covers before taking the towel he'd wrapped her in and drying himself off.

"My hair is wet, and I'm wetting the pillow," she complained.

"I don't really care, baby. All I want to do now is to lick you all over."

He dropped the towel on the floor and dove under the covers with her. Her skin was cold against his, and he hugged her close to warm her up.

"Your body is always so warm," she mumbled into his chest. "It's like snuggling up to a furnace."

"Glad to be useful."

She felt so small in his arms, fragile, and for a moment, his heart skipped a few beats as it was seized by worry. Damn, despite Bridget's reassurances that Nathalie was strong and healthy, that uneasy feeling wasn't going to leave him until she woke up on the other side of her transition.

On some subconscious level, Andrew wished she wasn't pregnant. It would've made everything so much easier—an unpleasant and disturbing thought that he pushed away as soon as it materialized. The child was a blessing. He should never think of her as anything less than a miracle. Nathalie would be fine and so would their daughter.

"Did the flood spoil it for you too?" Nathalie moved her thigh to rub against his deflated manhood.

"No, of course not. It was cold," he lied. No reason to tell her he was worried. Nathalie needed him to be strong for her. "But keep rubbing me like that a few seconds more and see what it gets you."

She smiled mischievously. "I'll do better than that." Her soft hand closed around his hardening cock, and Andrew forgot what caused him distress a moment ago. Up and down and back up again her palm went, until he was as hard as a wooden club. A few more and he would embarrass himself all over her hand like a teenager.

"Are you warm enough?" he asked a moment before flinging the blanket off Nathalie and exposing her sexy, nude curves to his ravenous eyes.

"I was," she complained.

He covered her with his body, kissing her long and deep before sliding down to pay careful attention to her nipples. Just as he'd promised, he lapped gently at each turgid nub, his hands plumping her breasts just as gently.

"Okay?" he asked between licks.

"Perfect," she breathed, arching her back and offering him more.

He took one nipple between his lips, applying the barest of pressure, and then resumed his licking. Nathalie's fingers raked his hair, encouraging him to continue, but he had other plans. With a last feathery kiss to each peak, he slid further down until his mouth was aligned with her mound.

For some reason, she had her legs closed, and all his tongue could reach was the top of her slit—right where her little clit begged for his attention.

After a few seconds of his ministrations, her thighs separated, and he pushed them further apart to expose her petals.

"Lovely," he smacked his lips. "My favorite nectar." He speared his tongue into her opening.

Nathalie gasped, her bottom lifting up. Andrew slid his palms under it and cupped each cheek, massaging lightly in sync with his tongue.

It seemed Nathalie had forgotten that she was free to make as much noise as she wanted now, and for a minute or two her moans were subdued.

Either that or he wasn't doing it right for her.

Andrew redoubled his efforts, pressing two fingers inside her as he lashed at her clit with his tongue. Nathalie hissed, then let out a deep, throaty moan before erupting in a scream loud enough to shake the entire building.

Or at least that how it sounded in his ears.

God Almighty, the woman had lungs. Andrew was positive that not only Fernando had heard his daughter, but so had every immortal in the building. Any moment now, he expected the front door to burst open with Guardians rushing in to save the poor woman who screamed as if someone was going at her with a butcher knife.

As she sucked in a breath, no doubt filling her lungs for another scream, he surged up and covered her mouth with his—his shaft aligning with her entrance completely coincidental.

Nathalie took it to mean he meant business and pushed up. The head glided effortlessly through her wetness, and he lost it, growling into her mouth as he pushed all the way inside her with one powerful thrust, ramming against her cervix.

Nathalie hissed, but he wasn't sure whether from pleasure or discomfort and forced himself to hold still. "Did I hurt you?"

She shook her head. "It's nothing. Don't stop."

So he'd hurt her.

Damn, the guilt had a very disconcerting effect on him, and he experienced something he'd never experienced during sex before.

Andrew went soft.

Nathalie wrapped her arms around him. "What's the matter, baby?" She sounded worried, which doubled his guilt. Not only did he hurt her, he was also probably offending her by his very unmanly reaction.

Andrew lifted his head and looked into her loving eyes. "I'm sorry. I hurt you, and I'm mad at myself. The guilt is delivering an appropriate punishment."

She grabbed his cheeks and brought his head down for a kiss. "Silly boy, who do you think you're punishing? I told you it was nothing, and it's not the first time that it happened. You are big, baby, and I love every delicious inch of you, fucking me like you can never get enough."

And... he was back.

God, it was such a turn-on to hear Nathalie talk dirty. It was as if she turned into a different woman. Gone was the sweet, good girl, replaced by a sultry seductress. Only with him, though, no one else would ever get to see that side of her.

Moving slowly, he was careful not to surge all the way, keeping his thrusts slow and shallow and stoking the flames one tinder at a time.

"Please, Andrew, don't tease me," she murmured, clutching at his shoulders and digging her sharp nails into his flesh.

He could never deny her anything, not in this or anything else. Increasing the tempo, he was careful not to hit her cervix again, but it was getting increasingly hard to control his movements, especially with Nathalie lifting up on every thrust, meeting him halfway.

"God, Nathalie, you're killing me..." Andrew hissed through clenched teeth as he let go, pounding into her like they both needed him to. With a shuddering groan, Nathalie's sheath convulsed around him, and his seed erupted.

Andrew went still, every muscle in his body tensing as he poured every last bit into her, some primitive instinct guiding him to empty it all as deep inside her as it would go.

Nathalie's climax went on and on, until Andrew collapsed breathless, at the last moment rolling off her but bringing her with him. As they lay sideways, their bodies pressed against each other's, Andrew was reluctant to withdraw, but even though he was still hard, he wasn't going for another round.

Nathalie wouldn't have objected, but then she wasn't as careful with herself as she needed to be in her condition. She needed him to make sure she didn't overexert herself.

A few moments later, she started moving against him, prompting him to continue.

He clamped his hand on her butt to still her. "None of that, baby. You need to rest."

She arched both brows. "Says who? I'm not tired."

"Says I." He pulled out.

With a sigh, Nathalie rolled onto her back and covered her eyes with her arm. "Don't tell me you're going to be like that the entire nine months. You're going to drive me nuts."

Andrew got out of bed and walked over to her side. "Come on, sweetheart, let's get showered." He snaked his hands under her knees to lift her up, but she slapped at his chest. "I can walk."

"Okay…" He backed off.

As Nathalie swung her legs over the side of the bed and stood up, her body swayed a little. Andrew caught her and held her against him. She let him for a couple of seconds, then pushed against his chest.

"I'm fine."

Reluctantly, he let go, and she stepped around him, heading for the bathroom. A glance at the rumpled sheets stole his breath away.

There were blood spots everywhere.

Panicking, he called after her, "Nathalie!"

The urgency of his cry brought her running back. "What's wrong?"

"Look." He pointed at the bed.

Her hand flew to her mouth. "Oh, my God. What is that?"

"Blood!" He waved his hand.

"I know that is blood. But whose?"

He glanced at her inner thighs then at his deflated shaft, and sure enough, there was blood on both.

"We need to call Bridget."

Nathalie nodded, looking just as scared as he felt.

Andrew made the call, then did a quick wipe down with a washcloth and got dressed. He waited for Bridget in the living room while Nathalie grabbed a quick shower.

Less than five minutes later, there was a knock on the door, and Andrew rushed to let the doctor in.

"Hello, Andrew, where is Nathalie?" Bridget asked in a calm tone as if she was on a social visit.

"I'm here." Nathalie walked in, looking white as a ghost.

Bridget sat down and motioned for Nathalie to join her on the couch. Nathalie sat on the very edge.

"Tell me what happened."

"There was blood on the sheet." Nathalie's voice quivered.

"How much blood?"

"I don't know. What is considered a lot?"

"Was there a puddle or just a few stains?"

"A few small stains."

"Did you experience any cramps?"

Nathalie shook her head.

"Yes, you did," Andrew reminded her.

She waved a hand. "That wasn't a cramp, just a little ouch."

"Care to explain?" Bridget said.

Nathalie's cheeked pinked, and she looked at Andrew. He wanted to tell her that this wasn't a good time to be shy, but figured she was shaken enough. Besides, he had no problem saying what needed to be said.

"During penetration, I bumped against Nathalie's cervix, and it was painful for her. After that, I was cautious, but we got carried away toward the end. Nathalie didn't experience any more pain, but I suspect it was the work of the endorphins."

Bridget smiled and patted Nathalie's hand. "You have nothing to worry about. During pregnancy, extra blood flows to the cervix, and any bump against it may trigger a little bleeding. It's normal, and is not a cause for concern."

Nathalie slumped against the couch pillows. "That was one hell of a scare."

Andrew squeezed in between his fiancée and the sofa's armrest, wrapping his arm around Nathalie's shoulders. She was still tense, and Andrew decided to lighten the mood. "I agree. It was terrifying. I thought here goes sex for the next nine months…"

Her small fist delivered a playful punch to his bicep. "You're such a cad, Andrew, I don't know what I see in you."

"A hunk of a man, baby. You're after my irresistible body."

That earned him another punch.

Bridget laughed and pushed up to her feet. "Now that we have determined that the emergency wasn't really an emergency, I'll leave you kids to fool around." She pointed a finger at Andrew. "Gently, mind you."

He nodded. "Absolutely."

CHAPTER 33: ROBERT

It was late at night when they'd arrived at Carol's home, a small cottage in a nice, middle-class suburb. The inside was just as unassuming—a small living area with a fake fireplace, a kitchen that was open to the living area, two tiny bedrooms, and one bath. Not what he'd expected from a wealthy clan member.

Still, he wouldn't have minded living there with her. It felt like home, or what he imagined a home should feel like. With where and how he'd grown up, his only points of reference were movies.

"Should I bring out things from the car?" He followed her around, not sure what he should do next.

"No. I'm going to call first and see if they want us to come in right away."

"Couldn't it wait until morning?"

"No. I don't want to get in trouble again."

"Again?"

She waved a hand. "I did a few stupid things in my time, and I didn't like the consequences."

That was interesting. Was his Carol a troublemaker? He wouldn't put it past her.

"What did you do?"

She picked up the receiver and dialed a number. "It's a story for another time."

Drumming her fingers on the counter, Carol waited for her call to be answered. When it finally was, she didn't start with a hello. "Brundar, we've just got to my place. What do you want us to do?"

She had called this Brundar fellow a couple of times from the road. Robert found it strange that her fitness coach was her liaison to whoever was in charge of the clan in Los Angeles.

"I'm coming to get you," Robert heard the guy say.

"What about the rental, and what about our stuff?"

"I can take the Doomer, and you can stay and take care of it, or you can come along, and I'll have someone drop you off at your place tomorrow."

Robert bristled. *The Doomer has a name, and he saved your friend's ass.*

"I'm coming with Robert."

The guy disconnected without another word.

"When he gets here, we'll transfer what we have in the rental to his car. I'll come back for the rest of my stuff tomorrow." Carol avoided his eyes as she spoke, and he wondered what she was feeling guilty about.

Whatever it was, it was too late to back out now. Besides, he would rather be a prisoner of the clan than get captured by the Brotherhood. There was no doubt in his mind where he would fare better—even if Carol's relatives planned to torture him for information.

They waited in strained silence, and when a car finally slid into Carol's driveway, Robert was glad to get out of there. The driver got out and met them halfway. He didn't look like what Robert had imagined a fitness instructor would look like.

The man standing in front of him was a Guardian. Robert was willing to bet his life on it. Even though no weapons were clearly visible, he could tell the guy was packing, a lot, everywhere. And the way he carried himself was with the surety of a man who feared no one.

He heard Carol gasp when the guy offered his hand for a handshake and wondered why. Had she been expecting a pair of handcuffs?

"Welcome to the clan," the guy said while Robert clasped his hand. "You have our gratitude."

It was on the tip of his tongue to say that they had a strange way of showing it, but he had a feeling he should tread lightly with the man standing in front of him. Despite his almost feminine beauty, Brundar exuded a deadly aura. Cold eyes, not even Sebastian's eyes were that emotionless, and that flat, robotic tone...

This wasn't a male to trifle with.

Robert nodded, and Brundar immediately withdrew his hand as if he couldn't wait to sever the contact. Robert's lips tightened into a thin line. The guy probably couldn't stand touching a filthy Doomer.

"I'm glad to see you back home," Brundar greeted Carol with a slight deep of his head. No handshake, no embrace, and Carol, who was a touchy-feely sort of girl, didn't initiate any either.

Robert realized that he'd misinterpreted the guy's

reaction. Brundar didn't like physical contact, and Carol was well aware of it. That was why she had gasped when the Guardian had offered his hand to Robert. It must've been a big deal for Brundar.

Robert felt a lot better.

"If you pop your trunk, I'll transfer our things from the rental," he told Brundar.

The guy nodded and pulled out a remote key from his leather jacket's inside pocket. The vehicle's back door lifted, and Brundar helped transfer the stuff without saying another word.

When Carol locked her front door and got in the back seat, Robert wasn't sure if he should join her or sit up front with Brundar. His dilemma was solved when Brundar pulled a syringe out of his other pocket.

"I need to knock you out for the drive." He hesitated for a moment before adding an explanation. "We can't trust you yet, and our location is secret. I'm sure you would've done the same in our position."

Yes, he would've, but it was a small consolation. "Am I going to be held prisoner?"

"Only until we question you and determine your true intentions."

Robert frowned; that didn't sound encouraging. "Are you going to torture me?"

"You have my word that no harm will come to you."

"But I'm still going to be put inside a prison cell."

Brundar shook his head, his long blond hair fanning around his disturbingly beautiful face. "You will be staying together with Carol in a very nice underground apartment."

"A fancy cell."

"Exactly."

Well, it could've been worse. He motioned at the syringe. "How do you want to do it?"

"Get in the back and put your seatbelt on."

As Robert got in and buckled up, Brundar leaned and without much preamble stuck the needle in his throat with the precision of an experienced medic. Robert felt a sting, then something cold entering his bloodstream, and then nothing at all.

CHAPTER 34: AMANDA

An air of excitement suffused the shuttle as Amanda and her crew got comfortable for the ride. The flight had been uneventful. But regrettably, there had been no opportunity to join the infamous mile-high club. With no privacy to be had aside from the one and only bathroom, she'd given up on the idea. Twenty-five females on board, twenty-six if she counted the captain, guaranteed that there had always been a line to the coveted porcelain throne.

Besides, Dalhu had spent the entire flight in the cockpit. It wasn't so much that he'd intimidated the girls, not after Amanda had introduced him as her boyfriend, but that he'd felt awkward as the only male among so many women.

She chuckled. Her unflappable, courageous warrior was intimidated by a bunch of human females. Even now, sitting next to her on the bus, he seemed uncomfortable, mostly physically, though. At six foot eight, he was too tall to fit in the narrow space between seats. His knees bumped against the back of the one in front of them, and he was forced to sit sideways, stretching his legs into the aisle.

"Pardon me." Yet another female stepped over his legs to get to a friend sitting in the back.

Amanda cast her an annoyed glance, and the girl blushed, scurrying away. Were these supposedly traumatized females stealing looks at her handsome mate?

She didn't like it. Not at all. It had started in the restaurant they had stopped for lunch at. At first, just a few quick glances that could've been interpreted as curiosity, but some had not been so quick. The chits were getting bolder by the minute.

In a huff, Amanda crossed her arms over her chest.

"What's the matter?" Dalhu asked.

"I think half of the hussies on this bus have the hots for you, and it pisses me off."

"Shh, they'll hear you," he whispered in her ear. "And I think you're imagining it. I'm flattered by your jealousy, though." There was a satisfied smirk on his face she wanted to wipe off.

"They can't hear me; they are human. And I don't care if Vanessa or Gertrude can. Maybe they will tell the horny bunch to keep their eyes off what's mine."

"Sorry, can't do that," Vanessa chirped from the back of the bus.

Dalhu looked way too smug, Vanessa wasn't helping, and Amanda's finger itched to flip the therapist off. Except, she had an image to uphold. She was there to provide help and guidance to these women, which necessitated keeping an image of professionalism and refinement.

About an hour later, the bus came to a stop at the employee lodging area of the hotel grounds. Everyone filed out, and Dalhu helped the bus driver take the luggage out and put it on the sidewalk. Twenty-two identical rolling suitcases, two different ones that belonged to Vanessa and Gertrude, a crate with Dalhu's work in progress, and Amanda's three designer trunks. It might've seemed excessive, but she'd packed Dalhu's things together with hers, and they were taking the space of at least half of one of the trunks.

While the girls were scrambling to figure out which suitcase belonged to whom, she stepped aside and pulled Dalhu out of the way. "I'm going to stay and get them settled. Do you want to come with me, or do you want to go to the hotel and come back for me when I'm done?"

"I'll go to the hotel."

Her man was so relieved to get away that he hefted the crate under his arm and pushed all three rolling suitcases ahead of him with the intention of getting there on foot—over a mile of uphill trek through the hotel's enormous parking lot.

Stifling a laugh, she called after him, "Wait!"

When he turned to look at her, there was fear on her warrior mate's face. Poor thing. He probably thought she'd changed her mind and wanted him to stay.

"Take the go-cart," she said, pointing at the vehicle parked a few feet away.

"Is it ours?"

"Of course. The keys are in the ignition. When you get there, look for Paul, he'll show you around."

"Sounds good to me." He loaded their things into the go-cart, kissed her cheek, and was out of there with screeching tires. Well, not really screeching—only in her imagination.

"Did everyone find their suitcases?" She waited a

couple more minutes while the last few stragglers located their luggage. "Follow me."

The hotel itself was no doubt lovely, and Amanda couldn't wait to see it, but it would have to wait for later. Right now she was more interested in the employee quarters, where her charges would begin their new lives.

Per Vanessa's instructions, no one was there to show them around. Instead, the chaperones had familiarized themselves with the layout by studying the blueprints.

The four three-story buildings were located behind the sprawling parking lot in the back of the hotel, further inland. No ocean view, but other than that fabulously appointed. Every apartment had four bedrooms, two bathrooms, and a living room with a kitchen. Outside, the four buildings shared a private swimming pool and a large grassy area for employee use only.

Since the hotel wasn't due to open for another month, her girls were the first personnel to arrive. That would give them an entire week to themselves before the other employees showed up.

In preparation for the long and grueling task of thralling her charges one at a time, Amanda commandeered the manager's office, and Vanessa the currently empty employee lounge.

It was going to be long and exhausting. The script they'd come up with was designed to fill several weeks of lost time. Not something that could be accomplished quickly or with more than one person at the time.

In fact, the plan called for two stages.

Amanda was going to do the heavy lifting with the lengthy scenario, adjusting it to fit each girl. Vanessa was going to take it from there and check if it had been absorbed and hadn't created undo confusion. Gertrude's job was to escort each girl, starting with Amanda's office, through Vanessa's approval, and out to the other side of the building. The ones already thralled and those who were still in line were not to mix until the last one had gone through the process.

Three and a half hours later, Gertrude escorted the last one out, and Amanda collapsed, clutching her head. The last time she'd suffered a headache that bad had been after her vodka-drinking competition with the Russian crew of the *Anna*.

Fates, she hoped the surly bunch was okay. Amanda had grown fond of Geneva, the captain, and the others weren't so bad either, especially when drunk.

"You look like shit," Vanessa said as she entered the office.

Amanda grimaced. "Thank you."

"I mean it. You should go and get some rest. Gertrude and I can handle it from here. The bus will arrive in a few minutes, and there is no need for you to come eat dinner with us."

"What if someone has a relapse? This was tricky as hell."

"I can handle it, Amanda. You've done your part."

Well, she had done the right thing and offered, but she wasn't going to keep arguing when all she could think of was the beautiful bed waiting for her in the presidential suite, and Dalhu's capable hands massaging her all over.

"You're right. I'm exhausted. I don't think I could perform another thrall if my life depended on it. I'm all tapped out."

With a smile and a hand wave, Vanessa left and

closed the door behind her. Enjoying the quiet, Amanda rested her cheek on the desk for a few moments, then pulled out her phone and called Dalhu.

"I'm ready to go." She added a sigh.

"You sound awful."

"I feel even worse."

"I'm out the door."

She'd known Dalhu would drop everything to come get her, he always did. "I'm waiting."

This time she was pretty sure she heard the screech of tires a moment before Dalhu burst through the door with a frosty can of Cola in his hand.

She hoped it was as cold as it looked. "Sweetheart, you're a sight for sore eyes."

"Me or the Coke?" He handed her the can.

"Both."

As Amanda popped the lid, the fizzing sound of the soda was the sweetest she'd heard all day. She drained the entire can then produced a very unladylike burp. "Sorry about that."

Dalhu waved his hand in dismissal, and she realized he'd picked up the gesture from Kian. The two were getting closer. They were almost friends; a miracle, considering her brother's initial vehement hatred toward Dalhu.

"How are you feeling?" Dalhu asked.

"Much better, thank you."

"Are you hungry? Do you want to grab something to eat, or can you wait a little?"

Hmm, she wondered what he had in mind. If it was a tangle between the sheets, she didn't mind postponing dinner for an hour or two. "I'm still full from lunch." A little white lie so he wouldn't insist she had to eat first.

His face lightened with a big smile. "Sunset is in fifteen minutes. Paul explained it's very precise here. You have to be on time or you'll miss it. We can take a walk on the beach and watch it."

After the grueling day she'd had, there were a number of things she would've preferred doing other than walking on the beach, but this was Dalhu's first visit to Hawaii, and he deserved to get his fill of its beautiful sunsets and sunrises.

She smiled at her mate. "Sounds lovely."

CHAPTER 35: CAROL

"Is he still out?" Brundar asked ten minutes into the drive.

With his head resting on her shoulder, Robert's deep breaths were tickling her neck.

"Like a light."

"Tell me if it seems like he is waking up."

"I will."

Carol felt strange about the unexpected role reversal. Holding Robert's big, unconscious frame from slumping forward, and adjusting his lolling head so it would rest on her shoulder and not hang loosely from his neck, she felt protective of him. Her inert motherly instincts must've flared into life. He was her charge now, and she would take care of him the way he'd taken care of her.

A frown creased her brow when she realized that during their time together she'd grown accustomed to relying on him. Not that it had been evident in their day-to-day life in Vegas. She had money, and he didn't, she was familiar with the environment, and he wasn't. And yet, having him around had made her feel safer than she'd ever felt before.

Robert was a warrior, big and strong, and although he didn't exhibit violent or aggressive tendencies, quite unusual for an immortal male, she knew he must've possessed them to survive the numerous battles he'd fought in. If the need arose, like it had when she'd fallen victim to the sadist, Robert would be there to protect her. There was not a shred of doubt in her mind that he would fight to the death to keep her from harm—even though he didn't love her.

She wasn't his fated mate, and yet he treated her as one.

Would it be so bad to keep him? Even exclusively?

With her natural inclinations and her colorful past, she couldn't imagine what life would be like with a single male, and one as unexciting as Robert to boot. But dependable and loyal had its merits. Besides, she'd survived these last few weeks without her addiction to sex and excitement kicking into hyper-drive.

Come to think of it, none of her other addictions had bothered her either. Not once had she felt like getting high, or numb, which was surprising given how incredibly bored she'd been. And things with Robert hadn't been so great either. They'd argued and bickered like some old human couple.

A bump in the road had Robert's head slide off her shoulder, and she pushed it back, cupping his cheek to hold it in place. Hanging from his slightly parted lips was a drop of drool, and she absentmindedly wiped it off with her thumb. Poor guy. He'd allowed Brundar to render him as vulnerable as a newborn kitten, basically putting his life in her hands.

Carol tried to figure out what was it about having him around that soothed her soul—enough to forgo her assorted variety of crutches.

Not being alone?

Carol hadn't felt lonely before; she had plenty of friends and relatives after all, to hang out with. They were all single and destined to remain that way, so there was never a shortage of people to talk to, or invite over, or go out and have fun with.

Having a ready and willing sex partner at her disposal?

She'd never suffered a shortage of those either.

Then what?

Someone to always have your back, she heard a voice whisper in her head. She had a whole clan to rely on. But it wasn't the same, was it? Having a mate, even not a fated one, was different.

"Still out?" Brundar asked again.

"Yes. How long?"

"Less than five minutes. Are you sure he is not faking it?"

She chuckled. "He's not." Robert would not have known how.

He was still unconscious when Brundar parked the car in the clan's underground parking, kept sleeping through the wheeled gurney ride to the basement, and rolled to his side with a sigh when Brundar lifted him off the gurney and put him in bed.

Carol was starting to get worried. "Wasn't he supposed to wake up already?"

Brundar shrugged and headed for the door. "Everyone

reacts differently," he said before stepping out and locking her inside with Robert.

If she wanted out, he'd told her she would need to call security, and someone would open the door for her. Until Robert was proven trustworthy, this was how things were going to be.

Not fun.

She glanced at the bar and sighed. There was an under-cabinet fridge, a microwave to heat things up, and even a Nespresso machine, but there was no stove and no pots or other utensils to cook with. Cooking would have to wait for now. A pity, she was in the mood to whip up something amazing and show Robert what she could do, maybe even invite Brundar and show off a little.

Other than the lack of proper kitchen, however, this place was a palace compared to the tiny solitary-confinement cell Kian had thrown her in after her last drunken tirade in a bar. It looked like one of the luxury suites in an upscale hotel, the kind she'd stayed in only when she'd scored with some rich dude who had footed the bill.

This one, though, had some additional perks. Like a PlayStation and a bunch of games stacked high in the entertainment cabinet, or the narrow bookcase loaded with what looked like hundreds of movies. She pulled out a few, checking for titles she hadn't seen yet. Most were action flicks she had no intentions of watching, Robert would probably have fun with those, but she found a few romantic comedies too. She was about to search the next shelf when she heard a groan from the bedroom.

Robert was waking up, and by the sound of it, his forced respite hadn't been pleasant.

Peeking into the bedroom to check whether he was

indeed awake or groaning in his sleep, she saw him lying on his back and clutching his head.

"Do you have a headache?"

He answered with another groan.

"Let me see if I can find some painkillers," she said even though there was a fat chance she would. Immortals didn't normally suffer from headaches, but she'd often felt achy after a workout and had taken some Motrin for it. She probably wasn't the only one who didn't like to tough it out. Incredibly, she found a bottle of Motrin in one of the drawers in the bathroom. The vanity was stocked with a good variety of items she was planning on checking out later.

"Here you go, sweetie." She handed Robert a bunch of pills and the glass of water that she'd filled up in the bar.

He took the pills and looked at them as if they were poison. "What is it?"

"Just Motrin. They will help with the headache."

He shook the pills in his hand. "Why so many?"

"You've never taken any?"

He shook his head.

"You're a big guy and an immortal. We need way more booze than humans to get drunk, and the same is true for pills. Don't compare these to those you've given me. They are not in the same league. Motrin is a very weak painkiller."

He cast her one more suspicious glance before throwing the eight pills she'd given him down his throat and chasing them with several big gulps of water. Putting the empty glass on the nightstand, he started fumbling with the buttons of his shirt—his fingers clumsy and uncoordinated from either the headache or the side effects of whatever

Brundar had injected him with.

"Let me help." She swatted his hands away. His shirt was off in seconds, and Carol continued with his belt and his zipper. "Lift up," she commanded, pulling his pants off when he complied.

"Now get under the covers." She waited until he did and then tucked him in.

"Aren't you coming to bed?" he asked groggily.

"I'm going to grab a quick shower first."

There was no response other than Robert's breathing getting deeper.

CHAPTER 36: ROBERT

Robert woke up with Carol's curvy body pressed against him, her back to his front, her sweet butt a perfect cradle for his morning stiffness.

She hadn't always slept in the nude.

The first few days after their escape, she'd slept in what looked like men's pajamas. It had been one of the first items she'd purchased. The top, which was a couple of sizes too big, was long-sleeved, checkered, and buttoned in the front. The long pants pulled on the floor and had caused her to stumble more than once. She'd forgone those first, sleeping only in the long top and panties, then the top had been replaced by a T-shirt, and then nothing at all.

That had also been the first night they'd had sex.

He'd taken it as a sign of recovery, or maybe her trust in him, when she'd admitted she liked sleeping in the nude and snuggled up to him.

Eyes still closed, he smoothed his hand over her soft skin, following the dip of her waist to the curve of her hip.

She was so small. When awake, Carol seemed bigger for some reason.

She sighed and turned around, planting a closed mouthed kiss on his lips. "How is your headache?"

Headache? "What headache?"

She chuckled. "Good. I'm glad you're feeling okay."

Carol had thought he'd been joking, but he really didn't remember anything. His last memory was shaking hands with Brundar, after Carol and he had arrived at her house late last night. Then he remembered the syringe. Was it last night?

And where the hell was he?

Robert lifted his eyelids and looked around the room. The lights were off, and if there was a window in the room it was tightly covered, but he could still see well enough in the dark to appreciate the luxury.

"This is nice," he said.

Carol chuckled. "Yeah, I know. They gave us the royal prison cell."

"This is a cell?"

"Not exactly. It's more like a luxurious apartment with a locked door. From the outside."

Yeah, he'd been prepared for confinement. Not a crappy cell and iron bars, after all he'd saved one of their own and deserved some gratitude, but not something as luxurious either. Apparently, the rumors about the clan's wealth hadn't been exaggerated.

"How long have I been out?"

"Long. We got here at about three in the morning, and it's after nine."

Six hours of sleep. Must've been the effect of whatever Brundar had injected him with. He was surprised no one had paid them a visit yet. They must've known he and Carol were still sleeping.

As Robert lifted his eyes up to the ceiling and saw the camera, anger bubbled up from somewhere deep in his gut. The fuckers watching the feed had seen Carol naked.

"There is a camera up there," he pointed.

"I know. I saw it when Brundar brought you in. It's off. But the one in the living room is on."

"How do you know it's off?"

"Someone spray-painted the lens with black paint."

Robert felt the tension leave his shoulders. "I need to thank that someone. Other than me, no one should see you nude."

She snorted and slapped his chest. "Don't be silly; they are all my cousins. They can see me naked all they want." And to prove the point, she got out of bed and sauntered to the living room where the camera was on.

"Where are you going?" Robert called after her.

"To bring a change of clothes. Brundar just dumped everything in the living room, and I was too tired to put it away last night." She brought two duffle bags and dropped them in the walk-in closet. "Aren't you going to help?"

Not bare-assed, he wasn't. Robert pulled on his jeans and followed her to the living room. "Leave it. I'll take care of the rest. Go get dressed."

She cast him a look he found hard to decipher, shrugged, and sauntered back to the bedroom, her round bottom swaying enticingly with every step. He would've followed her if not for the damn camera.

She was naive if she thought her clansmen were oblivious to her feminine charms just because they were related. Humans married their cousins, so that couldn't have been too big of a no-no. Not to mention the stories about sexual abuse by fathers or uncles or even brothers.

Robert couldn't fathom anyone doing such a thing to his own blood, but there were plenty of perverts out there, and as proven by the sadist, immortals weren't immune.

He picked up their two other bags and carried them to the closet when the phone rang. Carol picked up the one in the bedroom.

"Yes, sure. Give us fifteen minutes." She hung up.

"Brundar called to say they are coming to ask you some questions." Pretending to search for something on the floor, she avoided looking him in the eyes.

What was she hiding?

Damn woman. He should remember that Carol only looked naive and innocent. Anyone strong enough to withstand what she'd been subjected to and not reveal every last detail of her life, had a heart of a warrior.

"Who are they?" he asked as he pulled out a shirt from his duffle bag.

She closed her eyes and took in a fortifying breath. "Kian, the clan's regent, and Edna, our judge."

They were sending the big guns, impressive. "What about Brundar?" The warrior seemed to regard him favorably.

"Probably."

Robert narrowed his eyes at her. "He is not your fitness instructor, is he?"

The corners of her lips lifted in a small smile. "He is my instructor alright, and what he teaches requires me to be fit, but I'm supposed to do it on my own."

What could a Guardian teach Carol that required her to get in better shape? Not that there was anything wrong with the shape she was in. Robert liked her soft, padded body.

Unless…

No, the idea was ludicrous. There was no way Carol was training to become a Guardian. Yes, she was tough, but she was also lazy and undisciplined—definitely not Guardian material.

Robert chuckled. "You're in the Guardian program, aren't you? You've been holding out on me," he teased.

She gasped. "How did you guess?"

He winked at her attempted joke. "Your fighting moves betrayed you." He imitated one of her bored poses.

"You don't believe me?" Carol bristled.

He shook his head. "Prove it to me. Show me your moves."

She worried her bottom lip and then shrugged. "It's a self-defense class, and if I'm good, I can graduate to the program."

Even a class like that was not something he would've expected Carol to join willingly.

He lifted a brow. "Do you want to?"

"Not really. I enjoy taking the classes because it's something to do, and I'm good at some of the stuff."

"Good for you. It's important to have basic fighting skills." He wanted to ask her more questions, but it had to wait for later. They needed to get ready for their important visitors.

They were dressed and ready when the knock came, but they hadn't had enough time to make coffee. He wondered how formal these guests were, and if they would mind him using that Nespresso machine. It looked simple enough to operate.

The door swung open, and for a moment Robert was confused, his eyes following the stout, strange looking man entering the room and carrying a large tray. He looked distinguished enough in the suit he was wearing, but the clan's regent wouldn't come in with a tray.

Must be a servant.

Robert's eyes darted back to the door and those following behind the servant—a tall, striking male and a plain-looking woman with the wisest eyes Robert had ever seen. He didn't know who impressed him more, the regent or the sage.

"Hello, Robert." The guy offered his hand and Robert shook it. "I'm Kian, and this is Edna."

She offered her hand too, and Robert shook it with utmost care. Her hand was so delicate that it seemed breakable. "Thank you for helping our Carol." She smiled a sad smile that reminded him of that famous painting, The Mona Lisa.

When Carol came forward, Kian pulled her into his arms for a quick embrace. "You gave us a big scare, girl. Don't do it again."

She chuckled. "I don't intend to."

The women embraced next, and Robert couldn't help noticing that Carol had been more at ease in her regent's arms than in Edna's. Had they been lovers? A surge of jealousy clouded his vision, but then he shook it off. Carol had told him that clan members didn't hook up with each other, and he had little reason to doubt her. Especially since Sebastian had said the same thing.

Then again, there were always the deviants.

Taking a quick sniff, Robert was relieved. No one in the room smelled of arousal or hostility. Suspicion, though, there was plenty of that in the air.

The servant cleared his throat and waved his hand at the coffee table, bowing slightly at the waist. "Coffee is served, mesdames and messieurs."

"Thank you, Okidu," Kian said as he took a seat in one of the chairs facing the couch. Edna took the other, leaving the sofa for Robert and Carol.

The servant bowed again. "Would there be anything else, Master?"

"I'll let you know if there is. You may leave."

The regent turned to Robert. "We owe you a debt of gratitude, Robert. You can name your price."

Offensive jerk. As if Robert had rescued Carol for personal gain. He'd sacrificed everything for her. His home and his so-called family, as shitty as they had been, were forever lost to him, and he was left with nothing.

He put his hand on Carol's thigh. "My prize is sitting right next to me." He held his breath as he waited for Carol to refute his claim, saying that this was only temporary until she fulfilled her promise to him.

Kian nodded in approval. "I appreciate your nobility, but let's be practical. You've abandoned your brethren and the only home you've ever known. I'm well aware that you couldn't have taken anything with you, and that you need our help in starting a new life."

Unfortunately, Robert couldn't afford a proud refusal. "I need papers to work legally in the States, and if you can help me find a job, I would really appreciate it. In the meantime, though, I'm asking for asylum. By rescuing Carol, I became a deserter. You can imagine what would be done to me if I were ever caught." He wasn't going to spell it out with Carol and Edna in the room, but he saw understanding in the regent's eyes. The man was a warrior. "I have no doubt they are searching for me, but maybe with time they will give up."

Kian chuckled. "No one is looking for you, Robert, because they think you are dead."

Robert frowned. "Why would they?"

"You didn't tell him?" Kian asked Carol.

She shook her head. "I was afraid to." She lifted her palm when Kian's features darkened and he eyed Robert with suspicion. "Don't get me wrong, Robert is a kind and considerate male; a miracle given where he comes from, but these were his friends. He only hated his sadistic boss."

A shiver went through her, and Robert instinctively wrapped his arm around her shoulders. Whatever her deception was, she'd done it out of fear.

"What happened?" Robert directed the question to Kian.

"Before you helped Carol run, we were planning a rescue operation. When she called to tell us that she escaped, she mentioned the other women held captive at the base. We attacked, liberated the women, and destroyed the monastery."

"What happened to the men?" It was a stupid question, but he had to ask.

"You'd be glad to know that your sadistic commander is dead, but most of your friends are not. There were some casualties, naturally, but the rest are in stasis."

"Stasis?" He had no idea what that was.

Kian shook his head and lifted his coffee cup. "I can't believe they don't teach you guys the most basic stuff about your own immortal bodies. You know that other than death by venom you cannot die unless your head is cut off or your heart is removed from your chest, right?"

Robert nodded.

"Stasis is a suspended state achieved by injecting your enemy with venom but not until his heart stops completely. In that state, the body can survive indefinitely and be revived in some distant, utopian future when our peoples achieve peace or at least learn to coexist."

Robert snorted. "Never going to happen."

Kian's handsome face twisted in a grimace. "That's my opinion as well, but I'm overruled."

The overruling must've come from the goddess. That was what happened when a female was in charge. Females were soft-hearted. Not that he was ungrateful. Thanks to her, the lives of his friends had been spared.

Robert felt conflicted. On the one hand, he was glad no one was coming after him; on the other, he mourned those warriors who were his friends. Even if not technically dead, they were just as good as.

But he was happy that the captives were free and even happier that the sadist was no more.

Aside from getting captured, Robert's biggest worry had been the fate of the other girls. With Sebastian favorite whipping toy gone, his ex-commander would've probably killed them. Carol was indestructible, but they were not.

"Penny for your thoughts," Carol said, her pixie face pinched with stress.

Robert clasped her hand to reassure her he wasn't mad. "I'm glad Sebastian is dead, and I'm glad the girls are free. I'm not happy about my friends being in stasis, but it's better than being dead."

Kian looked puzzled. "Who is Sebastian?"

"My sadistic ex-commander.'

"I thought his name was Sharim."

"It was. He gave himself a new one when we came here. Mine isn't Robert either, but I want to keep it."

"What's your real name?" Carol asked.

He shook his head. "It belonged to a different man. That male is gone."

He saw approval in Edna's eyes. She hadn't said a word throughout the entire conversation, and he was starting to think that she had only come to observe.

The regent was the one who would conduct the interrogation. He shifted his eyes to Kian. "You wanted to ask me some questions."

"I think we've covered the basics." He glanced at the woman. "Edna is going to perform her own kind of evaluation."

Robert turned to the woman. "Ask away."

She smiled her sad smile again and pushed to her feet. "Carol, would you mind changing seats with me?"

"Sure, no problem." Carol looked as puzzled as he felt, but did as Edna had asked.

The woman sat next to him, her knees almost touching his, and lifted her hands. "Give me your hands, Robert."

Not knowing what to expect, he did.

"I'm going to probe you, and it's going to feel uncomfortable unless you open up to me and let me in. I'm not a mind reader, I can't read thoughts, but I can read emotions and intents. That's why Kian brought me here."

Robert braced himself for whatever was going to happen next. He had nothing to hide, but there were things he'd done that he wished he hadn't. Not that he'd had a choice. Still, he was man enough to accept responsibility. He could've disobeyed orders and paid for the refusal with his own life. He'd chosen to live.

Edna's presence inside his head was indeed uncomfortable. Remembering her instructions, he tried to relax and let it happen. The pressure eased, feeling more like a gentle flow. Robert closed his eyes.

"I need you to keep your eyes open," Edna said.

"Okay." He lifted his lids with an effort.

She took forever. By the time it was over, he felt lightheaded and nauseated.

Edna looked drained.

"So many layers." She smiled weakly. "Your countenance is deceptive, Robert. You give the impression of being a simple man, but you're not."

From the corner of his eye, Robert saw Kian tense. What the hell was she talking about? He *was* a simple man, and her words were making him look bad in Kian and Carol's eyes. It sounded as if he was some kind of a mastermind who was hiding who he really was.

"It's not that you're hiding something, it's more that you're hiding from something. I can't tell you what it is, though. You need to figure it out for yourself. You care for Carol and would always protect her, but you don't love her. Not yet."

She smiled at Carol's crestfallen expression. "Not every love ignites with a flare, some start as a spark and need a lot of tending to grow."

Carol nodded.

What was it with that woman? Carol wanted him to love her while she'd stated over and over again that she didn't love him?

"What about the Brotherhood?" Kian interjected, clearly not interested in hearing about love and flares and other romantic nonsense.

Edna shifted her wise eyes to the regent. "Robert has no ill feelings toward the Brotherhood. Not everything he did for them sits well with him, but he is okay with most. I've gotten the impression that he regrets losing that way of life. But that's not unusual for someone who suddenly finds himself displaced."

Kian waved a dismissive hand. "What's the bottom line, Edna, can he be trusted or not?"

"I don't know."

The regent looked disappointed, but not as much as Robert.

"What now?" he asked Kian.

"We have another way to test you. But he won't be available until the evening."

"He, as in the guy who is going to torture me?"

Kian chuckled. "The only torture he is going to inflict on you, are his corny jokes. Prepare to suffer."

CHAPTER 37: ANANDUR

Onegus had received the update early in the morning, and he and Anandur headed out to meet up with Turner's team.

Their first meeting had been last night, and the introductions had been made in a rented shack of a house that was to serve as their temporary base for this mission. Thanks to the case of Coronas Anandur had bought on the way, he'd gained the men's approval even before they had a clue as to who he was and what he could do.

Their commander, however—a guy named Javier who didn't speak a word of Spanish, or much English for that matter, and communicated mainly through a variety of grunts—hadn't been too thrilled about the booze before a mission.

Anandur had disliked him on sight. Sticklers for the rules were, as a rule, not his favorite people.

Even more annoying, the guy had gotten it in his head

that he was the leader of this mission and could give orders to Onegus and him. Anandur would've told him to shove it if not for Kian's explicit instructions to cooperate with the humans.

"Listen up," Javier called for everyone's attention.

"Here is the plan."

Wow, the guy could actually speak.

Onegus and Anandur had gone over the update several times before arriving at the shack; it had been concocted by Turner, no doubt. The guy's logic was solid, there was no argument about that, but Anandur wasn't thrilled about the increased risk to the crew and the new victims Alex had collected on the way.

"Overtaking the yacht while the cargo and the customers are still on board is too risky. We have to assume that the customers are armed, and the women, crew and cargo alike would be used not only as human shields but as a means to gain the upper hand." Javier paused and unfolded a nautical map, then pinned it to the wall so everyone could see.

Grudgingly, Anandur had to agree. However, he was more concerned with Alex than the mortal criminals who could be disabled with a thrall. The first thing the scumbag would do was to grab a girl and threaten to snap her neck if his demands weren't met.

The operation would be over before it ever began.

"According to the inside information that Anandur provided, we know that the customers, together with their purchased cargo, plan to disembark in Acapulco. We let them. Our team will follow and apprehend the customers on land and free the women, while Onegus and Anandur will wait for the yacht to depart and catch up with it at sea, using a stealth-blade helicopter."

He pointed at the map then looked at Anandur. "Make sure the yacht is in international waters before you board."

When the briefing was done, Javier approached Onegus. "You sure the two of you are enough to apprehend the owner of that boat? What if he grabs a woman and hides behind her? You need a sniper. Any of you good with a gun?"

"I am." Onegus flashed Javier one of his charming smiles, but it didn't do a thing for the guy. His lips remained tightly pressed, and his frown deepened. The dude needed to lighten up.

"Two men are not a team. I've been in this business long enough to know that. Unexpected shit happening is the norm, not the exception, and having backup is the only way to go."

Damn, the dry stick was right. Problem was, any human assist they brought along would freak out when fangs and super strength made an appearance, rendering them useless.

Onegus smiled again. "I'll confer with my friend and let you know what we decide."

Javier nodded his approval. "Take your time. The yacht is not expected to arrive until evening."

On the shack's front porch, and out of human earshot, Onegus rubbed his hand over his light stubble. "He is right. I think we should get another Guardian here."

Anandur sighed. "We could use someone like Arwel. Even a drunk immortal Guardian is better than a couple of human soldiers. But with Bhathian gone, the keep is left with only Brundar, Arwel, Yamanu and Kri. These are not good numbers. I don't feel right pulling another Guardian away from there."

"Agreed. The next question is whether we take a couple of humans with us or not. Instinct tells me not to. This is between us, and one of our own. We just have to hope that the Russians will be smart enough to stay out of the way."

"Let's hope so." Anandur followed Onegus inside and watched him deliver the news to Javier. The guy wasn't happy, but ultimately it wasn't his call.

"What are you going to do with the customers?" Anandur asked.

Javier's smile was chilling. "They belong to us. It's part of the compensation."

Onegus and Anandur exchanged looks, then both shrugged. Whatever Javier was planning to do with these lowlifes, it would be a fate they no doubt deserved.

"Javier, one more thing you should know before we part ways. The girls you free may not cooperate with you. They may even think that they are going with the customers willingly. Knowing the perpetrator, we suspect that he drugged and hypnotized them. Hold them here until we arrive so we can check what was done to them."

Javier's brows lifted. "Hypnotism? You guys think I buy that crap? It's all make-believe."

"It's real, my friend, believe me." Anandur clapped the man on his shoulder. "I can demonstrate. If you want proof, that is."

Javier looked like he might but then shook his head. "I don't give a fuck one way or the other. I trust Turner, and I'll follow his instructions whether I understand them or not. My job is to catch the bad guys, free the girls, and bring them here, and then take them home. I don't need to know anything else." He walked away with a disgusted expression on his severe face.

"Spoken like a true soldier," Onegus said quietly. "Admirable."

"Are you jealous? Would you like us to be such an obedient bunch and not ask any questions?" Anandur teased.

"I can dream."

CHAPTER 38: ANDREW

A strong sense of déjà vu assailed Andrew as he watched the display above the elevator doors, the numbers getting smaller as he neared the dungeon level of the basement. Not that the posh apartment Amanda and Dalhu had shared way back then looked anything like the word implied, but it still held the new Doomer behind lock and key as securely as any prison cell.

Once again, Andrew's lie-detecting skills were needed, and he wondered whether the transition had sharpened or diminished them. He hadn't had a chance to put them to the test yet.

Without paying attention to where he was going, Andrew's feet carried him to the right place, and he knocked on the deceptively ordinary-looking door. The thing and its jamb were reinforced to withstand an immortal male's strength. The Doomer couldn't break free.

Andrew was curious to meet this latest defector.

The guy was either a hero or a mole, and it was

Andrew's call that would determine the Doomer's future. He was used to the burden of responsibility. His lie-detecting skills had been put to good use during his long years of service.

Kian opened the door, and Andrew walked in. As first impressions went, the Doomer looked like a decent fellow; clean-shaven, his eyes betraying his worry but lacking hostility or deceit. He was about Andrew's height, the new post-transition one, and had an average build for an immortal male; wide shouldered and muscular, but lean. Like their human counterparts, only those who pumped iron religiously bulked up into bodybuilder territory.

"Robert the hero, I assume." He offered his hand. "I'm Andrew."

The guy looked embarrassed as he shook it with a strong hand.

"Carol?" Andrew tilted his head sideways to peek behind the two big males blocking her from view. He'd seen pictures of her as part of the briefing for her rescue mission, but he'd never met her in person. Like every other clan member, she must've been at Syssi's wedding, but they hadn't been introduced, and he didn't remember her.

She was even prettier than her picture, with a riot of blond curls cascading around her small face, and big blue eyes. When she got up to greet him, he was surprised at how soft she looked. About Syssi's height but a little more padded than his sister, she was the classic temptress; childlike yet sexy, innocent looking but tough as nails. She had to be to come out unscathed from her ordeal. Still, he was well aware that warriors carried scars on the inside as well as on the outside, and Carol might be scarred as hell and just hiding it well.

"That's me. The big troublemaker who caused a war."

"You were just the catalyst. It was bound to happen with or without you." He offered his hand, and she shook it.

Her smile was genuine. "Thanks for letting me off the hook."

"Shall we begin?" Kian asked. The guy had no patience for small talk.

"Do I need to sit next to him?" Robert asked Kian.

Andrew took a seat across from the Doomer. "No, you don't. I'm curious why you asked, though," he said.

"Edna," both Kian and Carol answered.

"Oh, so I'm an afterthought..." he teased. "You brought the big guns first."

"You weren't here in the morning." Kian apparently had taken his affront seriously.

Andrew didn't mind, on the contrary, it was good practice to hear another expert's opinion. "What did she have to say?"

"She was undecided."

Andrew glanced at Robert again, searching for what had been missing from his first impression. For Edna to be unsure, the guy had to be complicated as hell. And yet, he seemed perfectly ordinary. Luckily for Andrew, looks could be deceptive, but words, when spoken to his face could not.

"Okay, Robert. I'm going to ask you a bunch of questions, and I want you to answer them as truthfully as you can. Think of me as a lie detector, just better."

"You can do it? Discern a lie from truth?"

"Without exception."

Robert pointed at Kian. "And he trusts your judgment?"

"Completely," Kian answered.

The guy grinned happily. "Then I'm good. I was worried you guys would never believe me."

"Truth," Andrew said. "Do you want me to ask the questions or do you want to do it?" he asked Kian.

"Go ahead. You're the expert."

"Very well. First, Robert, I want you to tell me a lie." Andrew needed to test his skill before proceeding.

"About what?"

"Anything. What color are my eyes?"

"Blue."

"You were supposed to lie, Robert."

"Sorry." The guy rubbed his neck.

"What's my hair color?"

"Brown."

Damn, the guy was either not so smart or had a real hard time lying. "Again, you were supposed to lie."

"Okay, but you need to ask me something that isn't as obvious. I can't help it."

What could he ask Robert that the guy would be inclined to lie about?

Something about Carol, he wouldn't want to say anything negative about her. From the briefing, Andrew knew that she was a pothead, but Robert might not know it. What else? She didn't work, didn't volunteer, and spent most of her time hanging out with friends and clubbing.

"Is Carol a hardworking person?"

Robert hesitated. "Yes," he finally answered.

A clear and resounding lie. Hallelujah. "That was a lie. Congratulations."

"Hey, not nice," Carol pouted.

Kian crossed his arms over his chest and lifted a brow.

"Fine." With a huff, she mimicked his pose.

It was time to start the serious questions.

"Why did you rescue Carol?"

"I couldn't stand the torture. She was so brave, but I was afraid her mind would snap, and she would become catatonic. No one can go through what she did, day in and day out, not even a trained warrior, and not lose his mind."

"Truth."

Kian shifted in his seat, and Andrew had to avert his gaze. The guilt was as overwhelming as it was irrational. If they could've been faster, they could've spared her days of torture. But that had been impossible. They had done all they could.

"Did you know that by helping her you were leaving everything behind for good?"

"Yes."

"Truth. You had no ulterior motives?"

"I did. The most compelling motive there is. An immortal female of my own."

"Truth. Did you demand from Carol that she be with you in exchange for your help?"

"I did. I asked for three months, hoping she would grow to care for me and consider staying."

Andrew glanced at Carol. She looked conflicted, as if she hadn't made up her mind yet.

"Truth. How did you like your life in the Brotherhood?"

Robert shrugged. "It was all I knew. I hated the battles, even though I did what was required of me. Getting the second in command position with Sharim was a reward, and it worked out fine until he started torturing the first girl and then Carol. I hated him then. I wanted him dead."

"Truth. Was there anything that you liked doing?"

"Since Sharim's wasn't a real combat unit, he put me in charge of all the administrative work and procurement. When he started collecting girls, he put me in charge of seeing to their needs. I liked doing that. I'm organized and methodical. I was good at it."

"Truth. If you could, hypothetically, would you go back to the Brotherhood?"

This time Robert didn't answer right away. It took him a couple of minutes. "Depends on whether Carol decides to stick with me. I'd rather be in the Brotherhood than alone. If I could have a different commander, that is."

"Truth."

Andrew looked at Kian, checking if his brother-in-law was satisfied with Robert's answers.

Kian lifted a finger, indicating he was taking over. "Unlike Andrew, my questions are more direct and require a yes or no answer."

Robert nodded.

"Are you a mole?"

"No."

"Truth."

"Did you come here to gather information about us?"

"No."

"Truth."

"Would you ever consider selling information about us to gain access to the Brotherhood or for any other reason or purpose?"

"I'm not that stupid."

"I need a yes or no answer."

"No, I would never disclose any information about you or your clan for any reason you can think of. I'm not a mad dog. I wouldn't bite the hand that feeds me."

"Truth."

Kian clapped his hands on his thighs. "Okay then. He pushed up to his feet and waited for Robert to do the same. "Welcome to the clan, Robert." He offered his hand.

"That's it? No more questions?" Robert asked as they shook on it.

"I don't have time now. But later we will discuss what job you can take on. You're not completely free yet, there is a probation period during which you'll be wearing a locator cuff and will be restricted to the keep, but you no longer need to stay here. I'll have Ingrid find you an apartment upstairs."

"Thank you." Robert shook Kian's hand again then shook Andrew's. "And you too, Andrew. I appreciate you coming here to help me out."

"You're welcome, but I did it for this guy, not you." Andrew pointed at Kian. "Now, if my services are no longer needed, I would like to bid you farewell and go up to my fiancée who I haven't seen since morning, and who is waiting for me impatiently."

Kian offered Andrew his hand. "Thank you, as always, invaluable." He slapped Andrew's back.

"What do we do now?" Carol asked.

"You wait here for William, who is going to bring the cuff, and then for Ingrid to show you to your new place."

"Thank you." Carol gave Kian a quick hug and then hugged Andrew. "You too."

"No problem." Andrew kissed her cheek, belatedly remembering that immortals were funny about other males touching their mates, him included. He glanced at Robert, but the guy was either too relieved at the moment to notice or didn't share that affliction.

CHAPTER 39: ANANDUR

The wait was nerve-wracking.

The human team was spread out, hiding in several strategic locations around the harbor and waiting for the customers and their purchased human cargo to disembark.

Until the yacht left the harbor again and their part in the mission began, Onegus and Anandur were stuck waiting in their hotel room.

For lack of more productive things to do, Anandur watched the live feed from the drone following the yacht. At least he would know exactly when it docked. The big question was the time of departure. Tonight or next morning, and if it stayed overnight, would Lana attempt to contact him?

Anandur could only imagine how betrayed the crew must've felt. They'd been expecting a rescue by now. Lana was probably cussing him out, using every Russian curse known to men. With a sigh, he glanced at the laptop screen again.

A moment later, Onegus stood up. "I'm going to take a nap. Wake me up in an hour, and then you go. Watching that thing serves no purpose. The yacht is not going to move any faster. In fact, there is no reason for you to stay up either. Kian or William are going to call us when the boat finally docks."

"What if they think the same thing?"

Onegus lifted a brow. "Kian? William? I don't think so."

With that his commander toed off his boots, lifted the comforter off one of the beds, and crawled in. Thirty seconds later, his breaths slowed and deepened.

Lucky bastard. Anandur wished it was that easy for him. He tried, but it was no use. Too anxious and too agitated, he couldn't sleep even though it was the second sleepless night in a row. Not a big deal. He could go without for another forty-eight hours and still subdue one fucking civilian without anyone's help. So why the hell was he so worried?

It made no sense.

Maybe it was a premonition? If Syssi got them, others could as well.

He was being ridiculous.

What was next? Calling the tarot hotline and asking for a reading?

When the call finally came, Anandur was still wide awake, while Onegus was sleeping like a baby and ignoring his cellphone.

Anandur grabbed it. "What's up?"

"Where is Onegus?" Kian asked.

"He is right here, snoring."

"Well, good for him. Just wanted to let you know the boat will be docking in about half an hour. You should get ready."

"Why? We need to wait until she leaves again."

"I want you to check on the girls immediately after Turner's team gets them, and do whatever you need to help them out. I don't want the girls waiting around for your return. The sooner they get home, the better."

"What if the yacht leaves while we are busy with the girls?"

"You'll still have plenty of time until she reaches international waters. Your pilot is ready to take off on a moment's notice."

"Okay. I'm going to wake Sleeping Beauty up and wait for Turner's team to report."

What Anandur really wanted to do was hoof it to the harbor and take part in the action, maybe get a word to Lana. But like an obedient soldier, he was following orders. Which in this case meant he wasn't going to do anything stupid.

More than two hours had passed by the time Javier called. "We got them. Four girls and three scumbags."

"Anyone hurt?"

"The fourth scumbag. Do you care?"

"No, not really. How are the girls taking it?"

"Hysterics. We locked them in one of the bedrooms, and we are awaiting your arrival. I hope you know what you're doing because those are four terrified little girls."

Anandur's blood froze in his veins. "What do you mean little girls?" he growled in a voice that could barely pass for human.

"Sixteen, maybe seventeen. I didn't ask. They shriek like banshees whenever anyone gets close."

"Son of a bitch," Onegus spat.

Too distraught to try and sound human, Anandur handed Onegus the phone. Little girls. He was going to kill Alex, slowly. There would be no trial for that dirtbag motherfucker.

"We'll be there in fifteen," he heard Onegus say

Anandur trained his eyes on Onegus, the twin projectors illuminating his commander's face. "I can run faster than that."

Onegus frowned. "You need to take a deep breath and calm the fuck down. I've never seen your eyes glow like that. Javier might be mistaken. Or he might have exaggerated to get a quick response from us. Sixteen or seventeen could easily be eighteen or twenty."

Not that it made much of a difference. An eighteen-year-old girl was still a child in Anandur's eyes, but the reality was that most girls that age were already sexually active, which made it just a little less atrocious. Not as far as the intentions of those men, but as to the girls' own perception of what had happened. Partying on a luxurious yacht, they had no idea what fate had been awaiting them.

Anandur stomped his feet into his boots, grabbed his wallet and his watch and headed for the door. "I'm waiting in the car," he called out to Onegus, who had rushed into the bathroom. As from this morning, their gear was stored in the helicopter, and they had nothing to take with them from the hotel.

A few minutes later his commander slid into the passenger seat of their rented car, and Anandur took off. By the grace of Lady Luck, they reached their destination without getting pulled over by the police.

There was a communal sigh of relief as they entered

the living area of the small house, though audible only to their immortal ears. Each of the men had probably thought he was the only one glad to see them come in and do something about the four hysterical girls.

"Follow the sobs," Javier pointed to the second door off the hallway. "They think we are the bad guys, and that we murdered their boyfriends and are going to do inconceivable things to them."

Anandur wasn't surprised.

The girls had been under the impression that they were on vacation and going out with guys to party in Acapulco. Instead, they'd been attacked by a bunch of commandos, their so-called boyfriends subdued, and all of them taken to what looked like an abandoned shack.

The key was in the door, and as Onegus twisted it in the lock and depressed the handle, the shrieks got louder. When he pushed the door open, they found the four girls huddled in the corner like a pile of scared kittens.

"Look at me," Onegus said in a soft voice that nonetheless carried a tone of command. He was already working the thrall, pushing it as a gentle wave to induce calm.

A handy little trick Anandur would've loved to master. Unfortunately, his thrall was pitifully ineffective, especially on humans who had whipped themselves into a frenzy.

The shrieks stopped, and four pairs of red-rimmed, teary eyes looked up to Onegus.

He crouched, perhaps in an attempt to look less intimidating, and smiled. "You are safe, and you are going home to your families."

One gathered the courage to ask, "Who are you

people? And why did you kidnap us?"

He pointed to the living room. "These men, the ones you are terrified of, rescued you from a horrific fate. The men you were with were not nice guys. They didn't mean you well. They purchased you from the yacht owner either for personal use or for resale."

"Oh, my God," one of the girls whimpered.

"What do you mean purchased us?" the brave one asked even though he saw understanding dawn in her eyes.

"We've been monitoring his activity for a while now. He tempts pretty girls like you to come on board and party, then sells them to sex-slavers."

She glanced at the shocked expressions of her friends and shook her head. "I can't believe we were that stupid. What were we thinking? We were on vacation in Cabos, a little getaway to celebrate the end of finals week, and this really handsome guy invited us to his yacht, and we thought nothing of it…"

Naturally, they had been under Alex's thrall.

The fact that these were college girls, not sixteen- or seventeen-year-olds, was a huge relief. Anandur thanked the merciful fates.

"He drugged you. That's why you didn't question anything and followed him without thinking, and he kept drugging you while you were on board." Onegus gave them a plausible explanation. "Look around you. Do you have a purse with you? Luggage? Would you have followed these men you thought were your boyfriends without a purse, a phone, a passport, or some other form of identification?"

The girls exchanged glances, then shook their heads, the horrifying realization dawning on their young faces and leaching the color out of them.

273

The one who had done all the talking was the first one to bounce back. "So you're from the government? Like the FBI?"

Onegus shook his head. "We are a secret private organization dedicated to stopping this horrendous trade." Minute by minute, Onegus's calm tone was melting away the girls' anxiety.

Anandur watched the stress leave their faces. The leader who'd asked the questions even got up and sat on the bed, and then the other three joined her.

Onegus was doing a wonderful job, his gentle thrall unraveling Alex's and adding a hefty dose of reassurance.

"Here." He handed the leader a few sheets of paper and a pen. "Write your names and home addresses, and these guys out there will take you home."

She took the papers and handed them out. "Are you going to accompany us?" she asked hopefully.

"I wish I could, but we still need to apprehend the yacht owner and bring him to justice."

The girl smiled for the first time. "Good luck. And if you need me to testify against him, I'll be happy to."

"Thank you, we might call on you, but we probably won't need to. We already have enough evidence to put him away for eternity."

And wasn't that the truth—eternity having a whole different meaning in Alex's case.

CHAPTER 40: LOSHAM

Nothing helped Losham's melancholy. Not the pretty girls, not their soft hands on his body, not even their gasps and their moans and their whimpers.

The only time he felt like doing anything at all was when he was plotting revenge. And the more he plotted, the more ambitious in scope his plotting became. His father, the exalted Navuh, would be very happy with him. For once, Losham's need for revenge aligned with Navuh's ultimate goal of world domination.

Losham had used to scoff at his father's grandiose ambitions, not to his face, naturally. Navuh wouldn't have executed him, he was too valuable, but a beating and prolonged torture were a given.

He often wondered if Sharim had inherited his deviant tastes from his grandfather. Navuh's private harem was inaccessible even to his sons, ensuring no one knew what went on in there. For all Losham knew, his father could've been even worse than Sharim.

Navuh's offspring hadn't been raised by their mothers. The five sons he'd fathered had been taken care of by nursemaids and tutors. The daughters had been given into the care and tutelage of the other Dormants.

To father Dormant sons who could later transition into immortality, Navuh's private harem must've been comprised of immortal females, and not ordinary Dormants who had been turned by Navuh either, but the daughters of gods. Navuh's five sons possessed abilities almost as powerful as their father, which meant that they were of much purer blood than the rest of the men whose genetics had been diluted by generations of breeding with humans.

Losham would've loved to have known his mother. If she was still alive, that is, and hadn't been executed for displeasing his father in some fashion. Losham must've inherited his brilliant mind from her. Navuh was smart, but not nearly as smart as Losham.

Sitting in the antechamber to his father's reception hall, Losham glanced at the huge portrait of Navuh. His father cut an imposing figure, and it was on Losham's advice that he had it hung there and not in his private residence as had been his original intention.

Anyone cooling his heels in the waiting area was forced to look at the intimidating male who seemed to be staring at them from the canvas. Combined with the long wait, by the time they were admitted, they were properly subdued.

Obviously the portrait had no effect on Losham, and he didn't mind sitting and waiting for hours until his father deigned to see him.

That form of humiliation didn't work on him either.

Navuh could pretend all he wanted that he was too

busy for an audience with Losham, his top adviser, but Losham knew exactly what the despot was doing behind the imposing double doors.

Absolutely nothing.

Losham, on the other hand, had everything he needed to keep working while appearing inactive and resigned. The gears in his brain kept turning at an uncommon speed, while his memory ensured that none of his conclusions was ever forgotten. Everything was stored and organized in the appropriate compartments.

A side door opened and Navuh's secretary emerged, but he knew the guy hadn't come to escort him in. Losham hadn't been waiting long enough.

The secretary bowed his head. "His Excellency, Lord Navuh, is very busy today. He will see you as soon as he can." The man bowed again and scurried back through the side entrance to the reception room; the one dedicated for servant use.

Up until Sharim's untimely demise, Losham hadn't been interested in taking over the world of humans. There was no need, no real gain to be had, just a lot of headache and additional work. It was better to be the puppeteer and manipulate the human leaders to do the work for him.

History was abundant with various despots who had striven to achieve that goal, but even though some of them had commanded armies of hundreds of thousands of soldiers, ultimately they had all been defeated.

Contrary to popular belief, what humans referred to as good usually triumphed over what they referred to as evil.

What those despots had lacked, though, was an adviser as brilliant as Losham. He wasn't presumptuous, nor was his ego overinflated. He'd known most of those leaders and their closest lackeys personally. Some had been highly intelligent, but Losham was in a league of his own.

His biggest asset, though, something none of them had had the luxury of, was time.

He could plot and plan then plot and plan again, setting things in motion, then sit back and wait to see his machinations come to fruition.

And that was his second biggest asset—patience.

An asset the great Navuh lacked.

That was why his father would not approve of Losham's plan unless he presented it with a slight variation: The estimated timeline.

Losham wanted Annani and her spawn gone, eradicated, and whatever they'd given the humans destroyed, annihilated.

It wasn't logical. He'd run through the scenarios of possible outcomes, and none of them were good. In fact, destroying Annani and humanity's technological and social achievements was detrimental to the Brotherhood's future. The new technology and global communication made life much easier, even for Doomers.

Destroying it served no other purpose than the need for revenge.

The side door opened and Navuh's secretary emerged, his robe flying behind him as he rushed over. "Our exalted leader will grant you an audience now, but Lord Navuh regrets to inform you that he can spare only ten minutes of his valuable time."

It was the same nonsense every time; a posturing Navuh apparently couldn't do without. Not even once had his father cut their meetings short. He was too smart not to listen to everything his best advisor had to say.

Instead of rolling his eyes, Losham assumed a respectful expression and bowed his head. "Our Lord's wishes must be obeyed. I'll keep it brief."

CHAPTER 41: ANANDUR

"Ready?" Onegus asked, his voice coming out of the speaker inside Anandur's headset. The helicopter pilot had switched to silent mode almost immediately after takeoff, but it was still pretty noisy in the cabin.

They hadn't followed the boat until it became late enough for Alex to be asleep, and with international waters only twelve nautical miles or so from the coast, it meant that the *Anna* had passed that line hours ago.

The high altitude of the drone following it ensured that even immortal ears couldn't detect it by sound. The helicopter's silent mode, however, wasn't silent enough. If awake, Alex would hear it, and the mission would be compromised. The moment he realized that he was under attack, the jerk would use the crew as a shield.

Anandur didn't know the guy well, but anyone who could sell people into sexual slavery wouldn't hesitate to snap a woman's neck; which meant a long swim. The pilot was keeping the craft steady about three nautical miles away from the yacht.

Fortunately, the water was warm.

"Ready," he replied.

Onegus went first, rappelling down and jumping the few remaining feet into the water. Anandur went next. Given the mild temperature they'd decided to forgo wetsuits, which would've restricted their movements. Now that he was in the water, Anandur regretted not putting at least a sleeveless top on. The straps holding his equipment secured to his back chafed like a son of a bitch.

Onegus was a powerful swimmer, but so was Anandur, and it took discipline not to turn this into a competition. It reminded him of the trek up the mountain not so long ago, when Kian and Andrew had butted heads about Kian rushing ahead of the humans who couldn't keep up. Shockingly, Anandur had been the one to talk sense into those two. A lot had happened since. Funny how centuries could pass with nothing significant happening, not as far as the clan's future, that is, and then suddenly everything was changing at an unbelievable pace.

An hour later they caught up to the boat.

With practically no wind, and waters as calm as could be, they were banking on the captain engaging the autopilot and going to sleep. The boat's slow speed was a good indication that that was indeed the case.

The good news was that there were no lights in the common areas or the other rooms on this side of the yacht. Hopefully, both the crew and Alex were sleeping in their own beds and not having an orgy at his cabin.

Not a far-fetched scenario according to Amanda.

She'd been their main source of information about the

crew and their habits, as well as the yacht and its layout. After searching the boat from top to bottom, looking for the drugs she'd suspected Alex of smuggling, Amanda was well familiar with where everything was and who slept where and with whom.

Anandur unstrapped the grappling hook launcher and glanced at Onegus who had done the same. The hooks were going to make noise; there was no way around it. They had seconds to get to Alex before he grabbed a crewmember.

Onegus nodded and pointed his launcher up toward the railing. "On three. One. Two. Three." They shot at the same time, their hooks clunking noisily against the metal railing. Damn, unless the scumbag slept like a dead man, there was no way he hadn't heard that.

Anandur gripped the rope and climbed faster than a monkey, arriving a second ahead of Onegus. This time, he wasn't straining his muscles to the extreme in competition with his superior, and the prize wasn't satisfaction over winning. He was competing against time, and the prize was getting the crew out alive.

Their bare feet made hardly any noise as they ran toward Alex's cabin, arriving within seconds at his door. As planned Anandur burst in, while Onegus covered him with a throwing knife in each hand.

"Fuck, Alex isn't in his bed," Anandur gritted before running for the bathroom, his heart pounding in his chest not from exertion but fear. Alex must've grabbed whoever had been sleeping with him and dragged her in there.

But there was no one in the bathroom either.

Could he have slipped Turner's watch and stayed in Acapulco?

Alex could've done so easily if he'd suspected their

presence, thralling whomever he'd bumped into to forget he'd ever seen him. He'd pulled a similar trick with the private investigator in Marina Del Rey.

"Not in the closet," Onegus said.

"Not in the bathroom either."

Damn, the possibility of Alex giving them the slip was gaining credence. Nevertheless, the safety of the crew demanded they ascertained Alex wasn't on board first.

"Fucking hell, I wish we could split up," Anandur said as they left the owner's suite. One could rush to Geneva's cabin on the upper deck, while the other to the crew quarters on the lower deck. But assuming Alex had a gun, they needed to cover for one another. A bullet in the right place might give Alex enough time to either escape or deliver death with a blade. Working together, one of them could take the bullet while the other jumped Alex.

"Geneva first," Onegus said and broke into a sprint. It made sense. Her cabin was the closest.

Again, Onegus covered while Anandur burst through... and was greeted by a barrel of a gun. But it wasn't Alex who was pointing the thing at his heart. It was a blurry-eyed Captain Geneva. Sitting in bed and clasping the weapon with two steady hands, she meant business— provided her ancient Russian handgun would actually fire. The thing belonged in a museum.

"Put the gun down, Geneva. We can't find Alex. Is he on board?"

For a second or two, her eyes traveled the length of his mostly bare body, still wet and dripping water on the carpet, then shifted and gave Onegus the same once-over. She shook her head. "Anandur, you shit-head, we thought you weren't coming."

"I'll explain later. First, answer my question."

She waved the gun, and both he and Onegus instinctively ducked. "Of course he is here, where would he be?"

"You sure he didn't slip out and stayed in Acapulco?"

"Pfft, if he did, then he is still swimming. He was here before I went to bed."

"Fuck, let's go, Onegus."

"Where are you going?" she called after them.

"We need to find him before he grabs one of the crew and uses her as a bargaining chip," Anandur answered while grabbing the handrail on the glass staircase and using it to swing himself to the level below, then repeating the same move to descend another level. Onegus was right there with him as they ran to the first crew cabin and burst through the door.

Two startled women jumped out of bed, and a moment later the rest of the crew rushed out into the hallway, gawking at the two half-naked, wet men.

"Anandur!" Lana called and threw herself into his arms, kissing him on both cheeks. "You came." Then she scowled. "Two days late!" and she delivered a slap that would've knocked out a human.

He caught her hand as she prepared to deliver another one. "You can beat me up later. First, we need to find the scumbag. He is either swimming toward shore or hiding here somewhere."

Light footsteps running down the stairs had everyone whip their heads around, but it was just the barefoot Geneva, still clutching her gun.

"You found him?" she asked.

"He is not here." Damn, they had a problem. If he was

still on board, hiding somewhere, Alex could sneak up and grab one of the girls while Onegus and Anandur searched for him. And telling them to get into one room and lock the door wouldn't help either, not unless it was reinforced.

Anandur cast a glance at Onegus, who was probably thinking the same thing. "We need to call the chopper and have them airlifted."

Brilliant idea, but someone had to take the yacht back to the harbor, and neither he nor Onegus had ever driven a boat like this. Give him an oar, and he could row with the best of them, but this modern day behemoth was too complicated to figure out on his own.

Geneva snorted. "I'm not leaving. I'm the captain."

Anandur cocked a brow at Onegus. "What do you think?"

"That the chopper can take only five. I thought they could maybe squeeze together, but I think there would be a weight problem."

The Russians weren't small women. Tall and heavily muscled, they probably weighed the same as average-sized males—Marta possibly more.

"Okay, Geneva, you stay, but the three of us stick together, understood?"

Her lips forming a tight line, she nodded. "He is just one man," she said, but he heard the uncertainty in her voice. The woman was too smart not to notice Alex's peculiarities. She knew something was up with him, just not exactly what.

Onegus hailed the helicopter pilot and relayed the plan. The women would be taken to Acapulco and wait for Geneva to bring the boat back, hopefully with none of them hurt and Alex subdued.

The women got dressed and were ready to go faster

than Anandur expected, and as the group emerged on the upper deck, the chopper was already hovering above with the rope dangling down and dragging over the wooden planks.

"Can you climb the rope, or do you need to be pulled?"

The women were athletic, but rope climbing required a lot of upper body strength. If they couldn't, he would have to go first and pull them up one by one, then go down again, which would leave Onegus and those waiting below exposed.

Lana harrumphed. "Watch." She jumped up and grabbed the rope high, letting it fall on the outside of her leg then stepping on it using the opposite foot to anchor it. Her weight distributed between her arms and her feet, she climbed at an admirable speed.

"Okay, I'm impressed, who's next?"

"I go." Renata jumped and caught the rope, climbing just as expertly as Lana had.

Sonia went next, then Kristina, and the last was Marta.

The women must've had military training. No mud-wrestlers learned to climb rope like that. For the first time, doubt drifted through Anandur's mind, and he questioned the whole mud-wrestling tale.

They should've checked the Russians' story. He couldn't believe no one had thought to do so. Except, what reason could the women have to lie? It wasn't as if the profession of mud-wrestling prostitution was such an honor badge.

"We should check the closet," Geneva said as the helicopter took off.

"I did," Onegus said.

"Did you check behind the fake panels?"

"No. But don't you need to close them from the outside?"

She shrugged. "I don't know if he is hiding in there, and if he is how he managed to close the panels from the inside. But if it were me, I would've used the best hiding place on this ship. Don't forget that he thinks the crew is loyal to him and will not rat him out. Unless someone knows there is a hidden compartment behind the false wall, no one would think to check there."

Good point.

Onegus turned on his heel and headed for the stairs, with Geneva following close behind him.

Anandur caught her arm to get her attention. "We go in there together, but if I tell you to get out, you don't wait even a split second to do so. The thing we fear the most is Alex grabbing a hostage. If he is in there, Onegus and I can handle him, but I don't want you to become collateral damage. Understood?"

She nodded.

"I want to hear you say it, and for the love of your God, don't try to be a hero."

She cast him a quizzical glance. "I'll get out of the way. You have my word."

"Good." He clapped her on the shoulder.

The ridiculously large walk in closet housed the equivalent of a clothing store, and none of the items were from Wal-Mart like Anandur's. He wasn't familiar with the cost of men's high fashion but estimated that tens of thousands of dollars had been spent on this wardrobe. Maybe even more. Such a waste.

He pointed Geneva to a safe corner, far from the entry

door, where no one could grab her from behind without going through Onegus and him first. Then the two of them pushed the clothing aside to clear a wide section of the back wall.

Alex's scent was all over the place, but it didn't mean he was on the other side of these panels. The scent lingered on his clothes, even the laundered and dry-cleaned stuff.

Examining the seams between the panels, they didn't find any that looked uneven or warped. Maybe Alex had used one of the panels closer to the side walls, not the center ones.

With that in mind, Anandur pushed the clothes back to the middle and away from one side, but these panels also looked undisturbed. Maybe they should stop pussyfooting and just pry them out and see whether he was there or not.

Onegus started clearing the other side, when Anandur heard the unmistakable sound of a gun being cocked. He leaped at Onegus to get him out of the way, but he was a split second too late. The bullet tore through the fabric paneling and into Onegus's chest.

As the commander hit the floor, Anandur shouted to Geneva, "Get down!" and dropped over Onegus to shield his body from the volley of bullets that followed, spraying the closet. Some went into the walls; others ricocheted off the harder surfaces.

A moment later the fake wall exploded, and Alex leaped out, holding a gun in each hand and shooting straight ahead to clear the way. In another split second, he would realize that his targets were down on the floor and then it was game over.

Anandur did the only thing he could to turn the barrels away from Geneva, he grabbed Alex's legs and pulled, toppling the scumbag to the ground. What he hadn't expected was the guy's quick reflexes.

Alex turned mid-air, landing on his ass instead of his face, and pointed the gun at Anandur's head with an evil smirk and a glint in his beady eyes.

Damn, it was going to hurt. But if Anandur moved out of the way, the scumbag was going to shoot Onegus.

Alex must've realized Anandur's dilemma, taking a second to gloat before pulling the trigger. That second was his downfall.

A shot that was louder than all of those that had come before it was fired from behind, hitting Alex in the back of his skull. He dropped, his head hitting the floor.

Geneva lowered her gun and closed her eyes. "I'm sorry I killed him, but it was either him or you."

"Thank you for saving my ass, but he is not dead. Yet."

He should probably thrall her now.

She frowned and walked closer, placing two fingers where Alex's pulse was supposed to be. "He is dead. What about your friend?" Voice calm, Geneva was all business. Who was she? What was she? No civilian would act that casually after killing a man.

"Not dead. Just injured."

To prove him right, Onegus groaned and turned on his back, clutching his chest. "Son of a bitch, that hurts."

"He needs a doctor. Call the helicopter back."

Fuck, he needed to think fast. Amanda had said the Russians were so guarded that they were difficult to thrall unless they were drunk. Anandur had trouble thralling even a willing subject, let alone a resistant one.

Onegus could probably handle her, but he was in no

shape to do anything other than lie on his back and moan in pain until his body repaired the damage, which would take another ten minutes or so. Alex's head injury would take longer, but Anandur still needed to cuff him as soon as possible, and it would be damn hard to explain why he was putting handcuffs on a dead man.

"Geneva, there are things you don't understand, and I can't explain. What I need you to do is go up and change course to bring this boat back to Acapulco."

"What about them?"

"Leave them to me. I know what I'm doing."

Geneva pinned him with a hard stare then shrugged. "No problem. I don't need to know." She turned around and walked out of the closet. "The less I know, the better," he heard her murmur as she left the cabin.

Definitely ex-military. Or maybe the KGB?

Anandur pulled a pair of reinforced handcuffs from one of the many compartments in his waterproof equipment belt and cuffed Alex's hands behind his back. He grimaced as he checked the injury. It was a nasty one, shredding part of the skull and doing a number on the inside, but the bullet had already been pushed out which meant healing was progressing well.

Onegus sat up and caught the bullet as it fell out of his chest, then put it in his belt. "A souvenir." Holding a hand over his injury, he pushed up to his feet and headed for the bathroom. "I'm going to wash up. Can you find me something to wear?" He waved a hand at the racks upon racks of clothing.

"Sure, any preferences? Italian couture, French?"

"Surprise me."

"Yes, dear."

After securing Alex's ankles with another pair of handcuffs, Anandur pulled a couple of T-shirts, jeans for Onegus and pajama bottoms for himself and joined the chief Guardian in the bathroom.

The guy had done the smart thing, taking a quick shower and washing off not only the blood from his chest but the ocean water as well. Anandur handed Onegus the clothes and jumped in the shower for a quick wash down of his own.

It felt good to pull on clothes over a clean body.

Grabbing several washcloths, he dipped them in warm water, then went back to the closet where he'd left Alex and cleaned the guy as best as he could.

Onegus shook his head. "This scumbag doesn't deserve it."

"I know. I'm not doing it for him. I don't want Geneva and the others to see it. I still need to convince the astute captain that her shot wasn't fatal."

"Don't worry about it, I'll take care of her and the others."

"Good luck. You heard Amanda; the super-suspicious Russians are resistant to thralling."

Onegus flashed him one of his charming smiles. "You really think any female can resist this?" He pointed at his pretty-boy face.

CHAPTER 42: KIAN

"How did it go?" Syssi asked Kian when he returned from collecting the crew's testimony.

The boat's crew, together with the two Guardians and the accused, had flown to Los Angeles the morning following Alex's capture. Kian had the women stay together in an apartment a few miles away from the keep. The building belonged to the clan, but it was only a rental asset owned by a subsidiary; no direct connection to the clan.

Taking Syssi by the hand, he led her to the couch and pulled her onto his lap. "Now everything is great." He nuzzled her neck. "I love coming home to you."

She smiled. "You're funny. You work from home and hardly ever leave the keep. It's me that comes home to you."

"Semantics." He kissed her softly, hoping she'd drop the subject and continue to more pleasant topics—the kind that didn't involve talking.

But his Syssi wasn't going to let it go until he told her

everything she wanted to know. Better get it out of the way.

"So what did they say? Do you have what you need for the trial?" she probed again.

"We already have more than enough to convict Alex ten times over, but I've taken Edna with me to run a light probe on them."

She frowned. "Why? Did you think they would lie?"

"No, but Anandur got a little suspicious. He said that they didn't act like civilians during the mission. Too cool-headed and disciplined. At some point, they must've had military training."

"So?"

Kian rubbed a hand over his jaw. "They never mentioned it. Why tell Amanda about the mud-wrestling and the prostitution but not about military service?"

"Do you think they might be spies?"

"No, it doesn't add up, and Edna confirmed that other than their part in Alex's trade, she sensed no guilt in them. It seems that they are telling the truth about wanting a new life as legal aliens doing legal work. They might be deserters from the Russian army. That would be a better explanation than the mud-wrestling story."

Perhaps he was paranoid, but Kian was contemplating having Andrew ask the Russians a few questions. Just to make sure.

"You're right. Does it matter?"

"To us? No."

"Didn't they want citizenships, though?"

"They were happy enough with the alien status, and it sure as hell wasn't easy to pull off either."

The truth was that their testimony was superfluous at this point. Enough incriminating evidence had been collected by Turner's team, who'd questioned the four girls and the lowlifes who'd purchased them. But a deal was a deal, and Kian wanted to give the Russians what had been promised without them feeling like they hadn't earned it.

"When are they leaving for Hawaii?" Syssi asked.

"Tomorrow. Anandur is escorting them."

"I wish we could go," she said with a wistful look on her face.

Kian smoothed his palm over his wife's long hair, hating that he couldn't give her everything she wanted. He wouldn't have minded a tropical getaway with his beautiful Syssi, away from the keep and the clan and the responsibility that came with his job. But someone had to do it, and that someone was unfortunately him. Or fortunately, depending on who you asked. "We are going to Scotland soon. It's a mini vacation."

Syssi scrunched her nose. "I would love to see Scotland, but three days, including travel time and a wedding, is not enough to do any sightseeing. We'll probably never leave the castle grounds. But I'm excited about exploring it. Amanda says it's beautiful."

The truth was that he hadn't visited the Scottish keep in so many years he would probably have trouble recognizing it. Sari had been renovating the place extensively, one section at a time—specifically the windows and doors, plumbing and electrical systems, the bathrooms, and of course top of the line security measures.

"We will go to Hawaii some other time when things are less hectic here."

Syssi's face twisted in a grimace, but it only made her look cuter. "As if that is ever going to happen. If it does, we wouldn't know what to do with ourselves."

True. And how pathetic was that?

"It is what it is, love. Nothing I can do about it. Besides, you're busy too, especially now with Amanda gone."

Syssi sighed and rested her cheek on his chest. "I can't wait for her to get back to the lab. She makes running it look so effortless while it's nothing but."

He rubbed her back. "If you need help, don't be shy and ask for it. Hannah is a capable girl. I'm sure she can ease your load."

"Not really. It's the juggling of university research and our own for the clan. And now we have William's game to integrate as well."

"Can I do anything to help?"

She lifted her head and kissed his lips. "That's so sweet of you to offer, but you'd be just as lost as I am. Amanda has been doing it for such long time now that she doesn't need to stop and think before tackling every little issue."

Proud of his baby sister, Kian nodded. He knew she was a gifted teacher, but it was good to hear that she was also a great manager.

As Syssi cupped his cheek, running her thumb over his lips, Kian took it as a sign that the time for talking was over and pushed to his feet with Syssi in his arms.

"Are you sure I need to be present at the trial tomorrow?" she asked as he carried her to the bedroom.

He could understand her reluctance to participate. It would be difficult to hear the testimony and even more difficult to vote on the sentence, but he was going to ask for the most severe one they had, entombment, and a unanimous vote was needed. Local clan members would be present physically, and those abroad would vote virtually.

"I'm sorry, sweetheart, but there is no way around it."

She pouted. "Can't you give me special dispensation? Aren't you the boss?"

So now he was the boss, funny.

Outside of the bedroom, he found himself saying 'yes, dear' more often than not, which was fine by him. Whatever made his Syssi happy, he was more than glad to oblige. She loved submitting to him sexually, but she also loved that he never argued with her over anything. What she wanted, however she wanted it, she got it.

As long as it was up to him, it was hers.

There had been only one point of disagreement between them about what she'd considered extravagant gifts, but they had worked out a compromise. The next super-expensive piece of jewelry he'd buy her would be on their fifth wedding anniversary. In the meantime, she wanted gifts that were more about the heart than the wallet.

Problem was, he had no idea what she'd meant by that. Hopefully, not love poems or other crap like that because then he was screwed. Spending money was so much easier than coming up with ideas.

CHAPTER 43: ANANDUR

"It's beautiful here." Lana threaded her arm through Anandur's as they strolled along the beach.

"Yes, it is." He hoped she wasn't attaching any romantic meaning to it. He'd merely wanted to say goodbye properly, not rekindle what had never been between them. He liked her, the sex had been awesome, but that was it.

He glanced at Amanda and Dalhu who were strolling a little ahead of Lana and him, leading the procession of those who wanted to see the sunset—which was everyone except Geneva.

They had their arms wrapped around each other, her hand lovingly stroking his back. Anandur couldn't help but compare their relationship to that of Kian and Syssi, or that of Andrew and Nathalie. The two other couples were so in love that the air between them sizzled, melting into rainbow-colored goo, not to mention their crazy rush to get married.

Not these two.

On the surface, both appeared more reserved, their

expressions of love more subtle—like this little backrub Amanda was giving Dalhu. But whoever had been privy to what they had gone through to be together knew that only true love could've motivated two people to go to such extremes.

"Penny for your thoughts," Lana nudged him.

Considering that he was saying goodbye, he couldn't share his musings with her. Bringing up the subject of love was a bad idea. "I'm glad you like it here, and that you and your friends are getting along with the other trainees in the program."

It had been Amanda's idea to include the crew in the training the other women were going through in preparation for their jobs at the hotel. He'd thought she'd lost her mind and had told her as much. It was like putting an ex-rapist, even a reformed one, together with rape victims.

She'd dismissed his concerns.

The other women had been thralled to forget what had happened to them, and the Russians were too ashamed of their part in Alex's trade to ever bring it up. Just to make sure, though, he'd warned them against ever talking about it with anyone, reminding them that they could still go to jail for their part in the crime.

Lana and the others had sworn to take it to their graves.

Hopefully, that wouldn't be anytime soon. They had a new lease on life, and he wished them success in achieving their dreams.

"I hope you'll be happy here. Find a nice guy, start a family," he said, and then glanced at her almost fearfully, not wanting to see her hurt.

She nodded, looking thoughtful but not sad. "God

willing. I always wanted children."

"Oh, yeah? How many?"

She pretended to think about it, looking up to the sky and holding a finger against her lips. "At least ten, maybe twelve."

"Seriously?"

She laughed. "No, but four is good."

"You know, raising good kids is not easy. Some grow up rotten despite your best efforts."

Like Alex.

His mother was a good person, and what he'd done had broken her heart. It had been difficult to watch her on the monitors, as she'd cast her vote. She'd looked so defeated, so devastated, crying inconsolably when he'd been taken to the catacombs.

Her pleading to make it merciful had convinced Edna to reduce the severity of the punishment. With the help of Brundar's venom, Alex had been put into his tomb already in stasis instead of suffering through many days until his consciousness faded. He didn't deserve the mercy. It had been granted to his mother.

One thing was sure; any wistful thoughts Anandur had ever entertained about becoming a father were gone. Even if one day the fates smiled upon him and brought him his one true love, he wouldn't want children with her.

Lana shrugged. "There is a saying in Russian about people making plans and God laughing at them. It doesn't sound good in English. But you understand, yes?"

He nodded. "Shit happens all the time."

"And good things too. I want to say thank you, Anandur. I know you helped us to get information, but I also know what you give us is more than it was worth."

"You're welcome. But the thanks should go to my boss. He was the one who came up with the idea of letting you run the dinner cruises for the hotel."

"I know, and I said big thank you to Kian, and the others did too." She chuckled. "He didn't like the hugs and the kisses on the cheeks. Maybe we are not the type of women he likes?" she asked hesitantly.

Go figure women.

She didn't mind that Anandur had been using her to get incriminating information on Alex, but was hurt thinking Kian didn't find her or her friends attractive.

"Kian is a newlywed, and he has eyes only for his wife. You could've been the finalists in the Miss Universe competition, and he would've felt awkward about getting hugs and kisses from you. Besides, the guy is crazy jealous and hates it when any man even looks at his wife for more than a second. He would've exploded if some strange guy hugged her. So, naturally, he thinks the same is true for her."

Lana sighed. "So romantic. I hope I find a man who will love me like this."

Shit, now he was feeling like an ass. "I'm sorry that I can't be that guy."

She shook her head. "It was nice. Especially the sex..." She winked. "But I didn't feel butterflies in my belly when we were together or cry when you were away. It wasn't love."

"Hm, butterflies and crying. I'll file it under what to expect when falling in love."

A pair of pale blue eyes pinned him with a hard stare. "You laugh because you never loved a woman. When you do, you call me and say; Lana, you were right."

CHAPTER 44: NATHALIE

"I'm starting to show," Nathalie groaned, observing her profile in the mirror. From the front the change wasn't noticeable, but from the side the bump was pretty obvious.

She smoothed her hand over her protruding middle. The seamstress was coming to do the final fitting, and she was willing to bet the dress was going to be too tight in the waist.

"Don't be silly, your belly is just as flat as it was before." Syssi waved a hand. "It's all in your head. You're a month and a few days pregnant. The baby is still smaller than an almond."

Syssi was kind, but the scale didn't lie. Nathalie had gained a pound and a half since last week. "My pants are starting to feel tight."

Syssi smirked. "You know, when they say that you should eat for two when pregnant, I don't think they mean it literally."

There was a knock on the door. She was expecting the

dressmaker, but it was Bridget, her other bridesmaid. Syssi and Bridget were getting their final fittings too. Amanda, her third, had gotten her own dress, which was fine by Nathalie. She didn't want them to look the same anyway. They had agreed on a color, but each had chosen her own dress design.

"Hello, girls." Bridget entered the master bedroom and closed the door behind her. "Why the sad face, Nathalie?" She sat on the bed, watching Nathalie's reflection in the mirror.

"Just look at it," she said as she rubbed her middle again. "The whole rush was so I wouldn't show at my wedding."

"Pfft, it's probably gas."

Syssi gasped. "Bridget!"

"What? I'm a doctor. Intestinal gas is natural and nothing to be ashamed of."

Nathalie frowned, thinking about the burrito she'd had for lunch yesterday. Maybe she was bloated because of the beans? But what about the weight gain?

A muffled cellphone ring sounded somewhere in the room. Nathalie scanned for the source, but then remembered it was still in her purse. She'd rushed home to make it in time for the fitting and dropped her stuff on the dresser instead of pulling the phone out and charging it. The battery was probably in the red zone. It had been one of those days in the coffee shop, and her plans to leave early and avoid stressing over getting home on time had been thwarted.

Syssi tossed her the purse, but the ringing stopped. A few seconds later it resumed.

She pulled the phone out and glanced at the number.

It was Bhathian.

Her heart somersaulted in her rib cage. Did he have

news about her mother? Had he found her?

That would be the best wedding present ever.

"Hello?"

"Nathalie." His voice sounded gruffer than usual, and her heart sank down to her gut. Bhathian didn't have good news.

"What happened?" she asked, choking on the words that left her constricted throat and went out of her dried-out mouth.

"Eva gave us the slip again. Someone else had been withdrawing money from her account."

"Can't you ask them if they know where she is?" What she meant was; thrall them to get her mother's whereabouts, even if whoever was doing the withdrawals was reluctant to share that information. There were all kinds of rules governing who could be thralled and who couldn't, but she was certain that these were extenuating circumstances.

"I did. Sister Juliana of the Casa de Martinho orphanage said that Eva donates her monthly salary to the orphanage and has been doing so for six years. They have a signed authorization."

Nathalie's legs felt wobbly, and she sat on the bed next to Bridget. "Maybe someone in the orphanage knows where she is?"

"I went there and asked. No one has any information about her."

She hesitated only a moment before asking, "Did you make sure they were telling the truth? I know they are nuns and all, but they might be protecting her anonymity."

"There was no deception. They really didn't know."

"So it's a dead end."

"I'm afraid so."

"Are you coming home?"

"I already have a plane ticket to Scotland. I'll stay until then and just hang around. Maybe the fates will smile upon me."

She nodded. "The fates already did. We found each other. Finding her has been a long shot. Don't let it get you down, Bhathian. We have plenty to be grateful for, and we shouldn't tempt fate by not showing our appreciation for the gifts we've been given."

He sighed. "I have such a smart daughter. You must've inherited it from your mother."

His words cheered her up a bit, and she smiled. "I love you too."

She heard him suck in a breath and realized it was the first time she'd told him she loved him.

"I love you, Nathalie. You brought sunshine into my dreary life."

Tears stung the back of her eyes. Papi used to call her his sunshine too. She was so fortunate to have two fathers who loved her.

"I guess I'll see you in Scotland?"

"You sure will."

"Goodbye, Bhathian." It had been on the tip of her tongue to call him Daddy, but it was too soon. She still felt like she would be betraying Papi.

"I'm so sorry." Bridget patted Nathalie's knee.

With their bat-like super hearing, they must've heard Bhathian's grim news as clearly as she had while holding the phone to her ear. There was no privacy with those people.

"Me too," Syssi said. "Do you want a glass of water?"

"Yes, please." Her mouth felt so dry that her tongue

was sticking to its roof and her words were coming out slurred.

Syssi left and a moment later came back with a tall glass of water. She handed it to Nathalie. "The seamstress is here. Should I let her in? Or do you need a moment?"

Nathalie gulped half the glass on a oner and hiccupped. "Sorry about that. Let her in. There is nothing like trying on a beautiful dress to chase a bad mood away."

Bridget high-fived her. "When the going gets tough, the tough try on clothes. In my case it's shoes."

The dress was gorgeous, and her new plump breasts looked amazing in it. Question was, whether the snug waist would fit.

It did, but the seamstress had pulled the zipper up with difficulty.

Nathalie groaned, her belly muscles straining the seams to bursting. "I knew it. It's too tight."

The damn tears she'd barely managed to contain after Bhathian's call were threatening to spill out. Her mother was not going to be at her wedding, and now she was also too fat for her dress. In a week, she was going to have a protruding belly, and her dreams of a white wedding would be crushed.

It wasn't about hiding her pregnancy.

She didn't care if the whole clan knew she and Andrew were expecting. It was about a silly girl's dream of wearing a beautiful princess-style dress with big fluffy skirts and a tiny waist.

"It looks great," Syssi said.

"Yeah, but in a week's time I might not be able to squeeze into it at all."

The seamstress, Mrs. Bella Shultz, shook her head and pushed her horn-rimmed glasses higher on her nose. "You need to be comfortable at your own wedding and not squeezed like a sausage. I'm going to let it out a little, but this is the last modification." She pointed a finger at Nathalie. "I'll bring the dress tomorrow. You'd better watch what you're eating until the wedding. No beans, no cabbage, no cauliflower, not even bread. Anything that causes bloating is out."

Bossy old lady, but she was right. From now and until she walked down the aisle, Nathalie would be eating salads with no dressing and dry chicken breasts.

Yum…

CHAPTER 45: ANDREW

Exhausted after the long flight from Los Angeles to Edinburgh, Nathalie had fallen asleep as soon as they'd gotten comfortable in the limousine. At first the drive had been smooth, but as they neared the castle it had gotten bumpier, jolting Nathalie's head, which was resting on Andrew's shoulder.

If not for Syssi's irrational fear of a helicopter ride, they could've already been at Sari's keep. Frankly, though, he was grateful. Andrew hated the damn things. Then again, he hadn't ridden in one since his transition so his weird reaction to helicopter takeoffs and landings might be a thing of the past.

He'd test it some other time.

Syssi hadn't been too happy about flying the clan's private jet either, but Kian had managed to convince her that it was just as safe as a commercial airliner. He must've believed that because Andrew would've known if he'd lied, but the truth was that flying in style was riskier.

The small planes weren't as safe. Still, he'd chosen not to say anything, and neither had Brundar or Anandur. They either didn't know or had preferred to keep quiet.

"I can't believe the old man is still sleeping," Anandur whispered from Andrew's other side.

Nathalie had been worried when Fernando hadn't woken up throughout the entire flight. She'd stayed awake to watch over him, checking every few minutes if he was still breathing.

"The sedative Bridget gave him knocked him out. It was a relief to see him wake up when we landed, even though he went back to sleep as soon as we got into the limo."

"It's a damn shame we only get to stay a few days. Most everyone is already there, partying and drinking." Anandur leaned away, giving Andrew a little more room.

Andrew adjusted Nathalie, so she rested more comfortably against him. "Kian can't leave the keep for longer than that. As it is, I don't know how he has the guts to entrust its safety to the human security team. It makes me uncomfortable as hell."

Anandur chuckled. "Safety is an issue for him when he has to protect people, not things. And all of our people are here."

"True."

"I heard the guys in the office threw a surprise bachelor party for you."

"It wasn't anything fancy. Just pizzas and beers at Barney's."

Anandur leaned in close and whispered, "What about the strippers?"

"There were none. To the horny bastards' great

disappointment, Barney refused to allow strippers at the bar." Andrew could just imagine the tantrum his fiancée would have thrown if there had been naked women at his party.

"That's a shame." Anandur leaned back and crossed his arms over his chest.

Absentmindedly, Andrew wrapped one long strand of Nathalie's dark chestnut hair around his finger, then let it spring back and uncoil. Beautiful hair. Beautiful woman. She was going to be a magnificent bride.

He'd stolen a glimpse of her wedding dress when the seamstress had dropped it off. It was a huge fluffy number with endless petticoats, lace, and little pearls sewn all over. Nathalie had refused to let him see her in the dress before the wedding because according to some stupid superstition, it was bad luck.

Andrew wondered at her convoluted logic. She'd come to every fitting he'd had for his new custom-tailored tux, and that had somehow been okay. No bad luck involved.

Damn, his back itched, and he couldn't scratch it without disturbing Nathalie. "How much longer?" he whispered.

"Almost there," Anandur answered.

It seemed like they were climbing higher and higher up the mountains, the serpentine Highland road dangerously too narrow for the large limousine taking them up to the castle. It was dark, there were no lights on the road, not even the headlights of other cars, and the asphalt hadn't been fixed in a long time, probably since it had been first laid. The road was so full of potholes that it was a wonder Nathalie could sleep so soundly, or that Kian could type away on his laptop.

Syssi was reading a book, her glowing eyes providing the illumination. Must've been an exciting story. It was just too weird. He was still getting used to the various quirks of their new physiology.

The limo made another sharp turn, and he had to brace himself not to slide over into Anandur. If he were still human, Andrew would've been anxious. But the limo's driver was an immortal, and his eyesight and reflexes were just as exceptional as Andrew's, probably better. He was in total control of the vehicle.

A few minutes later the road ended in a short bridge. Across from it loomed the castle walls, but the massive gate had been left open and the limo glided by, going through the inner wall gate and into the castle grounds proper.

The sprawling stone building was surrounded by grassy lawns and flowerbeds. Andrew was impressed. Unless those Scottish immortals had thralled some human gardeners to take care of their greenery, they must've been into horticulture.

He kissed Nathalie's forehead. "We are here, baby. It's time to wake up."

She lifted her head and looked out the window.

Illuminated by a clear moon, the castle and its gardens must've been clearly visible even to Nathalie's human eyes, but she didn't say anything. Was she still sleepy?

"What do you think?" he asked.

"That I'm dreaming. It looks like something out of a fairy tale."

Andrew chuckled. "I don't know about that. I always imagined fairy-tale castles as gloomy and imposing. This one looks inviting." Only three stories high, not including the attic or the basement he was sure a building this old had, it was wide but not tall. The windows must've been new because they were large and ornate.

Several people spilled out the front doors and rushed to greet them. He must've met all of them at Syssi's wedding, but he only remembered Kian's other sisters, Sari and Alena, and a few of the Guardians who'd come back to help with Carol's rescue.

Lots of hugs and kisses and a few happy tears later, they were escorted to their rooms and left alone to freshen up. Nathalie's father was in a room across the hall, close but with no shared wall, thank you very much. Although with how thick the walls were in this old stone structure, the soundproofing between rooms was probably damn good.

"Look at this bed." Nathalie walked over to the monstrosity that had stepping stools on both sides to climb onto it. "Why do you think they made it so tall?"

Andrew shrugged. "It's Scotland. It gets really cold here in the winter. Maybe the further it is up from the floor the less drafty it gets."

"I don't think so. Not with this fireplace. You can stand inside it."

Just for the fun of it, he did, then peeked inside to see if it was the genuine article or a modern imitation. It was the real thing.

He walked back and took Nathalie's hand. "Come on, baby, let's freshen up. They are waiting for us with dinner."

Andrew would've gladly skipped the meal and jumped into the inviting bed for a quick romp with his beautiful bride, cuddling with her under the ultra-thick comforter and sleeping for a few hours.

But he couldn't be rude to the people who had organized his wedding and had also paid for it. He'd argued that he wanted to cover at least part of it, but Kian wouldn't hear of it. When Andrew had asked for Sari's phone number, Kian had refused to do that either.

The fight over who would foot the bill hadn't ended there. When Andrew had called his parents, his dad had thrown a fit over it as well. He'd said that he was happy that his two children had found the loves of their lives, but he'd insisted that he wanted to pay for the wedding. At least one of them.

He'd even demanded to talk to Kian.

His dad's efforts had been just as ineffective as Andrew's. There was no reasoning with his stubborn brother-in-law. His father had even threatened not to come to the wedding, but Kian had called his bluff.

Tomorrow, when his parents arrived, Andrew would have to smooth things over between his dad and Kian, or the two stubborn mules would keep arguing and upset Nathalie.

He wasn't going to let it happen.

She would have her princess-in-a-castle dream wedding, and nothing was going to tarnish her day.

With a sigh, he opened the door to the adjacent bathroom, and his jaw dropped. "Nathalie, you have to see this."

She pushed by him. "Wow. This is like something straight from a fairy tale."

Someone had gone all out with that bathroom. Whimsical murals adorned the walls and the ceiling, ornate porcelain legs supported the bathtub and the vanities, and everything that could've been possibly gilded was. Gilded mirrors, gilded faucets shaped like swan necks, and gilded towel holders: A Disneyland-style, fairy princess bathroom.

"Do you think they did it for us?" The tired look gone

from her face, Nathalie's eyes sparkled with excitement.

"Kian mentioned that they were renovating the castle a section at a time. Perhaps they did this one after hearing your wish for a princess-style wedding."

Nathalie turned in a circle and laughed. "That's why Sari was so eager to escort us to our room. I was wondering why she was so bubbly, but I assumed she was the easily excitable type, which didn't really make sense. Her job here is the same as Kian's in Los Angeles. You need a level head to hold a position like this."

The gesture was so over the top that he didn't know how to react. What do you say to someone who'd had done so much for you?

A thank-you just wasn't enough.

Nathalie seemed to ponder the same problem. "How are we going to thank her for this?"

Giving Sari his firstborn was out of a question but... "Maybe we can name our daughter after her? Just the middle name, that is."

Nathalie smiled. "I like it. Sari. It's a unique name. It sounds exotic."

Andrew grimaced. "It sounds like an Indian dress."

"What if we spell it differently?"

"We could, but I still vote for saving it for the middle name."

An idea had been brewing in Andrew's mind for the past week, but he was waiting for the right time to approach Nathalie about it.

His hand reached for the pendant he was wearing under his shirt. He'd picked it up from the jeweler the morning of their flight and hadn't shown it to Nathalie yet.

Andrew didn't feel like it was a proper substitute for

the tattoo that he'd carried on his body. The white gold pendant, hanging from a thin chain around his neck, was just a piece of jewelry, not a memorial for his friends.

But if he named his daughter Phoenix, Andrew would not only pay tribute to their memory, but in some small way invite them to share in his legacy. His immortal daughter would carry their unit's symbol into eternity.

He hoped Nathalie wouldn't object.

A disturbing thought must've crossed her mind because Nathalie's smile wilted. "We shouldn't talk about names until the baby is born. It's bad luck," she whispered.

Andrew gathered her into his arms. "When did you become so superstitious? First the dress that I wasn't allowed to see, and now this baby naming thing. Is it something new?"

She nodded into his chest.

"Why?"

"Because I'm scared. I feel like I've been too lucky and my luck is about to run out. I have all I've ever dreamed of, and I'm afraid of losing it." Her words came out in a shaky whisper.

Wrapping his arms tighter around her, Andrew kissed the top of her head. The truth was that he had no words of reassurance for Nathalie because he'd often felt the same. As if happiness was a rare commodity, a finite resource, and if you had a lot of it, fate or God or the universe wouldn't let you keep that much for yourself. Some would be taken away.

Instead, he said the only thing that was the honest truth and was hers to keep forever. "I love you, Nathalie. And I always will."

CHAPTER 46: NATHALIE

Nathalie's full bladder demanded her attention, waking her up far too early for someone who was supposed to still be jet-lagged. She wanted to stay cuddled with Andrew under the blankets, but it refused to be denied. Seven or eight weeks pregnant, and she was already suffering every imaginable symptom.

Was it because she was older?

Thirty wasn't that old for having her first baby. Women were starting families at an older age now. Heck, her own mother had been forty-five when she'd gotten pregnant with her. But like everything else in Nathalie's life, it seemed nothing ever came easy.

Which reminded her that Andrew's parents were due to arrive. Beside her Andrew was snoring lightly, looking calm and content as can be, while she felt like throwing up, and it had nothing to do with morning sickness.

Nathalie was a nervous wreck, but it wasn't marrying

Andrew that had her panties in a wad, or even imagining walking down the aisle with hundreds of people watching; it was the prospect of meeting Andrew's mother.

God, how she wished she could indulge in a glass of wine or two to calm the jitters. If everything had gone according to schedule, Andrew's parents had arrived at the airport about half an hour ago, and the helicopter sent to pick them up would be landing at the keep shortly.

Just great. The dreaded first meeting with her future mother-in-law had to occur the morning of the wedding.

Dr. Anita Spivak, the accomplished and saintly pediatrician, intimidated the hell out of her, and that was even before she'd met the woman face to face. Nathalie didn't know what was more impressive about Andrew's mother, the fact that she was a medical doctor, no small achievement by any standards, or that she was volunteering in Africa, a dangerous and unforgiving place.

She would be so unimpressed with her future daughter-in-law. A baker who didn't finish college and had gotten pregnant out of wedlock. What if Anita suspected Nathalie of doing so on purpose to entrap Andrew?

Ugh. She'd better take care of that bladder.

Barefoot, she padded to the bathroom and took care of that first, then debated whether to go back to bed or jump into the shower.

She was too strung up to fall asleep again.

Too much was going on.

As if the upcoming meeting with Andrew's parents weren't enough, Bhathian's connecting flight had been canceled. The last she'd heard from him, he'd said he was scrambling to find an alternative. Hopefully, he would make it on time to the wedding.

If not, she was going to make everyone wait.

As per Bridget's instructions, Nathalie didn't wash her hair. Appointing herself as Nathalie's stylist, Bridget was going to wash it later. Amanda had put herself in charge of her makeup, and Syssi was going to help with the dress and whatever else was needed.

Wrapped in a thick towel, Nathalie went back and nudged Andrew, feeling a little guilty about waking him up after only a few hours of sleep. "Andrew, wake up, baby, we have tons of things to do."

His lips lifted in a smile. Opening his eyes, Andrew moved with that new unnatural swiftness she was starting to get used to. In a second, her towel was gone, and she found herself under his big, warm body, his morning erection poised at her entrance.

"Good morning, gorgeous." Andrew buried his nose in the hollow between her neck and her shoulder. "You smell so good." He kissed the soft spot then nipped it, sending shivers straight down to her center. Any other morning, she would have loved to continue their play, but not today. She was too stressed.

"We can't, Andrew. Your parents will be here any minute now, and you're still in bed. You need to get up."

He swiveled his hips, the tip of his shaft sliding against her wet entry. Damn, even when stressed out of her mind, the man never failed to turn her on.

"How about a little quickie? Two minutes. I promise."

Nathalie slapped his shoulder. "Save it for the wedding night, tiger. Now hop into the shower and get ready."

"Yes, ma'am." Andrew made a pouty face as he rolled off her, then pointed a finger at Nathalie. "I'm holding you up to it, and I'm going to collect even if you are exhausted and fall asleep."

Nathalie climbed down the insanely tall bed and collected her towel from the floor. "I promise, I won't. And if I do, you have my permission to do wicked things to me while I'm out."

"Ooh, kinky, I like." He waggled his brows.

"Gross, if you ask me, but fine." She wrapped the towel around her body and headed for the closet. Andrew was still at the same spot she'd left him, no doubt ogling her ass. Incorrigible. But as always, he managed to make her feel better. "Get moving, Andrew, we don't have all day."

He was done in less than five minutes. If there was one thing that years of military service had taught Andrew, it was how to use time efficiently in the bathroom. She didn't want to know what else it had taught him. But as long as it had kept him alive she was grateful for it.

"Ready?" He clasped her hand.

"As ready as I'm going to be."

Andrew peered down at her face and frowned. "Why are you so anxious? You're not getting cold feet, are you? Because if you do, it's too late. I'm marrying you even if I have to do it caveman style." He pulled her along, his long legs quickly eating the distance between their room and the main staircase.

She had to strain her leg muscles to keep up. "Oh, yeah? And what's that? I've never heard of a caveman wedding."

"Because there is none. I'll throw you over my shoulder, proclaim in a loud voice, so every male in my tribe hears me, that you're mine, and carry you to my cave, where I tie you to whatever cavemen use for bedposts and have my wicked way with you."

If it were only that simple.

But then she wouldn't have her dream wedding.

She tugged on his hand to get his attention. "Slow down, Andrew. I can't walk that fast."

"I'm sorry, baby." He stopped and wrapped his arm around her waist. "You walk at whatever pace is comfortable for you, and I'll follow your lead."

"Thank you."

The helicopter pad was in the back, next to the stables and the barns and a large vegetable garden. Sari's people must've either striven for self-sufficiency or liked to keep busy with farm work.

It was a beautiful, cloudless morning, and the long walk was invigorating. Andrew kept his promise and didn't rush ahead, giving her plenty of time to look around. Whenever a barn's or a stable's doors were open, Nathalie peeked inside, curious to see the animals, but only a couple looked like they were used for that purpose; most housed a more modern form of transportation—cars.

At the helipad, they joined Syssi and Kian.

"I'm so excited." Syssi pulled Nathalie away from Andrew. "I can't wait for my parents to meet you. They are going to love you."

"You think so? Why? I'm no one special."

Syssi's eyelids peeled wide. "Are you kidding me? The girl who managed to put an end to Andrew's bachelor status? My mother is going to kiss both your hands and thank you."

That was nice to know. Apparently, any female would do, as long as she managed to drag Andrew to the altar. On the one hand, it was a relief to know that she didn't need to be anybody or prove anything to be accepted; on the other, it was an insult because she didn't need to be special or wonderful or anything other than someone with ovaries.

"Besides." Syssi leaned and whispered in her ear. "You're a knockout, and you can bake. A killer combination."

That was much better. Hopefully, Syssi's parents would share their daughter's opinion.

CHAPTER 47: ANDREW

"You look beautiful, sweetheart." Andrew kissed Nathalie's cheek, careful not to dislodge the huge rollers Bridget was putting in her hair.

Nathalie made a face. "I look ridiculous, but thank you."

Andrew glanced around and chuckled. Their bedroom suite had been converted into a bridal command center, bustling with activity and saturated with estrogen.

He was definitely not invited, and his presence was tolerated with the understanding that he was just picking up his tuxedo and going to Kian and Syssi's suite—the groom's and his best men's headquarters.

Kian had promised Cuban cigars, and the best Scottish whiskey money could buy. Great, but Andrew would've rather stayed with his bride and watched her getting ready.

Even with a helmet of rollers that made her look like an alien spacewoman, his Nathalie was stunningly beautiful.

And to think she'd been worried his parents wouldn't like her. Who in their right mind wouldn't? She'd enchanted them by simply being herself.

She was perfect.

"Andrew, stop standing there like a doofus and move it." Syssi gave him a gentle shove.

"I don't get why I need to go. Kian stayed with you before the wedding, and you guys walked down the aisle together."

He'd caught a guilty look on Nathalie's face before Syssi shoved him again.

"I need to pick up something from my room. I'll be right back," Syssi called to the girls as she opened the door and walked out with him. "You shouldn't complain, Andrew. Nathalie just wants a traditional wedding."

He swung the tuxedo bag over his shoulder. "I was just teasing."

"Don't. Not today. She is too stressed. Bhathian called earlier."

"I know. He should arrive more or less on time."

"If everything goes well, he is scheduled to land in an hour. Which means he'll be here in two or more. I told Nathalie that forty-five minutes' delay is not a big deal, and that everyone would just spend more time schmoozing, but it didn't do any good. She is still stressing."

Andrew sighed. "This was supposed to be her dream wedding. I thought she would be floating on a cloud. I don't get why she can't relax and enjoy herself."

Syssi kissed his cheek. "Don't worry about it. Go and have fun with the guys. The girls and I will take care of Nathalie. We can't give her wine, but we will get her to loosen up with some goofing around."

"Can you videotape?"

She slapped his back. "Get out of here already."

"Didn't you need to get something from your room?"

"Nah, it was just an excuse to escort you out. See you at the altar, big brother."

Cigar smoke and male laughter greeted Andrew as he opened the door to Kian's suite. The guys were out on the balcony, but they had left the French doors open, and all the smoke was getting inside.

Sari was going to kill them for stinking up her castle.

"Andrew, my man, I have a cigar with your name on it," Kian waved him over. He hadn't been joking. A red bow was tied to the big-ass cigar, with his name printed on it.

"A bit much? Wouldn't you say?" He took the cigar and the cutter Kian was handing him. Andrew had asked the guys not to throw him a bachelor party, and this was the compromise; a wedding day guys' get-together.

"Don't look at me. I sent this clown to buy them." Kian pointed at Anandur.

Anandur shrugged and took another swig from a bottle of whiskey. "Seemed like a good idea when the sales girl offered to personalize the cigars. Gave me more time to admire her bosom."

Arwel chucked an empty cigar wrapper at him. "I'm sure you did more than admire it."

Anandur huffed. "A gentleman doesn't tell."

"Too bad you're not a gentleman," Kian said.

Anandur arched a brow. "Have you ever seen me treating a lady with disrespect? Give me one example."

Kian frowned but came up with nothing.

"Aha, you can't. I'm a perfect gentleman." With a slight bow, he handed his bottle to Andrew. "And I'm even sharing my booze in a very gentlemanly manner."

Andrew pushed the hand with the bottle away. "Keep it. I'd rather have a beer."

The guys went silent as if he'd committed blasphemy.

"Beer? On your wedding day? Shame on you, Andrew," Arwel slurred, letting his thick Scottish accent take over, and handed him an unopened bottle of whiskey. "Don't drink it all. Your lovely bride will not be happy if you show up drunk." He finished his declaration with a burp.

CHAPTER 48: NATHALIE

Nathalie's phone rang, but there was no way she could reach it. Her beautiful dress required careful maneuvering around furniture. Besides, her nail polish was still wet.

Syssi answered. "Bhathian. Are you calling from the airport?" He must've responded in the affirmative. "Great, we are waiting for you." She smiled at Nathalie and gave her the thumbs up. "No. No way. Nathalie won't let us start without you," she told him. Bhathian must've argued because Syssi kept shaking her head. "I can't give her the phone, she has wet nail polish on." Syssi rolled her eyes as she listened. "A suit is fine. Not everyone is wearing a tux."

From Syssi's side of the conversation, Nathalie surmised that Bhathian didn't have a tux. "Tell him he can come in jeans if he wants to. I don't care. As long as he is here for the ceremony nothing else matters."

Syssi smiled. "He says he loves you."

"Tell him I love him too."

Naturally, Syssi didn't have to say anything because

he'd heard her. In this room, Nathalie was the only one who'd heard just half of the conversation. She would have to endure that, and other human limitations, for the next seven and a half months.

"He is going to be here in about an hour," Syssi said for her benefit.

"That's great. Just half an hour delay." Nathalie waved her hands in the air to speed up the nail polish drying and hardening. She hadn't planned on having her nails painted, preferring the natural look of a good manicure, but when Amanda got something into her head, there was no changing her mind. It was better to just go with it.

The second coat of nail polish and the topcoat were dry by the time Bhathian called to say he'd arrived and was downstairs waiting with everyone else.

Bridget and Amanda fussed with some last minute unnecessary touch-ups to Nathalie's hair and makeup, while Syssi went to get Fernando, who'd spent the afternoon watching William and some of the local boys play video games.

Nathalie had been so worried about Papi's reaction to another new place and new people, but he surprised her with how well he was handling everything. If she hadn't known better, she would have thought he was improving. Sadly, the doctors had told her that dementia wasn't curable, and the best she could hope for was to slow its inevitable progression.

The door opened, and Papi walked in, looking debonair in his tuxedo.

His face lit up, and he clasped her hands. "My Nathalie! You are the most beautiful bride I've ever seen. You look like a princess."

A tear stung at the corner of her eye, but she was

afraid to touch it and ruin Amanda's masterpiece. "Excuse me, Papi." She pulled her hand out of his grasp, grabbed a tissue, and gently dabbed at the tiny drop.

"Hey! No crying, girl!" Amanda waved a finger at her.

"I'm trying, but it's hard not to get emotional with all these crazy hormones floating around."

Amanda smiled wickedly. "You leave me no choice. I'd have to walk behind you and tell you annoying jokes. And if that doesn't work, I'd have to kick you. You can't get mushy while pissed."

Fernando frowned. "No one kicks my daughter."

Amanda smiled sweetly. "I was just joking, Fernando, I love Nathalie." She leaned in, as if to air kiss Nathalie's cheek, and whispered in her ear, "I'm so going to do it." Out loud she said, "Big smile, girl. Show Andrew and everyone else how happy you are to become his wife forever and ever."

Amanda might have meant it as a tease, but it had been exactly what Nathalie needed to hear. She and Andrew were getting married, and everything else, small or big, was inconsequential. Still, she was grateful that Papi was there, and that her biological father was there as well.

As the bunch of them spilled out of the bedroom, Nathalie glanced at the ornate, tall ceiling and couldn't believe she was getting married in a real castle.

The curving staircase was magnificent, but she wondered how she was going to manage the descent in her full dress. Real princesses and the actresses playing them must've trained for hours perfecting the skill of walking gracefully with their heads held high and not getting their feet tangled in their skirts.

"Girls?" She glanced at Amanda and then at Sissy.

They understood immediately, and each picked up a side, together with the countless petticoats under it. Luckily, the staircase was built on a grand scale. The three of them, including her dress, could stand side by side.

When the last step was behind her, Nathalie felt like she'd overcome the final obstacle. From now on, everything was going to be wonderful. The smile came naturally; a big grin everyone would see even from under her veil.

Amanda and Syssi let go of the skirts, and Papi took his place at her side. She threaded her arm through his, and together they waited a few moments for the bridesmaids to enter and join the groomsmen.

It was good Papi wasn't paying attention to the details because the ceremony was only loosely based on the traditional one. For starters, one of her bridesmaids was married, and then the three had entered together and not one at a time. The thing he was sure to notice, though, was that a woman was officiating. A glowing, otherworldly woman.

The first notes of *Here Comes the Bride* sounded from the pipe organ, and Nathalie patted her father's arm. "It's our cue, Papi, let's go."

As they entered, a hush fell over the assembled company. They advanced at an easy pace toward the altar, where Andrew was grinning from ear to ear and looking more handsome than ever.

You're stunning, he mouthed.

Nathalie grinned back, her eyes trained on her man to the exclusion of everyone else, including the small, glowing figure up at the altar.

"Look, Nathalie," her father whispered in awe. "An angel came to marry you. You two are blessed."

"Yes, we are, Papi."

CHAPTER 49: ANDREW

"Good morning, Mrs. Spivak," Andrew said jokingly and kissed Nathalie's warm cheek. The pagan ceremony hadn't called for a name change, and he wasn't sure Nathalie wanted to take his even after the civil one. But it was fun to say.

Nathalie groaned and turned around, presenting him with her best asset. Poor girl. She'd been exhausted after the wedding and the reception, and he hadn't had the heart to hold her up to her promise.

His Nathalie had gotten her dream wedding, and she'd had fun.

After discarding the petticoats that had been weighing her down and restricting her movements, she'd gotten comfortable and danced the night away. Toward the end, her feet had been so sore that he'd had to pick her up and carry her up to their room. Not that he hadn't planned to do so anyway.

Andrew would've let her sleep the day away, but people were leaving and wanted to say goodbye.

"I don't want to get up," she moaned. "Every muscle in my body hurts."

Damn, his plans for morning sex with his wife would have to wait. He pressed his erection to her luscious behind. "I'm sorry, sweetheart, but you have to."

"Why?"

"Because my parents are leaving and want to say goodbye, and so are Syssi and Kian and many others."

She turned back around. "Is anybody staying?"

Wrapping his arms around her, he cupped her butt cheeks and gave them a gentle squeeze. "Dalhu and Amanda are flying out tomorrow, and Bhathian the day after. I think that in three or four days we will be the only ones left."

She smiled a sleepy-eyed smile. "And we will be off on our honeymoon."

He kissed her soft lips. "What do you want to do first? Explore the countryside or stay in bed for a few days? I vote for staying in bed."

"I'm sorry about last night. I didn't keep my promise."

He rubbed her back. "You were exhausted, I would've been an asshole if I didn't let you sleep."

She sighed. "If I were immortal, I would've had the energy. But as a human, I can't keep up with you.

The last thing Andrew wanted was for Nathalie to feel less than perfect the morning after their wedding. "As an immortal, odds are you wouldn't have gotten pregnant. After the transition, fertility rate drops to an almost zero level. We've been given a precious gift. The extra wait is a small price to pay."

More than anything, Andrew hoped that he wouldn't

be proven wrong. So many things could happen between now and then, but he refused to let worry spoil the moment.

"I know. I'm just tired and achy and envious. You are strong and healthy and gorgeous, and you're going to stay like that, while I am going to get fat and even more tired. It's unfair."

"What can I do to make it up to you?"

She shook her head. "Ignore me. I think I'm moody because I'm crashing from yesterday's high."

"I don't mean right now. For the next eight months. Is there anything I can do?"

"Just keep loving me and telling me I'm beautiful even when I look like a hippo."

"That goes without saying, and my princess is never going to look like a hippopotamus."

"An elephant?"

"You're going to look like a beautiful woman who is pregnant with my child."

That seemed to appease her, and a small smile bloomed on her face. "Is it true that men find pregnant women sexy?"

"I don't know about other men, but I find you incredibly sexy. You want me to prove it to you?" He pressed his erection against her belly.

Regrettably, he didn't get the response he wanted. Instead, Nathalie reached for his pendant. "It came out perfect."

"It's okay, but it's a poor substitute for the tattoo."

"What else can you do? Nothing will stay permanent on your fast-regenerating skin. Do you want me to get one?"

"A tattoo? No way."

She pouted. "Why not? I can have the experience and

then it will fade away after the transition, same as yours."

"But that's exactly the point. It will fade, so why bother. I have a better idea, but only if you agree."

"Shoot."

Andrew hesitated. Nathalie would not refuse his request even if she didn't like it. If he thought she'd only agreed for his sake, he would scrap the idea himself. "What do you think about the name Phoenix?"

"For our daughter?"

He nodded.

"It's beautiful, but I told you that I don't want to name her until after she is born."

Andrew released the breath he'd been holding. Nathalie had spoken truthfully. She really thought the name was beautiful. "How about a list of potential names? Is that considered bad luck as well?"

Thinking it over, she first frowned and then shook her head. "I think it's okay. So we have two for the list; Sari and Phoenix."

"Phoenix and Sari. Sari would be on the list of middle names."

Nathalie snuggled closer and kissed his neck. "I think Phoenix is perfect, and it will definitely go to the top of the list."

"You are the best, my Nathalie." Andrew closed his eyes and gave a silent prayer of thanks for the gifts he'd been given.

First and foremost, for the gift of life—his human one. He'd been spared when so many hadn't. He hadn't expected to survive and yet he had. Same for immortality. He hadn't expected to come out alive on the other side, and yet here he was, healthy and strong.

But maybe he'd been given those gifts not because he'd wished for them or earned them, but because Nathalie had. She was so much more deserving than he.

It made perfect sense.

God or fate had entrusted Andrew with Nathalie's wellbeing, and he was going to spend his days and his nights making her happy, holding her, and loving her, for as long as they both lived. Which, hopefully, meant as close to eternity as it got.

:

Eva & Bhathian's story is next

Book 11 in The Children of the Gods Series
Dark Guardian
Found

FOR AN EXCLUSIVE PEEK
Join The Children Of The Gods VIP List
And gain access to preview chapters
and other exclusive material through
the VIP portal at
itlucas.com

Made in the USA
Las Vegas, NV
14 November 2022

59453348R00187